BIDDING TO SIN

Victoria tried to struggle but was firmly pinned by Arlene's weight and superior strength. She panted heavily, but said nothing. Arlene grasped her hair in one hand and pulled her head to one side. Then she bit her on the neck. Grasping a thick fold of skin and muscle firmly between her teeth, she sucked hard to draw the blood to the surface. Victoria made a croaking sound that was growing towards an agonised shriek by the time Arlene released her grip. The love-bite shone like a bloody brand, though the skin was not broken.

'Now,' said Arlene, 'just think how you're going to explain that away. Just ask yourself, while I'm fucking you, how you're going to explain that to your man.' And she reached down to Victoria's sex and pushed her fingers deep inside her, as far as they would go. She ignored Victoria's cries of fear and pain. But when those cries turned to spasms of arousal she worked with them, bringing them slowly up, step by step. The body underneath her squirmed and struggled, but that was only natural. This woman, for whom sex had become a dull and boring thing, had a lot to learn and it would be a steep learning curve. And Arlene wasn't going to ring the bell until the lesson was over.

BIDDING TO SIN

Rosita Varón

This book is a work of fiction.
In real life, make sure you practise safe, sane and consensual sex.

First published in 2006 by
Nexus
Thames Wharf Studios
Rainville Road
London W6 9HA

www.nexus-books.co.uk

Typeset by TW Typesetting, Plymouth, Devon

Printed and bound by Clays Ltd, St Ives PLC

ISBN 0 352 34063 0
ISBN 9 780352 340634

Contents

1

The Wrap

When Melanie went back to her office to pick up the yellow post-it note she'd been on the point of forgetting – the one bearing Charles Bermont's weekend telephone number and the memo-to-self scrawled in her usual urgent capitals: 12.30 SAT. WITHOUT FAIL – she wasn't surprised to see Kirsty through the glass partition. Seated at her desk, her back towards Melanie, Kirsty was now the sole occupant of the cluttered open-plan area the Creative Design Team referred to as their studio. There was something poignant about her appearance there amidst the still-life of abandoned drawing boards, half-empty coffee mugs and dark video screens, and something vulnerable about that long slender neck and delicately poised head, both emphasised by the old-fashioned way the fine blonde hair was tied up on top. But Melanie had noted these things before. What riveted her attention now onto the slim, graceful figure that seemed to defy the severe metal spine and brutal backrest of the typist's stool it perched on was the sudden awareness that the girl was masturbating.

Melanie stopped in her tracks. Kirsty was obviously unaware of her presence. She couldn't have seen Melanie come in without turning in her seat, and she'd evidently been too engrossed to hear the door. She must have believed the entire suite to be as empty as it had become just minutes before, when everyone else had trooped off to the local to conclude their usual 'Friday Afternoon Wrap' in the time-honoured way. She herself had pleaded a last-minute task and said she would join them later.

With widening eyes and drooping jaw, Melanie watched as the girl's hand massaged her breast through her clothes. Although the other hand wasn't visible, the sinuous movements of the shoulder and the corresponding tensing of the stockinged thigh, spread sideways and well exposed to view below the hiked-up skirt, told clearly enough where it was and what it was doing. Melanie stood transfixed. A small voice within told her that she was intruding on something very private and that it wouldn't do to stand and watch. But a stronger instinct refused to let her turn and depart the scene. A thrill of excitement passed through her loins, followed by a glow of empathy for her incontinent subordinate.

Then, something seemed to startle Kirsty, to bring her abruptly back to the land of the living. Perhaps she glimpsed a reflection somewhere, or detected a subtle change in the ambience even though the door linking Melanie's office to the studio was closed. Or perhaps some sixth sense kicked in. Whatever it was, Kirsty tensed and froze, her head canted upward. It put Melanie in mind of a young roe deer she and Mark had once come across grazing in a wood. The animal had suddenly stiffened and raised its muzzle to the air, aware of a threat but not knowing where it came from until, sighting the human intruders, it had stared at them for just a second before turning and loping quickly away. The analogy held. Kirsty swung around on her stool and looked straight into Melanie's eyes.

For what seemed like an age the two women stared at each other, immobile. Kirsty – whose other hand could now be seen between her thighs, pressing against moist

2

white panties – turned pale. Then she flushed bright red and was on her feet, almost a blur of ungainly motion as she headed for the door, knocking over a chair and sending a coffee mug crashing to the carpet in her panicked flight. Before Melanie had regained enough presence of mind to call her name through the partition, to tell her that it was all right and nothing to get upset about, the girl had disappeared from the studio and could be heard running along the corridor, her rapid footfalls quickly fading amidst the swishing and huffing of hydraulic hinges. The sounds echoed in Melanie's brain as she stood there trying to get her thoughts together. When she did, she was worried. And, being worried, she was angry. Damn! she thought. Why did this have to happen just at this time? A few minutes ago everything had been going swimmingly. Now she had a problem. Damn!

By the time she rejoined the others in the pub, Melanie was once again the poised efficient manager, the linchpin of Bermont and Cuthbertson's resurgence as a major player in the world of media design. Okay, she had a new and totally unforeseen problem concerning one of her best and brightest team members, but problems were her bread and butter. She would deal with this one as she always did, by calm appraisal, careful planning, decisive resolution. As for the rest of the team, here dispersed around the bar sipping their pints, they were starting to gel into the first-rate creative force she knew they were capable of becoming, and this was the time in the week when she rewarded them, when she encouraged them, over a relaxing drink and a friendly chat, to wind down and ease themselves into their respective weekends.

The Wrap had been one of her innovations. From about 3 p.m. every Friday, work ceased as she joined them in the studio to discuss the past week's output and the next week's challenges, well larded with small talk and banter, until it was time to hit the weekend trail via the Rose and Crown. As the female boss of an almost entirely male team, Melanie felt a certain responsibility to keep their spirits up. As well as always dressing well and looking good for them, she made a point of injecting her particular brand of feminine warmth and vigour into their working relationships. Not infrequently, and especially on Friday afternoons, this sparked into mild, good-natured sexuality evidenced by knowing looks, inviting gestures, and witty innuendo. It never strayed beyond the bounds of decorum – after all, everyone knew that Melanie and Mark were an item of long standing – but it kept things lively. It added spice to the working day. It stimulated the creativity upon which everyone in the company depended. And besides, Melanie just loved the attention.

'Where's Kirsty?' someone asked when Melanie was at last seated with a glass of Chardonnay in front of her.

'She was feeling unwell,' Melanie lied. 'I told her to go straight home and get some rest. We'll need her to be on good form next week when – I suppose I should say *if* – the Castadiosa contract comes in.'

'Oh, poor little Kirsty,' said Dean, mockingly. 'Can't have her mixing with us rough fellas, can we?'

'Leave her alone, bitch!' put in Adrian with feeling. 'Perhaps she'd mix a bit more if she didn't have to put up with your catty remarks all the time.'

'Make up your mind, sweetheart,' rejoined Dean. 'Which will it be, bitch or cat? Canine or feline?' He leered at Adrian. 'Just name your quadruped of choice.' Adrian dropped his gaze and sipped his beer.

Dean and Adrian were the two gays in the team, but they were anything but a pair. Creative minds of the highest order, they were also, in their different ways, rather prickly characters, especially towards each other. Dean, a slightly rotund five foot five with delicate hands

4

and tiny feet, was anything but the 'rough fella' his remark had implied, but he more than made up for that by his perpetual verbal aggression expressed as ironic wit. Adrian, by contrast, was tall, handsome and beautifully proportioned. He was the kind of good-looker women were immediately attracted to, until they realised that the gleam in his eyes was not for them but for their hunky male escorts. Dean knew he wasn't Adrian's type either, but he never let up with his provocative double-edged invitations, partly because this never failed to discountenance his colleague, and partly because he hoped for a result one day. Their feuding was one of the problems Melanie had inherited when she took over the Creative Design Team, and it had taken her months to convert their destructive animosity into creative competitiveness.

'Now, now!' chided Melanie. 'You've been good boys all week. Don't spoil your weekend before it's even started. Besides, we're still technically in office hours, and there'll be no cat-fights on *my* watch.'

They smiled at her submissively. It was testimony to Melanie's authority as a manager that she could make remarks like that without giving offence. There'd been much scepticism at her appointment to such a sensitive and critical post just under a year ago. Even Charles Bermont had had reservations and it was only Phillip Drew's insistence that had persuaded him to give her a try. Now, Charles was forever congratulating himself on his wisdom and foresight. 'There was something about the woman that convinced me she was the man for the job,' he'd say. Then he'd start to chuckle at his own unoriginal wit, and would not stop until his interlocutor was chuckling sycophantically along with him.

Melanie owed much to Phillip Drew, and she thought of him now as she tasted her wine. How often had they drunk Chardonnay together, savouring its tartness against the sweet softness of each other's lips? Well, not

5

that many times, actually! For the first year of her MBA course Phillip had been just a tall, striking figure occasionally glimpsed entering a lecture theatre or seminar room, a reputation for business success and inspirational teaching, a name on the hard covers of some of the best management science text books. He'd been a legend, a vision of mature masculine beauty that could make your knees buckle if you came upon him too suddenly in the corridor, a dream that could wake you in the night with a sweet ache in the loins and a wetness about the labia.

It wasn't until halfway through her final year that she'd had any direct dealings with him. To begin with she was just one among the many admiring students who attended his lectures and hung upon his every word. Later, she'd dared to add her name to the list of those wishing to do a project under his supervision. Her joy when she learned that she'd been selected was matched only by the fear she suddenly felt at the thought of the weekly, hour-long, one-to-one tutorials she'd have to undergo. How would she survive them? How would she be able to concentrate on the project? She sipped her wine again as she remembered how nervously she'd approached that first tutorial, torn between hope and dread, and how radically, naturally, wholeheartedly he had resolved her predicament at a stroke!

By the time she found herself outside the door of Phillip Drew's office at the appointed hour, Melanie had psyched herself up for what she knew would be the most important event of her entire MBA course. She was sure of getting her degree – her grades so far had been too good for actual failure to be a serious possibility – but was she strong enough to see this challenge through and, if not, could she expect to succeed as a woman of business?

The fact was, she was hopelessly infatuated with Phillip Drew, even though she'd never exchanged a word with him outside a crowded classroom. She cursed herself roundly for her susceptibility. After all, at 24 she was too old for a schoolgirl crush. She'd worked for several years in the tourist industry after leaving school, and had enrolled in the course to take her more quickly up a career ladder whose lowest rungs were already well below her. It wasn't as if she was inexperienced sexually, either. She'd enjoyed a string of lovers before Mark, and prided herself on her toughness of mind where men were concerned. She could be attracted without being bowled over, love without being disenfranchised, give, by and large, just as good as she got. And yet she was obsessed with this man! It didn't make sense! But it was too late now to do anything except face the music. She knocked on the door at the second attempt, her tense, white knuckles having fallen inches short at the first.

'Come in.'

The voice was loud and firm, even through the closed door. There was no retreat. She turned the handle and sidled into the room, helplessly aware of the poverty of spirit her body language was betraying. Quietly closing the door behind her, she stood peering across the room to the desk and to the man who sat behind it, head bent as he wrote into a large desk diary. Seconds lumbered past. At length, still writing and without looking up, he spoke.

'This tutorial will be a lot easier on our voices if you sit over here by the desk.'

The deliberate mockery of the remark was heightened by the dry flat tone in which it was uttered, and the pang of indignation it induced was enough to jar Melanie out of her timidity. There was defiance in her tread as she strode over to the desk and, whether he detected it or not, it made her feel stronger. She sat down on the light tubular chair that stood beside the desk and tried to compose herself as she waited for him to speak again.

At length, he closed the diary and turned to smile at her. 'You are Melanie Brooks,' he said. She nodded, not

7

ready yet to trust her voice under the penetrating scrutiny of those dark green eyes. He named the project, this time making it clear by look and intonation that he expected a response. She managed a fractured 'That's right.'

'Good,' he said.

He summarised the project, then asked her how she intended to tackle it. Melanie spoke for a few minutes and felt her nervousness recede. Her voice gained strength, her brain began to clarify. Her heart, however, yearned for this man more than ever and, as they exchanged ideas, she felt herself slowly splitting into two. One part of her was thinking and talking management science as coherently and intelligently as she could have wished. The other part was longing to be touched, and to touch in return. That part ached to reach out and stroke his face, his thick dark hair. It cried out for those lips to cease their meaningless work forming words and to form kisses instead, to come together with hers and feed her soul with the loving she craved. It longed to feel those arms squeezing her body against his, those hands cupping her breasts, grasping her buttocks, stroking her thighs. It inflated her nipples until they chafed inside her bra and made her fearful that he would notice them. It made her labia swell and spread so that the crotch of her panties pressed into her and moistened itself in her juices. It made her clitoris into a hard, insistent thing that begged for its own gratification, if not at his hand then at her own. And all the while she talked of this theory and of that, of one alternative plan of action and another, of so-and-so's findings and of such-and-such's survey results.

The clock on the wall showed that three quarters of the allotted hour had passed and they fell silent, having apparently exhausted the academic possibilities of this preliminary tutorial. Melanie now knew exactly how she would set about her project, and he, for his part, was satisfied that she had the necessary knowledge to make a good fist of it. He glanced at the clock, then at her.

'We'll meet again next week,' he said, 'when I'll expect you to have developed the plan we've discussed and taken at least the first step towards implementing it.' Then his face took on a serious expression with eyes cast down. 'You know,' he said, 'I was pleased that you opted for my project. I was impressed by the coursework you did for me, and I felt sure you would be ideal for the task. I'm wondering now, however, if you made the right choice.' He lifted his gaze again, and his eyes were piercing.

'You've already proved that you're capable of handling what must be an extremely difficult situation for you. On the evidence of this tutorial alone, I'd say you've got what it takes to go a very long way in business, to take on the toughest challenges and succeed. So if you were to change your mind now, it wouldn't in any way count against you. There are still some projects not assigned, and there are other tutors who would be delighted to supervise you in them.'

Melanie cringed. How much did he know about what was going on inside her? How much had she inadvertently revealed? And by what means: her words, her body language? Or had he picked up the raw scent of her desire? She felt a blush forming and tried to suppress it.

'You understand why I'm saying this, don't you? Not many people would have noticed, but I'm too experienced to let it pass me by. As I said, I'm convinced you can handle it, but to continue the project under the circumstances would be putting a considerable strain on your personal resources. It wouldn't be fair of me to allow you to go through with it without giving you the option of pulling out.'

Melanie's blush had conquered and was suffusing her face with crimson. She knew exactly what he meant, and she could have wept with the shame of it. The easy thing to do now would be just to nod and hurry from the room, never again to sit at his desk bandying management theory, feeling the warmth of his smile when she impressed

9

him with her grasp of the subject, marvelling at the breadth and depth of his knowledge as he expounded to her. It would be the easy thing, but it would also be utterly, utterly unbearable. Biting her lip to summon her resolve, she shook her head gently, and kept shaking it as she struggled to stammer out something comprehensible.

'You've obviously realised what I hadn't intended you should ever know,' she began at last. 'You must be used to female students having feelings towards you, and I don't suppose you think much of it, but I promise I won't let it get in the way of the project, and I hope I'll be able to hide it better in future.'

He studied her earnestly. 'I'm sure you will,' he said after what seemed like an age. 'If you're quite sure you're strong enough, I'll be happy to have you as my project student. It would also be valuable training for you, of course. When you're playing the game for real in the boardroom of some big multinational, you'll be very glad you learned to hide your true feelings.'

Melanie savoured her reprieve. She had no hope of ever experiencing the joys she'd imagined a little while ago, but she could still profit from an academic relationship with him for the rest of the term. That would be better than nothing.

'Of course,' he went on – and there was a new, more playful tone in his voice now – 'of course, it remains true that the circumstances place you under an unwarranted strain and, with examinations looming, a student needs to keep herself as free as possible of unnecessary stress.'

Melanie looked up at him enquiringly. He was smiling warmly now.

'And one must think of the tutor, also.' He let her digest this for a moment before continuing. 'Perhaps I'm more skilled at hiding things, but hasn't it occurred to you that I might find you very attractive too?'

Melanie gripped the edge of the desk. Could she believe her ears? Were her lurching emotions distorting her hearing?

'Having glimpsed your naked soul beneath your armour, I find I have a strong desire to see your body naked also.' He stood up. Prising her hand from the desk, he held it quivering in both of his. *'I feel sure you will grant me that. Self-control during tutorials is essential, but the more we exercise it, the more we are entitled to relax it afterwards, don't you think?'*

She didn't answer. A brief glance into his eyes, so radiant now with desire, was enough to convince her that he was sincere, that he wasn't mocking her for her weakness. She stood to face him. She knew she was betraying her resolution. She knew she'd given away too much, that she had, in relation to the terms she'd set herself before the tutorial, failed. But that didn't seem to matter any more. It didn't matter because what was happening transcended winning and losing, success and failure. She began to undo her clothing with her free hand. It was his will to see her naked, and she would submit to his will, in that, in everything.

'You're very quiet this evening,' said Mike Heppenstall. 'Something on your mind?'

Melanie switched off those delicious memories of her final term with Phillip Drew, those earnest, academic and entirely proper tutorials which were invariably followed by evenings and nights of joyful submission to tyrannical desire. She drained the last drop of wine from her glass and turned her professional smile onto Mike.

'Just the Castadiosa contract,' she said. 'It's going to be an important one for us, assuming Charles gets it signed this weekend as he promised. But you're quite right, Mike. I shouldn't be thinking about work. So, tell me what delights *you've* got in store for the weekend.'

But Mike had nothing interesting to impart. That didn't surprise her one bit. Mike was the dullest and weakest link in her team. The Castadiosa bid had been hard work for everyone, and he hadn't entirely pulled

11

his weight. Once the project started in earnest there'd be no room for passengers.

But now there was a much more pressing problem to occupy herself with: Kirsty. Damn that girl! she thought. But she smiled a big smile as she wished her team a good weekend and made her way out to her car.

2

Homeward Bound

When Charles Bermont set up the firm, he picked the best creative minds Iain Cuthbertson's money could buy. Things worked well at first and the firm earned itself a reputation in its first two years that had helped it survive the increasing uncertainties of the next two, when contracts began to fall by the wayside. That was when Charles called on his old friend Phillip Drew.

Phillip delivered a characteristically penetrating report on the company and its prospects, identifying the Creative Design Team as the problem. It had never really gelled; its individual talents had never come together as a team. The choices were stark: either start from scratch with the kind of creative guru who attracts talent like a magnet, or bring in a top-flight charismatic manager to meld the existing talent into an effective unit, dovetailing their strengths and cancelling out their weaknesses. Neither approach could be guaranteed, but he (Phillip Drew) considered the second to be the less risky. His final recommendation was: Find yourself a managerial wizard and offer twice the salary you were paying before.

That was what the report said. What Phillip said to Charles over a game of golf was: 'I believe I know just the person for you, old boy, but you'll have to have a little faith. She's young, she's inexperienced, and she's female.' Charles missed an easy putt on his next shot.

Now, driving slowly home through the city traffic, that same young female was thinking about Kirsty, her newest recruit and one of the key elements in the remedy she'd put together for the malaise that had previously afflicted its five male members. Kirsty had been slower to blend into the team than Melanie would have wished. She was talented, and the men respected her for it, but she was too quiet. Melanie had hoped she would take over much of her own role as feminine grit in the masculine oyster, but that, it seemed, wasn't her style. And now Melanie had caught her with her hand up her skirt and she'd run away in shame.

Melanie pictured her as she'd last seen her and smiled wryly to herself. She'd seen men masturbate often enough, and it was always a sure-fire turn on for her to watch Mark take his lovely cock in his hand and stroke its long thick shaft, or rub the slickening glans with his finger, but she'd never seen a woman do it before and hadn't expected the sight could have such an effect on her. The thought of it now brought a pleasant tingle to her loins. More than pleasant; urgent, insistent. Perhaps she could stop somewhere, just for five minutes . . .

But no. She had to get a handle on the problem before she could think of pleasure. She posed herself one of those multiple-choice questions the text books were so fond of:

Question: You catch a subordinate masturbating. Do you:
- *(a) go out quietly and come in again making lots of noise?*
- *(b) pretend you haven't noticed and just carry on as normal?*
- *(c) sack the person on the spot?*
- *(d) get your hands in your pants and join in the fun?*
- *(e) none of the above (please specify).*

Melanie liked to play this game when she had a problem. Not that the text books were much good in the really interesting cases like this, but it helped her focus. Option (a): well, that would have been the thing to do if she'd had her wits about her. Too late now, though. Likewise option (b); her stupid open-mouthed stare had made it pretty obvious that she'd seen exactly what was going on. Option (c) was a complete non-starter. For one thing, Kirsty was far too valuable and, for another, what the hell was wrong with a surreptitious wank when you think nobody's looking!

Option (d) would have been interesting, wouldn't it? What a difference it might have made if Kirsty had turned to see her with her hand in her own knickers! Again, it was too late, but the principle – of complicity and fellow-feeling – could be an important element in resolving the problem.

So that left option (e), as she knew it must. Well, the first thing she'd have to do would be to talk to the girl. Perhaps this was a good time to stop the car after all; Kirsty would be home by now, and the sooner she got her on the phone, the better. Melanie pulled off the main road and parked in a leafy suburban side street. She took out her mobile phone and scrolled through its memory bank until she found the number. As the phone dialled, she pictured again that elegant artistic hand with its slender fingers and pale ochre-painted nails pressing into the damp fabric of the panties. Melanie's free hand wandered to her own belly and by the time the answering machine picked up at the other end, she was gently massaging her mons through her skirt. She heard the recorded message – Kirsty's familiar soprano sounding as cheerful as if nothing untoward had happened – and waited for the tone.

'Kirsty,' she said. 'It's me, Mel. Listen, I'm sorry about this afternoon. I didn't mean to embarrass you, honestly. If you're there, please pick up the phone. We'll talk it through. Get past it. No sweat. Hell, we all do it, don't we! Please pick up, or call me later on my home number. I'll be in all evening. All night. Any time.'

It was the best she could do for the moment, but somehow she doubted Kirsty would call back. She was already beginning to suspect that there might be more to this than there seemed at first sight. Maybe Kirsty was unhappy in her job and this was just a symptom? Maybe she was in love with one of the guys and it wasn't reciprocated? Maybe she had some problem that had nothing to do with the office?

Suddenly, Melanie was aware of how little she knew about Kirsty, compared to the men. She felt guilty. She should have realised that a girl like that would need more attention, more support from her manager than the others. Melanie resolved to make up for any deficiency, starting as soon as she could get in touch with her. Right now, she wanted to get home and put the day's events behind her.

Oh yes, and she wanted to satisfy that urge that had arisen back there in the office and that wasn't going to go away of its own accord. Right here and now? Why not? She could hear the busy traffic on the main road a few yards behind her, but there was no sign of life in the side street. She stroked her mons again and felt the fire of lust flare up.

But no. Better idea. Mark would be home already and in the kitchen, preparing something good for dinner. Yes, that would be the place for it. She licked her lips as she started the engine and pulled away from the kerb.

Mark was, as she'd predicted, in the kitchen. He heard her come in but didn't look up as he called out his familiar 'Hi, Mel. Had a good day?' The aroma of shallots sautéing in butter and white wine accompanied his words out into the hallway.

'As if!' called Melanie. This was her usual response.

'Great,' replied Mark as he heard her footsteps behind him in the kitchen. She hadn't stopped to take off her coat, but this didn't surprise him. Before settling in for the evening, Melanie liked to patrol her territory like a she-lion returning to her lair after a day's hunt. She'd always start with the kitchen if he was in it, but she'd have covered the entire flat before taking off her day clothes and washing off the city grime in the shower. Even then, she'd need to party a little during their evening meal before her energy level subsided enough to keep her in one place, on the sofa, say, or on the rug in front of the fire.

She put her arms around him from behind and kissed his neck. He appeared barely to notice as he diced a chicken breast ready for the pan. 'I had a good day, too,' he said, even though she hadn't asked. She never did.

Melanie hoisted herself onto the work surface alongside him. 'If you promise not to breathe a word to anyone,' she whispered, 'I'll tell you something interesting.'

Mark promised.

'You know Kirsty, the girl in our office?'

'Of course,' said Mark. 'What about her?'

'Well, I went back to the office after the rest of us had left this afternoon, and guess what I saw.' Mark wasn't given so much as a second to indulge his fertile imagination. 'She was in there on her own, and she was –' she paused for effect '– masturbating.'

Mark whistled. 'That's amazing!' he said. 'I just never knew women did it too. My! You learn something new every day.'

'Okay, wise guy,' said Melanie. 'It may be an everyday experience for you, but *I've* never seen it before.'

'What a sheltered life you've led,' Mark chaffed.

'Well, I've seen it now,' said Melanie. 'She was sitting with her back to me, and she was doing – this.'

Melanie had thrown her coat onto a chair and she now demonstrated what she'd seen Melanie do. She let her left hand play with her breast, squeezing the nipple through her clothing. With her right hand she hiked up her skirt and reached in to press the soft flesh of her vulva through the bright yellow satin of her panties. She felt those flames again as her clitoris firmed to her touch.

Mark finally stopped what he was doing and turned to look. 'Hey,' he said with a knowing drawl, the realisation having dawned. 'It turned you on, didn't it? Go on, admit it. You watched her and it turned you on!'

'Oh, I admit it all right,' said Melanie. 'I'd never have thought it but it really did turn me on. I could hardly contain myself on the way home, but I know how you like to see me wank, so I held back. Wasn't that nice of me?' She pulled her skirt up further to let him savour the sight of her pale thighs bulging over the dark close-meshed stocking tops.

'Very considerate,' said Mark. He tried to keep one eye on the chicken, now searing with the shallots. He thought he could detect the aroma of her sex above that of the cooking food, but he might have been imagining it. In any case, it was making him horny, and he could feel his penis straining inside his pants.

'Of course,' Mark went on, 'there's nothing strange about a bloke like me finding that sort of thing erotic.' He licked his lips and rubbed his swelling member through his trousers as he watched her. 'But what does it say about you, huh?'

'I've a feeling you're going to tell me,' she said, pushing her hips forward and spreading her thighs a little more. Her fingers were now starting to work their way behind the taut cloth that barely covered her swollen labia.

'It's what I've always maintained,' he said, turning off the heat under the chicken for safety. 'Women get off on women. We men just can't supply all the erotic stimuli you need. You have to supplement our puny efforts with your own.'

Melanie was familiar with Mark's thesis. She'd frequently been tempted to counter it with tales of her trysts with Phillip Drew, but since these had taken place while she and Mark were already supposed to be an item, she felt it would be too risky. Instead, she'd accuse him of just making excuses for his own shortcomings, but now, after seeing Kirsty play with herself like that, she might just be prepared to acknowledge that he had a point.

'Well, how about putting up some competition,' she taunted. Her tumid vulva was exposed now. The crotch of her panties, having given up its attempt to protect her modesty, was rolled up in a thin yellow thong on one side, cutting into the crease between thigh and pubis. She ignored the discomfort of this as she teased out the fleshy ripples of her inner labia with her fingers. The sight of these thrilled her spectator, who took up her challenge and reached for his zip. An instant later, his long stiffening cock flopped from his open flies, and his hairy scrotum followed suit. He moaned at the relief of it, and also with anticipation of the sight she was preparing for him, her fingers already working at the little pink button of flesh that was quickly growing into the proud firm beak he so admired. She had the most prominent clitoris of any woman he'd known, and he loved to lash it with his tongue and roll it between his lips. Now, though, he would do those things only in his imagination, since it was for her to pleasure herself and for him to watch.

Melanie's fingers slid wetly along the length of her vulva again and again. She was aware of what Mark was doing with his cock just feet away from her, and it helped heighten her pleasure, but her mind's eye would not release those scenes of Kirsty in the studio. She saw again the sensuous motions of her body in tantalising rear view. Then she relived the moment when Kirsty turned to confront her voyeur, her fingers still pressing,

pressing between her legs. Melanie tried to bring that frozen image to life in her mind, to imagine those fingers moving and probing as hers were now doing, but the image remained stubbornly still. Nevertheless, she could feel her first orgasm begin to form in the depths of her belly and she slowed her stroking to delay and intensify it.

Her mobile phone lay by her side on the work top, still displaying Kirsty's number. Melanie placed her hand on it as if this might help re-animate her mental image of the girl herself. The smooth curvy feel of the phone gave her a thrill and, without thinking, she picked it up and pressed it against her inner thigh, at the same time inadvertently pressing the re-dial button. The cool hardness of the plastic against her soft warm flesh brought her orgasm quickly on. 'Mmm ...' she moaned, and again, 'Mmm ... Yes ...' Then, to the accompaniment of Kirsty's gentle voice reciting the recorded message once again, she was coming, and that mental image broke into sensuous motion, the fingers working in sympathy with her own. 'Kirsty,' Melanie moaned, half under her breath. 'Kirsty, Kirsty, Kirsty!' But her words were lost beneath Mark's throaty grunts, and she felt the warm spurt of his semen as it struck her groin and coated itself in sticky gobbets around her dancing fingers.

Their orgasms were the first of many that evening. Mark managed to finish the cooking despite his continued arousal – which Melanie exploited mercilessly with her hands and lips – and they ate and drank and made love for several hours. Mark was not at all put out that she'd been so aroused by another woman. When it came to other males he could be insanely jealous, but that was because he saw them as a threat to their relationship. Otherwise he was completely open-minded. For Melanie, though, it was something to marvel at, a hitherto unsuspected aspect of her sexual make-up, a new erotic avenue that she'd have to explore. She was grateful for Mark's encouragement in this, even if he had an ulterior motive, namely that it was bound to mean more exciting sex for him too.

During their respites that evening, Melanie called Kirsty's number several times. Each time she got the answering machine. Each time she left the same message: everything's cool, let's talk, please call back. But Kirsty didn't call back, and Melanie became more and more worried.

Mark tried to reassure her. She's just shy, he opined. She'll be over it by tomorrow. But Melanie wasn't to be cheered so easily. What if there was more to it? They speculated that she might fancy one of the guys and wondered which it might be. There were three prime candidates: Steve, Tony and Adrian. None of them would be a good bet for a girl like Kirsty: Adrian because he was gay, Tony because he was already spoken for, and Steve because he was the type who avoided romantic attachments with any girl likely to give him a problem when he got tired of her, i.e. after three or four weeks of vigorous but disdainful shagging.

Certainly, Melanie had never witnessed anything remotely resembling a budding romance, but a girl like Kirsty could harbour secret longings and nobody would be any the wiser. Her best guess was Steve, since she herself had been more than usually flirtatious with him that afternoon and he'd responded by strutting his stuff quite provocatively. That could well have been what had turned poor Kirsty on. However, Melanie didn't confide that to Mark; he might not have approved.

After one last attempt to talk to Kirsty, Melanie gave up for the night. Anyway, she was tired of thinking about the wretched girl, and almost exhausted by all the love-making she'd been indirectly responsible for. Almost exhausted, but when she and Mark finally lay together in their big double bed, the scent of sex on their naked bodies proved irresistible, and she submitted once more to the long stiff member that nosed imperiously between her buttocks and thighs as she lay face down. For a moment she thought it wanted entry to her anus, but after a few deliciously teasing strokes it moved to her vagina and slid home once again in a single easy movement. They lay still for a while before he began the slow deliberate tensing and twisting he knew she would appreciate after so many hot orgasms. The sensations filled her, radiating outward from her sex, relaxing her in body and mind. She would experience no orgasm this time, just the joy of his hard muscular body enfolding hers inside and out as she drifted towards sleep. She thought no more of Kirsty now, just of Mark, the man in her life. He wasn't Phillip Drew, but he was wonderful all the same, in his way.

3

Reaching Out

It was late morning on the following day, Saturday. Melanie pressed the top bell at the heavily reinforced front door of a converted town house in one of the not-too-notorious parts of the city. She waited, then pressed again, this time keeping her finger on the button for a good fifteen seconds. When she released it, she heard the electronic clicks and scratches that told her the door phone had been picked up. Then she heard breathing. Finally, a thin voice queried 'Who is it?'

'Kirsty? It's me, Melanie. I've got to talk to you.'

There was more breathing, then the voice came again, sounding weaker and further away: 'I've written a letter. My resignation. I'm sorry.' Then the speaker went dead. Kirsty had put down the door phone.

Melanie pressed the bell without pausing until the speaker came live again.

'Let me in, Kirsty, unless you want the whole neighbourhood to hear what you get up to when your boss's back is turned.'

There was total silence, but the speaker did not go dead.

'I'm not bluffing, Kirsty. I think you realise that.'

The buzzer sounded and Melanie pushed the heavy door open. She headed up the stairs to the top landing where a thin girl wrapped in a bathrobe stood framed in an open doorway. It was Kirsty, hair down, face bare of make-up. Melanie was glad she'd dressed down for this visit. She wore faded jeans and a dull-coloured sweater, her make-up was minimal and her hair un-styled. They were meeting on equal terms in that respect, at least.

Melanie followed Kirsty into the flat and closed the door behind her. She looked around. It was quite a large flat by inner-city standards, and the paucity of furniture added to the sense of space. The main room had a sofa, a coffee table, and a couple of beanbags, but very little else. The walls were partly covered with clusters of sketches in charcoal, pastel and watercolour depicting designs for fabrics, dresses and other garments, many worn by willowy human figures represented by a few lines and daubs of thin colour, yet surprisingly evocative of feminine grace. Beyond the main room Melanie glimpsed a small kitchen and a clutter of unwashed dishes. Another door – closed – evidently led to the bedroom and bathroom. The overall impression was of energy and imagination, but also of solitude and carelessness. It wasn't the kind of place Melanie could have contemplated living in. She shuddered a little, then turned to Kirsty, who seemed slimmer and slighter than ever as she hugged her bathrobe tight around her body.

'Kirsty, love. What happened yesterday doesn't mat-ter a damn. Nobody knows about it except us two –' Mark didn't count as far as Melanie was concerned; the only secrets she kept from him were her own '– and nobody will ever know. Something turned you on, and you did what any sensible girl would do. I'm only sorry I blundered in when I did. I embarrassed you, and I take the blame for that, but there's no need to be embar-rassed, no need at all. Hell, I've done the same as you lots of times.' She paused to see if her message was getting through, but Kirsty seemed hardly to be listen-ing.

24

'As for resigning . . . Resign! Over a trivial thing like that! If you've already sent that letter, I'll tear it up without even opening it. The team needs you, and we'll need you all the more next week when the Castadiosa contract comes in.'

Kirsty spoke at last. 'I know you're trying to make me feel better, Melanie, and I won't deny I felt embarrassed and ashamed yesterday, but it isn't just that. I guess that just helped me see things more clearly. I'm grateful to you for giving me the job, and I'm really sorry to be letting you down, but it just isn't going to work out. I know that now. It can't be helped.'

'Oh, Kirsty! You've only been with us a few months. Things are just beginning for you, and for the team. We're building something good at B&C, and you're as much a part of it as any of us. And think about your career. I'm not saying you have to stay with us forever, but you won't find a better opportunity just at this particular time, I'm certain.'

'You don't understand. It's me. It's the way I feel. I can't bear it, day after day, to see . . .' She stopped and bit her lip. Melanie thought she knew how the sentence might have ended.

'Are you in love, Kirsty? Is that it? Is it Steve?'

Kirsty started at this, and Melanie felt she was on the right track.

'Look, there's probably not much I can do to help, but whatever I can, I will. I'll be your friend. We'll hatch some little plot together and see if we can't land him for you.'

She could tell from Kirsty's look of horror that this wasn't the kind of girl-talk she needed. The poor girl must have got it bad, she thought. She remembered how she'd felt towards Phillip when she worshipped him from afar. She too would have thought it sacrilege to talk of plots and conspiracies. But Steve! She tried to see Steve in the same light as Phillip, but the attempt was laughable. This just made her feel further at sea, more remote than ever from understanding how Kirsty's mind worked. She began to realise that she was wasting her time here, that she simply hadn't a clue how to deal with the girl. The only card left was to plead for time.

'Give it a little longer, Kirsty, that's all I ask. You're upset now – and that's mainly my fault – so it's a bad time to make such a vital decision. Come in to work on Monday and we'll find time to talk about it some more. Believe me, I know how you feel, but quitting isn't the answer. Love comes and goes, but you have a great career ahead of you that'll see you through a lifetime of love affairs if only you don't throw it away now. Promise me you'll come in on Monday?'

Kirsty remained silent, the glint of a tear in the corner of one eye. Melanie felt defeated. She held back an almost overwhelming desire to take the girl by her flimsy shoulders and shake some of her own strength of character into her. But Kirsty was Kirsty, and Melanie couldn't alter that fact. With a final plea just to think about it and not be too hasty, she turned towards the door and left the flat.

Melanie slowly descended the first flight of stairs to the half-landing between floors and paused. Then she sat down on the top step of the next flight and let her mind run loosely over the situation in the hope that she might come up with a new angle. She played her little game.

Question: A discussion with a colleague has ended in a total failure of communication. Is this because:
  (a) you were speaking different languages?
  (b) the one doing most of the talking should have been doing most of the listening, and vice versa?
  (c) one of you knows something that the other one doesn't?

Option (a) was probably true in a metaphorical sense, she thought. Option (b) was even closer to the mark. Much closer. She'd done her usual thing, hadn't she. She'd gone in there with her own analysis at the forefront of her mind and had put all her effort into getting it across. Kirsty had obviously been reluctant to talk, but if Melanie had given her more opportunity, and more encouragement, might she not have opened up a little? Perhaps, referring now to option (c), she might have revealed something that Melanie hadn't taken into account at all.

As she pursued these thoughts, the front door of the building opened far below and Melanie heard the slow trudge of footsteps ascending the stairs from landing to landing. Eventually a woman appeared on the landing below where she was sitting. She was tall, brown-skinned, and in her mid thirties. She was dressed, like Melanie, in jeans and sweater. She was carrying two plastic supermarket bags full of groceries.

The woman looked curiously at Melanie as she approached the only door on the landing and, resting the bags at her feet, riffled in her handbag for her keys. Melanie noticed how handsome she was. She noticed too that her clothes, although casual, were of high quality in both fabric and design. They were also very close fitting, emphasising a full-bosomed athletic figure that almost made Melanie gasp.

The woman kept glancing up at Melanie as she inserted the key and opened the door. Then she picked up her bags and started into the flat. Before disappearing inside, she stopped and turned to Melanie once more. 'You know, honey,' she said in an accent that was pure Upper East Side, 'if that girl's thrown you out – and I can't see why she would – you can take tea at *my* table any time of the day.' She paused to see what effect her words might have on the dumb-struck Melanie. Then she went inside, adding as she did so, 'Just ring my bell,' and pointing to the number four painted on her door.

Then she was gone, the door was closed again, all was quiet. Melanie sat for three or four minutes more, her face, if there'd been anyone there to see it, a picture of dawning realisation, self-reproach for her stupidity hitherto, and – last but by no means least – erotic arousal. Finally, she raised herself to her feet and made her way back up the stairs.

Melanie tapped on Kirsty's door. It opened an inch or two and Kirsty's nose and tear-stained eyes appeared. Then it opened wide. Kirsty, still in her bathrobe, held a mug of coffee, and the aroma reached Melanie's nostrils to give an additional fillip to the strange new appetites that were awakening within her.

'I . . . I thought you'd gone,' said Kirsty in a whisper.

'I've just had an offer of tea,' said Melanie. 'But I think I'd really prefer some of that coffee right now. If you've got some to spare.'

Melanie was amazed at how wonderful it was to be touched in her most intimate places by another woman. Amazed, but by this time not really surprised. She was already so much ablaze with desire when she re-entered the flat that it had taken few words before the slim, fragile-seeming blonde had understood her purpose and they had shared their first kiss. But the sight of the naked body when the bathrobe slid to the floor, the ivory skin, the twin hemispheres of her breasts, round and deep, nipples prinked in anticipation, and that smooth round tummy with the neat tuft of hair where it tucked itself away between cream-coloured thighs, that sight gave Melanie a thrill that made her belly throb. Still clad in her crisply laundered jeans and loose woollen sweater, she had taken Kirsty into her arms, clasping those frail shoulders as gently as if she were taking up a fledgling that had fallen from its nest, but finding strength and vigour in them as the girl pressed herself against her and clasped her in return, first about the waist, then the buttocks. The softness of that skin enthralled her. She wanted to lick it, to pluck at it with her teeth, but her mouth was not yet ready to relinquish the pleasure of those soft sweet lips, that probing tongue.

'I'm new to this, Kirsty,' whispered Melanie when the kiss had temporarily spent itself. 'I need you to help me. To show me the way.'

'There is no *the* way,' replied Kirsty in a voice charged with restrained passion. 'There's only our way, what we want, what our instincts tell us to do.'

The kiss rekindled, but now Melanie could not endure to be fully clothed any longer. She started to pull up her sweater, then felt the delicious chill of the sitting-room air on her buttocks as Kirsty's nimble fingers undid her jeans and pulled them and her panties down to her knees. Then Kirsty was kissing her belly, stroking her inner thigh, teasing her pubic hair into a dark springy fleece. Melanie knew she was wet, and she knew that Kirsty would be savouring the scent of it. She wanted to bathe Kirsty's face in that fluid so that she might lick it from her lips and chin, as she liked to do with Mark. But this wasn't Mark. It wasn't even a man. It was a woman. It was Kirsty.

Melanie dropped easily onto the sofa as Kirsty finished undressing her. She looked at her own breasts as the girl stroked and fondled them, cupping them one by one in her hands as if to compare their weight. They were the same breasts she saw every day when she showered or undressed, yet now, with Kirsty's slender fingers dimpling their soft bulk or lovingly tracing the swelling rosettes, they seemed different. And then she realised that everything would be different now. Every part of her that Kirsty touched would be different. Every response, however often she'd made the same response before, would be different because it was a woman she was responding to. The tumescence of her nipples, as Kirsty kissed them and flicked them with her tongue, was different. The engorgement of her labia, where Kirsty's hand was now straying, was as never before.

Then Kirsty's head was between her thighs, pushing them apart as she pressed her face into Melanie's seeping slit. Melanie gasped. She put a hand out to Kirsty's head and ravelled her fingers in the unkempt blonde hair, then let it drift to Kirsty's face, lightly touching her cheek before drooping to where those busy lips played with her clitoris, where that warm moist tongue probed her cleft. It was as if she needed the evidence of her fingers' touch, as well as her other senses, before she could be sure this wasn't a dream, that it was really happening.

As Kirsty licked and probed and sucked, Melanie came. It wasn't a particularly spectacular orgasm – she was still too self-conscious, too aware of the novelty of her situation, for that – but it was a deep and honest one. Out there on the landing, before making up her mind to go back up the stairs to Kirsty's door, she'd had doubts about her course of action. She knew it was her only chance to keep Kirsty from quitting her job, from leaving her in the lurch with the Castadiosa contract, but she wasn't sure she'd be able to carry it off. That wasn't because of any moral scruple – with Melanie, pragmatism ruled – but through doubt that the unfamiliar homoerotic urges she'd experienced so far that weekend would extend far enough. She had no doubts now. Making love to Kirsty was divine. And there was still so much to come, so much to learn, so many new experiences!

Then she suddenly remembered. That telephone call! Hell! The note that had started this whole thing going, what had it said? 12.30? That was it. She was to call at

12.30 without fail. Melanie pulled Kirsty's head out from between her legs. The poor girl thought for a moment she was being rejected, but the truth, when Melanie checked her watch and told her about the call she had to make, turned her momentary pain into anger.

'What! We were just getting started! How can you think of business at a time like this? Am I such a poor lover? Do I bore you that much?'

Melanie tried to soothe her ruffled ego. 'You're a wonderful lover, Kirsty, really you are. You gave me a lovely little orgasm just then with your beautiful lips and tongue, but you've got to remember, I'm a raw beginner. We'll have to start slowly, but I learn fast and, believe me, I want to learn everything there is. Now that we've got together, I want you as often as I can get you. I want to taste every inch of you. But right now, I've got to make this call. Sorry.'

Kirsty grudgingly let her roll off the sofa and reach for her handbag where it lay on the floor. Melanie found the mobile phone and the crumpled note. Stretched out on the floor, she dialled the number.

A woman's voice answered the phone. Melanie recognised it as Charles Bermont's Personal Assistant, Jeanette. 'Hi, Jeanette, it's Mel. Charles was expecting me to phone.'

'Mr Bermont was expecting your call at 12.30. It is now nearly 12.45. I'll see if he's still available.'

Melanie ostentatiously mouthed the word 'cow' at the phone and gestured to Kirsty to join her on the carpet. This had the intended effect of making Kirsty feel included in the proceedings, a kind of co-conspirator. With a mischievous grin, she settled herself alongside Melanie's outstretched thighs and began stroking and kneading her buttocks.

'Hi, Charles,' said Melanie into the phone when she heard his voice. 'What's the news?'

The news she'd been led to expect was that the contract would have been signed after the morning's round of golf and that Melanie was to get her entire team started on it first thing Monday morning. But things had evidently not gone to plan.

'Bit of a hold-up, I'm afraid,' said Charles. 'Like our bid, but not convinced we can deliver. Heard a few unfavourable reports about one or two of last year's efforts. Assured them everything's hunky-dory now, but . . .'

Kirsty's fingers were probing between her buttocks. It tickled, and Melanie gave a little snort.

'Nothing to laugh at, Mel!' said Charles indignantly. 'This contract is a must-win. You know that!'

'Sorry, Charles,' she said, biting her lip. 'Touch of hay fever. Fully appreciate how important it is. Anything I can do?' Charles's clipped speech patterns were infectious.

'Matter of fact, there is,' Charles answered. 'Would you mind awfully coming down here this evening? We've arranged another meeting with Castadiosa.'

Melanie let out a squawk. Kirsty, who could perfectly well hear both sides of the conversation, had at that precise moment pushed her fingers deep into her vagina.

'I say!' said Charles. 'It's not asking too much, surely. We all have to pull together on this one. They know we've had our problems, and the fact is, you're probably the only one who can convince them we've got past them.'

Melanie was writhing on Kirsty's fingers like a worm on a fisherman's hook. It was all she could do to prevent her pleasure from expressing itself audibly. Charles took her silence for extreme reluctance and was starting to get angry.

'Look here, Melanie,' he went on, 'if we don't land this one we could be heading for serious trouble. Might even have to lay people off. Haven't had that experience yet, have you: telling your best workers they haven't got a job any more?'

Melanie managed to control herself enough to allay his fears. 'Heavens, Charles, if I'm needed there, I'll come. No question. I was just wondering how to break it to Mark. We'd planned a special evening together tonight. Anniversary, you know.'

This was totally untrue, but she had to regain the advantage somehow.

'Ah.' Charles's anger evaporated into sympathy. 'Quite understand, old girl. Sorry, and all that. Tell you what! Why don't you bring him along with you? We'll get the business over with, then we'll help you celebrate. Make a weekend of it. I'll send a car to pick you up. Four o'clock suit?'

Melanie felt the sharp edge of a fingernail against the soft flesh of her vagina. It was clear what Kirsty thought of Charles's idea. But there was no help for it; the deal was done. Melanie rang Mark and got his ready assent to the plan. 'I'm having coffee with a friend,' she said in answer to his inevitable question, then winced as Kirsty violently extracted her fingers in revenge for this further denial. Then she put away the phone.

'We've got a little time left before I have to leave, Kirsty love,' said Melanie, her voice heavy with apology. 'We can drink a little coffee, make some plans of our own for next time, and then . . .'

'And then what?' said Kirsty indignantly. 'I hate you! You drive me mad for months, flirting with the men all the time and ignoring me, then you come round here and shag me just so's I won't leave your precious team. You make phone calls in the middle of it – our first time! – and now you're going off for the whole weekend with your precious Mark!' Kirsty was showing a temper Melanie had never suspected she had. 'And now I suppose you want to kill time screwing around with me, with one eye on your watch so you won't be late. I could hit you! I could . . .'

33

Her temper faded as quickly as it had come, and Kirsty sulked. Melanie took advantage of the lull to put her arm around her shoulder and kiss her on the cheek.

'I know, Kirsty love,' she said softly. 'I'm a bastard, aren't I? I don't blame you for wanting to punish me, but –' she pinned Kirsty to the carpet by her wrists and rolled on top of her '– but I don't think you're tough enough to do it. Are you?'

Kirsty submitted without a struggle. 'No,' she whimpered, 'I'm not.' And then a gleam lit up her moist blue eyes. 'But I know someone who is.'

4

Tea and Retribution

Melanie tapped on the door marked four. It opened. 'Hiiii, honey,' said Arlene. 'You've come for your tea, right?' She beamed at Melanie and straightened her figure to maximum effect. 'That's the thing about you Brits, you just can't resist a nice cuppa tea.' She gave that last phrase something approximating the Yorkshire twang she'd heard on the TV adverts. 'Come on in.'

Melanie went in.

Kirsty had easily decoded Melanie's reference to an offer of tea. It was one of Arlene's favourite lines where 'Brits' were concerned, and she'd seen Arlene get out of her taxi from her kitchen window. The conclusion that they'd met on the stairs was an obvious one. Now, feeling distinctly miffed at Melanie's unfeeling behaviour, she'd sent her down to her friend, confidante and occasional lover, who, she said, would know what to do. Melanie had been persuaded that it was the only way she could make amends, so she agreed to do as she was told. Besides, she'd been intrigued by the sight of Arlene on the landing and was secretly glad of the entrée, despite being more than a little apprehensive at what she might be letting herself in for.

Inside, the flat was a complete contrast to Kirsty's, even though the general layout was the same. Here there was furniture where there had just been empty space, colour where there had been plain drab. The place had an air of comfort and warmth that Kirsty's lacked. It spoke of a large outward-going personality at ease with itself.

Melanie was invited to sit on the sofa while Arlene made tea. She chatted amiably and confidentially from the kitchen. 'That girl throw you out, honey? She ain't got her head screwed on right, if you ask me. Pretty little thing like you! But don't go taking it personally, now. Kirsty's got her head up her ass over that lady boss of hers. Got it real bad. Diddles herself to sleep 'most every night just thinking of her, and the boss-bitch not even noticing.'

Melanie was excited to hear herself referred to in this way. It stirred her to think that she could have caused such heartache, however unwittingly. She tried to picture little Kirsty in bed at night, 'diddling' herself to sleep.

'Say, what do they call you, hon?'

'Mel –' Melanie caught her tongue just in time '– issa,' she answered. 'Melissa.'

'Melissa, huh,' said Arlene. 'Nice name. I'm Arlene. You and me gonna be friends, I just know it.'

Arlene appeared with a tray of tea things. She put it on the coffee table in front of the sofa and sat on one of the armchairs opposite. Leaning over to lift the teapot ready to pour, she looked into Melanie's face and asked in rich suggestive tones, 'Tell me, Melissa. You like milk and sugar in your tea? Or do you like it dark and bitter?'

Melanie wasn't sure how to answer this. Something told her it wasn't the one-lump-or-two kind of question it masqueraded as.

'Let me put it another way. I can do frills and lace and long silk gloves. Or . . .'

She nodded towards a point behind Melanie's left shoulder and Melanie turned to look. On a chair against the wall lay a tangle of fine black leather. Melanie made out a halter with studs, a G-string, and a contraption that clearly had something to do with breasts but which was far too skimpy to be called a bra. And there was something else, something long and coiled, of scaly plaited leather, interwoven and glistening. It sent a sudden chill down her spine.

Melanie still hadn't stated her choice. She looked at Arlene, who looked back intently.

'Hmmm.' Arlene sounded thoughtful. 'Something in your eye tells me you just ain't up for frills today, Melissa. Frills are for good girls, and something tells me you ain't been a good girl just lately. Sometimes a girl like you gets herself a little bit outta line; in need of a little correction. Ain't I right?'

Melanie shuddered and looked again at that coiled thing. She knew from Arlene's voice that the choice she'd offered a few seconds earlier had been withdrawn. There was only one acceptable response to that last question, and it wasn't 'No'.

'Arlene can always tell when a girl been up to no good. But Arlene can bring her back to the path of righteousness.' She picked out each syllable of that last word, giving equal weight to all. 'I think you know that, don't you? I think you want Arlene to make everything all right again.'

Melanie's stomach turned over. She didn't know if it was fear she felt or longing. It was as if Arlene's words had opened an unsuspected vein of guilt deep within her, guilt for the way she'd treated Kirsty. And, yes, she did want to make it all right again. Just at this moment she wanted that more than anything else in the whole world. She nodded.

'Just take a sip of your tea now, honey, then we'll go into the other room.'

Melanie did as she was told.

* * *

37

The other room was Arlene's bedroom, but that wasn't immediately apparent on entering it. A heavy black curtain cut it in two and, as Melanie later learned, the usual appurtenances of a single woman's bedroom were crammed into the other half. What she saw as the door swung open and Arlene flipped a light switch might have been a stage set for a magic act, or a film studio where a vampire movie was due to be shot. As well as the curtain, the other walls were draped in black except where three or four full-length mirrors stood at intervals, reflecting the discreet pools of light cast by ceiling spotlights onto the reddish-brown carpet. In the centre of the space stood an object that Melanie failed to recognise for several seconds. It was a butcher's block, solid and squat, surfaced with deep cross-cuts of untreated hardwood packed together to receive the cleaver with a resonant *clunk* as it sliced through muscle and bone and sinew. She shivered at the sight of it. Perhaps Arlene noticed this because she took a thick plush tablecloth and spread it over the block. The tablecloth was deep red in colour – fresh blood to contrast with the old, congealed spillage that was the carpet – but it was, even so, less intimidating than the sight it covered.

'I call this my Chamber of Correction,' explained Arlene proudly. 'Many folks have left this room filled with gratitude for the uplifting experiences they've had here, for the privilege of having their misdeeds whisked clean away. It'll be the same for you, Melissa my dear. Of that I'm certain.'

Melanie caught sight of herself in a mirror. The unfamiliar lighting lent her face a gauntness she hardly recognised, but the reddish reflection from the carpet disguised the pallor she might have expected to see as she contemplated what was about to happen. She thought of turning her back and leaving the room, the flat, the building. But she thought of Kirsty, and of this spectacular compelling woman who was taking her by the arm and leading her into the centre of the room, and she knew she could not leave. It was going to be a challenge, but she'd always prided herself on her capacity to meet challenges head-on.

Besides, it was mostly play-acting, that was obvious. These lights, the lurid colour scheme, even the butcher's block, they were all just props in the little rituals some people needed to stimulate their flagging libidos. She, Melanie, had no need of such props, of course, but it would do no harm to play along if it pleased her new friend. No harm at all.

The block stood on a low dais fitted with a number of brass rings. Arlene directed her to bend across it and let her arms droop, allowing her wrists to be tied to the rings with soft broad leather thongs. When her ankles were similarly tied, Melanie's sense of the absurd came to the fore. Here she was, a full-grown woman who held down a highly paid responsible job and was respected by friends and colleagues alike, playing silly games in the bedroom of a perfect stranger she'd just met that morning! She smiled to herself as she settled her tummy onto the block and lifted her head to look into the mirror before her. She saw her face looking back at her, streaked silver from the high spotlights and gory brown from the carpet just a foot or two below. She saw also the reflection of the mirror on the other side of the room, and in it her own rear end, legs parted, faded jeans grading from daylight blue down to sombre purple where the shadows were deepest. She had to admit that however silly this game was, there was something thrilling about it too. And when Arlene, in businesslike fashion, leant over her to undo her jeans, sliding her hands under her stomach to get at the button and the zip, then pulling them down as far as they could go, and when she then pulled down the plain cotton panties, so redolent of the interrupted lesbian sex she'd just enjoyed with Kirsty, that thrill became all the more vibrant so that Melanie felt a tingle of expectation in her buttocks, in her quim, and in the slackening ring-muscle of her anus.

Then Arlene disappeared behind the curtain, leaving Melanie to contemplate the sight of her bare behind in the mirrors. Her buttocks shone white in the glow of the spotlight, but they cast deep shadows onto her upper thighs, and the cleft between them looked long and dark and deep. She felt a powerful wish to see into those shadows. If her wrists had been free, she would have reached back to probe there, to touch the hard puckered flesh around her bum-hole, to let her fingers slide along her throbbing slit and feel the wetness she knew was forming there. But she couldn't do that. She could move relatively freely over the block, even raising herself above it by arching her back, but there was no way she could free her arms and legs from their restraints.

From the other side of the curtain, she heard Arlene's voice, still soft and reassuring. 'This your first time, ain't it, hon? Don't need to worry, though. When some folks say, "If it don't hurt it don't work", I say, "Well, that just depends on how you go about it". When you're an expert like me, you don't need to go causing no pain. You can just bring it all out with a few gentle strokes, a few teasing flicks and switches to cleanse and purify. Loving chastisement, I call it.'

She re-emerged from behind the curtain and stepped into the spotlight. When Melanie saw her in the mirror the sight brought that tingle racing back through her body so that she squirmed in her restraints with sheer lust.

'So don't you worry none,' Arlene said. 'I may look like a devil. But I love like an angel.'

She looked demonic, that was for sure, but not like a devil exactly. More like a shaman, or a dancer in some exotic rite of expiation to a savage and demanding deity. Her hair was tied severely back so that the prominent bones of her handsome face were free to cast their own shadows in an intimidating mask of light and shade. Moulded black leather chaps covered her legs almost to the tops of her thighs so that, when her lower body was in shadow, the paler torso seemed to float out of the darkness like a genie out of a bottle. She wore the G-string Melanie had seen in the sitting room, a scant black leather triangle that emphasised the breadth and firmness of her hips and buttocks. But the most dramatic thing of all was her bosom. Her breasts, if they'd seemed large and full before when covered by her tight-fitting sweater, were scarcely to be believed now. The leather harness she wore both lifted them and compressed them at their base so that they projected forward, bare pale-brown cones of volcanic proportions, their points swollen on swollen rosettes that looked like darker, scarcely smaller breasts in their own right.

Melanie was creaming herself. She wanted to feel those breasts in her hands, against her face, any-how. She couldn't take her eyes off them, and when Arlene turned her back, she ached in her stomach until she turned around again. Then Arlene came forward to stand in front of her face.

'Take a good look, honey,' said Arlene. 'One day I'm going to let you fondle them, and suck them, and press them into your wet aching pussy. But not today. You can look all you like, but don't you touch. Understood?'

Melanie nodded. The swollen nipples bobbed tanta-lisingly in front of her face, but she made no attempt to reach them with her slavering lips.

Then Arlene picked up the whip she'd brought with her from the sitting room and moved into position. 'Remember what I said,' she said. 'It ain't gonna hurt.'

Reassured, Melanie relaxed her body, but she closed her eyes nevertheless when she heard the faint hum as this contradictory creature – seemingly half demon, half caring nurse or nanny – flicked the whip up and back, ready for the first stroke. She didn't hear the ferocious *whoosh* of the downstroke, however. Or, if she did, it was buried in the searing flash of sensation that streaked across her buttocks and raced through her body like an express train. All her muscles contracted at once. Her back arched. Her arms and legs straightened, lifting her from the block like a sprinter anticipating the crack of the starting pistol. Her head flexed back as far as it would go and her mouth opened wide as she sucked air noisily into her lungs. Then she let out a thin high-pitched squeal, holding the note at decreasing volume until her lungs were empty again. Then her body began to subside slowly back onto the block, where she lay gasping, as limp as a rag doll in a washing machine.

A hand took hold of her hair and rudely lifted her head. Arlene's face was inches from hers. 'I lied about it not hurting,' she said casually. 'Oh, don't get me wrong. I can do the loving chastisement thing all right. But, first time or not, a hard-hearted boss-bitch like you deserves to get the full treatment. Ain't that right, *Melanie*?' Arlene let go of her hair and her head flopped down.

So Arlene had known all along that she was Kirsty's unwitting tormentor. She, Melanie, should have realised. She'd been lulled into taking it all as a game, a silly sexy game, but there was, after all, more to it than that, and she was finding out the hard way. She felt the broad expanse of fire in her bottom slowly resolve itself into a throbbing stinging streak across the upper lobes of her buttocks. She felt the blood coursing through her body, making her extremities glow, her head sing. And she felt those sensations in her anus and vagina return with greater force, blossoming like some gaudy flower in a time-lapse film, growing, swamping the rest of her. At the same time, the centre of her consciousness seemed to migrate to her nether regions, so that soon she was barely aware of her torso, her arms, her head. Her whole being was in her bottom. She saw herself in the mirrors, just a pair of brightly lit buttocks, no longer white but pink, and with a raw red streak extending evenly across the top. She saw again the dark cleft between them and the deeper shadow underneath, but she no longer needed to see into that shadow, for she was there. She, Melanie Brooks, was in that cleft, inside that dripping, invisible cunt, and – and this is the strange part – she was calling for more. She could hear herself doing it, as if from a long way off. 'Again. Arlene. More. Please.'

'I knew I had you figured right,' said Arlene.

This time, Melanie didn't close her eyes. She watched in the mirror as the whip flipped back. She watched as a wave of accumulating muscular energy swept upwards from Arlene's calves to her shoulders and into her upraised arm. And, arching her back and raising her buttocks to meet it, she watched as that energy expended itself in a downstroke of awe-inspiring vigour. This time, she heard the roar of the whip. She saw its length flexing through the air as if in slow motion. And when it landed, just an inch below the first welt, it was as if someone were drawing a thin line of fire across that precise place. The fire eclipsed the sting of the previous stroke and set in train its own series of sensations which, more distinct than the first time, forked through her body picking out each muscle and organ. Melanie drank them in as a desert drinks in rain.

Just four strokes, each delivered with more force than the last, and that was enough. Melanie lay slumped on the block, gasping and moaning. She no longer asked for more. She didn't need any more, not now at any rate, not that. But she knew the game wasn't over yet. There had to be something else to come, something else she needed as she flopped across the draped butcher's table. She wasn't yet sure what it was, but she knew she needed it very badly indeed.

For a moment, sensing the stillness of the room, Melanie feared she'd been left alone, but when she lifted her head she saw that Arlene was still there, standing with her arms folded and breathing deeply as after a great exertion. Arlene wasn't looking at Melanie. She wasn't admiring her handiwork, that now brilliantly painted backside with its elegant stripes. She was looking across at something else.

Melanie turned her head in the direction of Arlene's gaze. Standing there, smiling wickedly and licking her lips, was Kirsty. She was completely naked, and her creamy skin glowed against the black curtain. Then she started to move forward. As she did so, Melanie realised what that odd shape was that seemed to be occluding her crotch, and in the same instant she began to understand what it was that she craved.

The dildo was almost as thick as Melanie's wrist and longer than any penis had the right to be. It was ebony black, and Melanie realised that it was held in place, not just by the thongs she could see extending up to Kirsty's waist, but by a similar projection enclosed in Kirsty's vagina.

'Oh, yes,' Melanie moaned. 'Oh, Kirsty. Oh yes.'

Kirsty took up her position behind Melanie and gently fingered the welts. Melanie gasped as fresh fires sped in all directions across her buttocks. Then Kirsty levelled the dildo with her hand, stroking Melanie's tumescent labia with it, sliding it along her slit, letting her juices coat its hard, ridged surface. Melanie moaned again. This was reaching her need. This was touching that insistent craving. This was how the game had to end. And yet . . .

Kirsty let the tip of the dildo rest at the entrance to Melanie's vagina. She waggled it up and down with her hand, and from side to side, but she did not slide it in.

'Is this what you want, Mel?' she whispered. Melanie was silent.

Then Kirsty pulled back a little and slid the slick plastic head up an inch or so. It came to rest at Melanie's anus, which, after the onslaught, was yielding and slack. She let the tip play there for a few seconds. She heard Melanie sigh deeply, and she knew what she would do next. But Melanie would have to ask for it first. That was only fair. After all she'd put her through, Melanie was going to have to beg.

'Is this what you want, Mel?' she asked again.

'Yes. Oh, yes!' Melanie couldn't wait.

'Yes what?' asked Kirsty.

'Oh, Kirsty! Please. Yes. Yes please.'

'Better,' said Kirsty. 'But what exactly, Mel? What exactly do you want?'

'Kirsty, please. Please. I need it now. Do it. *Please.*'

'Say it,' said Kirsty. 'Say what you want me to do.' She let the dildo play around the margin of Melanie's moist hole, which was opening and closing as if trying to grasp it and suck it into itself.

'Fuck me there, Kirsty,' said Melanie. Then, since what she desired still wasn't happening, 'In my bum, Kirsty. I'm begging you. Fuck my arsehole.'

And Kirsty was satisfied. She pushed forward with her pelvis so that the plastic dick slid into Melanie's eager rectum like an earthworm into its burrow. She felt the other end of the dildo in her own vagina, and it was good. And she knew it was good for Melanie, too, because the room was filled with her moans, her cries of 'Yes. Yes', and 'Kirsty. Darling Kirsty', and with those deeper choking sounds that come from the depths of a person's soul when they're being fucked as never before. And Kirsty was very, very satisfied.

5

Huntscroft

Melanie was in a taxi and her head was spinning. She was barely able to remember how she'd got there or where she was going, though she could remember other things well enough: Arlene's Chamber of Correction, for example, with its dramatic blacks and reds, the whip sizzling and zipping about her ears or coiling and uncoiling like a snake, and Arlene herself, exotic and exciting in her near nakedness. But most of all she remembered Kirsty and that ferocious anal orgasm that had almost blown the back of her head clean off. She was still limp and befuddled when they'd soothed her flaming welts with lotion, dressed her, and helped her down the stairs to the street and the waiting taxi.

Through the turmoil in her brain percolated the awareness that she had some sort of appointment and was going to be late. Too bad, she thought, vaguely conscious that such indifference to punctuality was out of character. Too bad. She relaxed back into her seat, wincing as her raw backside took her weight. Then she gratefully closed her eyes to let the scenes of the afternoon play themselves out once again on her retinas. She didn't open them again until the taxi pulled up outside her door.

'Where the hell have you been?' called Mark from the sitting room as she charged into the house and headed for the bathroom. 'It's ten to four. You'll never be ready on time.'

'Tell you later,' she called back. All she wanted to do was to get out of her clothes and into the shower. The sensations of the afternoon were fading now and, if she had to get back to normality, she wanted to get there under a cascade of water at just the right temperature – not too hot, not too cold. She entered the bathroom and closed the door behind her.

The door opened again as Mark, who was anything but content to wait until later, followed her in. She'd already taken off her sweater and bra, but he was in time to witness the unveiling of her gaudy backside.

'Wow!' he gasped. 'What ...? How ...? Who ...? That looks –' he searched for the word '– awesome! Absolutely awesome!'

'Thanks,' said Melanie, taking it as a compliment and stepping into the shower. 'It feels that way too.' She drew in her breath as the powerful spray-jet of tepid water hit her shoulders and ran down her back to her striped behind. She sighed loudly as the refreshing blast cleared her head.

'Did Kirsty do this to you?' asked Mark.

The question was premature as far as Melanie was concerned. She was in no mood to give an account of herself just yet. 'Tell you later,' she said.

Mark could not contain his curiosity. 'C'mon, Mel,' he pleaded. 'You can't leave me in the dark. Spill the beans; I need to know.'

He had a point. 'I'll tell you everything when there's time,' said Melanie. 'But just to give you a clue, I was right about Kirsty being in love. Only it wasn't Steve she fancied. It was me.'

'Ah-ha!' said Mark. 'I should have guessed. And what happened? Did her girlfriend take exception to you muscling in?'

'It wasn't like that,' said Melanie. 'Don't worry. I'll put you in the picture first chance we get. Now you'd

47

better go and tell that driver to wait a while. He's probably outside already.' Mark reluctantly obeyed.

Alone again, Melanie breathed deeply. She was feeling much more in control of herself now, but she'd found Mark's eager enquiries rather irritating. Something wonderful had happened to her, but she needed time to assimilate it. She turned up the temperature and soaped herself all over with her favourite scented shower gel. The glow in her buttocks began to suffuse her entire body like liquid gold and, when she finally emerged from the shower, she felt cleansed, purified and strong, on the threshold of a new life and ready to take it on her own terms. She didn't yet know just how fragile that feeling would prove to be.

When she next checked the time it was 4.30. Late, but not all that late, considering she was already dressed and made up. All she had to do was select a few weekend clothes and put them, along with some essential toiletries, into her overnight bag. Mark's was packed with his own things. Then she remembered Arlene's instructions for treating her weals. She took a jar of moisturising cream from the cabinet and was about to apply it, but then had a better idea. She'd let Mark do it. He'd like that, and it would make him feel more included, bring him in on the process of reconstruction she was going through. More importantly, it would help her re-establish her feelings for him after her strange new experiences. She called out to him.

'Mark, darling. Would you come here and do me a favour?'

Mark's voice replied. 'Sorry? What did you say?'

'Come here,' she called again, a little louder. 'I want you to put some cream on my backside.'

There was a brief pause, then, 'What's that? I can't hear you.'

Was he going deaf or something! 'Come and rub some cream on my sore bum,' she yelled.

48

'Cream? What are you worrying about cream for? We're eating out tonight, remember?'

For God's sake! she thought. There was music playing in the sitting room, but surely he ought to have heard her well enough. Her irritation returned, undermining the benefits of the shower. She applied the cream herself, smoothing it into the welts which had faded to an attractive rosy blush and responded to her ministrations with delicious pangs of sensation.

Minutes later, Melanie walked into the sitting room. 'I'm ready,' she said. 'We won't be all that la –'

She stopped in her tracks. Mark sat in an armchair sipping a beer and holding back a grin. Opposite him sat another man, dressed in a chauffeur's uniform. He was sipping mineral water. 'Good evening, Ms Brooks,' he said. 'I'm your driver this evening. My name's Craig.'

Melanie's glowering gaze switched back and forth between the two men. Mark's innocent expression was obviously contrived. Craig's might have been easier to read if his eyes were not hidden behind impenetrable dark glasses. Her irritation ratcheted up to annoyance, then quickly on to anger. Damn him! she thought. So that was why he was playing deaf. It was his way of punishing her for having a good time without him. But then, she ought to have realised he'd invite the driver in. It was exactly what he would do. Her wits must still be a little scrambled.

The car was a long sleek limousine with darkened windows. Inside, they had space to stretch out on the soft leather seats. Craig spoke to them as he started the engine and set the car whispering on its way. He told them it would take about forty minutes to get to their destination, a place he called Huntscroft. He then announced that he was about to raise the partition, which was soundproof, but if they needed to communicate with him they could use the intercom on the bulkhead. Then the partition slid up, blocking out most of what little sound the engine made and, being of darkened glass like the windows, almost obliterating Craig himself from their sight.

'As good a time as any, don't you think?' said Mark, rubbing his hands with anticipation.

Melanie knew what he meant, but she wasn't in the mood to indulge him. 'For what?' she asked.

'Come on, Mel! I'm dying to hear what happened with Kirsty.'

'Not here,' she said. 'Your hearing is obviously so bad I'd have to shout, and then Craig would hear through the partition, and it would be sure to affect his driving. Better wait till we're *really* alone, like on a life raft in the middle of the Atlantic, or a dune in the Sahara desert.'

Mark sighed. He regretted his little joke but wasn't going to apologise, or beg. She'd tell him in her own good time and he'd just have to wait. He leant on his armrest, increasing the distance between them, and fell silent.

Melanie was disappointed by his aloofness. He might have tried a little harder, she thought, and her anger quickened. She wanted to begin the process of getting together with him again, to incorporate him into her new life just as he'd been so central to her old one, but he seemed determined not to co-operate. A little diplomacy on his part, a little sensitivity, was all it would take. It wasn't much to ask, surely? Didn't he realise how delicate her state of mind was just at the moment? Could he really be unaware that the emotional fabric of her being had been so mangled and stretched that not only would it never return exactly to its original state but it could easily be torn or re-arranged by even the most trivial thing, like that silly trick he'd pulled, or like his crass impatience to hear all the lurid details? Why couldn't he see the danger, that figures once prominent in the tapestry of her life could find themselves relegated to the margins, or stitched out completely in favour of new ones?

They sat well apart on the sumptuous leather as the limousine glided along the motorway. For her part, Melanie resolved not to let this come between them, but for the time being she couldn't risk any initiative that might backfire and make matters worse. Not that it wouldn't have been fun to take advantage of the comfort and seclusion of the limousine to regale him with the story of her sexy adventure. She knew how to talk dirty to him and could have had him creaming his pants long before journey's end. But she needed to think. She needed to smooth out that crumpled fabric again before risking any such intimate re-engagement with the man she expected one day to marry. And so the journey continued in silence.

As the miles swept past beyond the smoky glass, Melanie's thoughts returned to the events of that afternoon and, from there, to the first time she'd experienced anal sex. It had been with Phillip Drew and, as now, it had been a momentous event, not least because it was the last time they were to meet. She'd finished her project and her exams, and there was nothing more to keep her in college. She should have gone home and begun applying for jobs, but something deep within her had prevented her from leaving, drawing her instead to Phillip's office like a disowned cat returning to its master.

When Melanie knocked on his door, she felt almost as scared as she'd been that first time. It had been several weeks since they'd met – weeks, for her, of concentrated revision with little room in her life for anything else. Even so, she'd thought about him often enough, and her memories of those weekly trysts had sustained her between bouts of study. Now she was free again, but that didn't mean she and Phillip could just take up where they'd left off. She'd known from the start that there was a time limit on their affair, and it had expired when she finished her project. So, by rights, she ought not to be here. They'd said their goodbyes and that should have been the end of it. But, for Melanie, it wasn't enough.

Phillip's face, when she walked into his room, confirmed what she already knew, that her visit was both unexpected and not entirely welcome. 'Melanie!' he said. 'I thought you'd have gone down already. To what do I owe the pleasure?'

'I . . . er . . . I just wanted to say goodbye,' responded Melanie with as much spirit as she could muster.

'I thought we'd done that already,' said Phillip. There was no warmth in his voice.

'We did,' she acknowledged. 'I know what we agreed, and I've no complaint. But there's something more I want from you, and I think you should give it me.'

'Oh?' said Phillip. 'And what makes you think that?'

'Because I know you'd want to if you knew how much it would mean to me,' said Melanie.

Phillip looked thoughtful. Then his expression started to soften and Melanie felt the temperature in the room rise perceptibly. 'You know, Melanie,' he said. 'I've always considered you an exceptional student, so I'm going to make an exception for you.'

That evening began much like the ones they'd enjoyed before, with food and good wine, and music playing softly as they talked. It was, Melanie explained, all she'd wanted. The last time had left her feeling incomplete, as though something would be missing from her life from then on. She told him how she'd consoled herself with memories of him during the long weeks of exams and how it had become a matter of importance to her that her fantasies should be realised once more so that she would finally be able to let go of them and get on with her life, her career, and her relationship with Mark. Phillip was all understanding.

Later, they were lying on the deep-pile rug in his living room. Melanie reclined between his naked legs, her head resting on his shoulder. She felt the heat and hardness of his pulsating prick against her buttocks, and the sensation brought her anus into life, a phenomenon she'd become accustomed to since knowing Phillip. Before him, that part of her anatomy had been taboo, a place to be avoided at all costs by the respectful lover. But Phillip had known better than she herself how sensitive it was, how responsive to the light touch of a finger or the glancing contact of a moist tumescent prick. And, little by little, she'd come to love the way he would first run that lovely prick between her labia to slicken it with her juices, then draw it teasingly along her anal cleft. Sometimes, he would bring its tip right up to her tight little sphincter, but, reading admonition in the sudden tensing of her body, would forsake it for the more conventional receptacle.

But, although she'd never articulated the idea to herself, it was precisely this that underlay the sense of unfinished business that had motivated her to re-engage with her former tutor that evening. And so, without fully understanding why, she manoeuvred herself so that his shaft lay between her legs and his pubic hair brushed her anus as they moved together. It was delicious. She sighed to let him know it.

'You like that, don't you?' said Phillip.

'I love it,' said Melanie with feeling. Her anus was slackening and tensing involuntarily.

'Perhaps you'd like me inside?' asked Phillip.

And that was when, with a sudden thrill of excitement and fear, Melanie understood what she had wanted all along. 'Don't hurt me,' she said, paying lip service to her former scruples.

He pushed her gently away so that she lay on her side. Then she felt his fingers reaching between her thighs. She gasped as two or three fingers slid easily into her vagina, then gasped again as his thumb came up to press against her tightly closed anus.

'Relax,' he said. 'Let your sweet little rosebud open for me.'

Her anus relaxed at the sound of his voice, and his thumb went suddenly in. The strange new feeling made her start. She wasn't sure if she liked it, and was on the point of asking him to stop. But then his fingers and thumb began to work together and she put aside the thought. Something was beginning to happen and she wanted to find out where it would take her.

She pulled her knees up to her breasts. With one arm Phillip clasped her legs against her body while his other hand pushed deep into her, front and rear. The feelings were multiplying within her, changing from discomfort and mild revulsion to a growing rapture that spread up through her torso and down her legs to her toes, making them tingle as if someone were stimulating them with electrodes. She let her hand drift down to her crotch and thrilled to the touch of her fingers against his and against her hardening bud. Soon, she was moaning and squirming, pushing herself back onto Phillip's hand again and again. It was fantastic, simply fantastic.

Phillip's thumb worked around and around in her bum-hole, slackening it, relaxing it. Then he withdrew it. 'Are you ready now?' he asked.

'Yes,' said Melanie. She clenched her anus tightly, then let it open again as she felt the head of his prick against it. At first, she doubted that it would go in but, after a momentary sense of pressure, she felt herself entered with surprising smoothness. Her rectum filled unsettlingly and, for a few seconds, her reflexes convulsed against the intruder. But she heard Phillip's gentle voice urging her not to resist, to let herself sink into the whirlpool of sensation that was about to engulf her, and her body obeyed, taking his cock deeper inside itself, relaxing so completely that she could almost imagine it was Phillip himself she was enveloping, the whole man, body, mind and spirit. And what bliss that was! What ecstasy! Every

*muscle in her body went limp, every bone turned to molten
plasticine as a deep orgasm, the deepest she'd ever
experienced, seized her and wrung her out like a dishcloth,
racing through her again and again as if it might never
stop until her entire body had turned to warm liquid and
drained away into the earth beneath. And when it finally
did, they lay as if glued together for what seemed like an
eternity until her body's natural reflexes reasserted themselves and ejected his detumescent penis in a final
satisfying peristalsis. Then she slept where she lay for
another hour or more. When she woke he was nowhere to
be seen, and she knew the time had come to let him go
forever. She let herself out of the flat and made her way
home.*

The limousine left the main road, negotiated a series of
minor roads, and eventually turned into a narrow
driveway that led through acres of woodland to a wide
lawn. Across the lawn stood a large Georgian mansion.
The car pulled up on clean white gravel in front of the
house.

Melanie and Mark stepped out from opposite sides of
the car. They thanked the driver, then headed, still
apart, still silent, for the house.

The large imposing door stood at the top of a flight
of three or four stone steps bordered by low balustrades
guarded by stone raptors, an eagle on one side and a
vulture on the other. Their expressions were stern and
admonitory, but Melanie, conscious now of how late
she was, paid no heed to anything but her goal of
getting inside and setting things to rights with her boss.
In fact, the only lateral thought that entered her mind
as they started up the steps was a hint of surprise that
Charles Bermont should own such an up-market country house. It didn't seem to fit with the other facts she'd
accumulated about him over the past ten or eleven
months. Not that there were many such facts. Up to

now, Melanie had definitely not been admitted to Charles's inner circle.

All the more reason to make a good impression tonight. Her respect for her boss fell within well defined limits, but she was astute enough to realise that he had considerable influence in the media business and that her career would be far more likely to flourish if she could count him as a supporter. Thinking thus, she would not have chosen to be nearly an hour late on this occasion.

They hadn't yet reached the steps when the door opened to reveal Charles Bermont himself. He walked jauntily down and stopped at the foot to greet them.

'So good of you both to come.' Charles was effusive. He dismissed Melanie's mumbled apology with a wave of his hand. 'Nonsense,' he said. 'Apologies all on my side. Such short notice. And on such a day! What!'

Melanie wondered what he meant by 'such a day'. Then she remembered what she'd told him on the phone. Too late. Before she could take control of the situation, Charles was shaking Mark by the hand and congratulating him.

'Must be galling to have business rear its ugly head on your anniversary, Mark old chap, but we had no choice I'm afraid. Vital contract for B&C. Absolutely vital. Make it up to you, rest assured. Make it a weekend to remember. What!'

Mark looked puzzled. 'Anniversary?' he queried. He glanced accusingly at Melanie, who was opening her mouth to speak. But the quick-thinking Mark got in first.

'Oh! Ah! Yes!' he said. 'Anniversary. So Melanie told you, then!' Mark had twigged that Melanie must have spun Charles a tale for some purpose best known to herself. She hadn't bothered to tell him, but then, she didn't seem keen to tell him anything at the moment. Okay, he wasn't going to let her down by exposing her lie, but he was damned if he'd let her get off scot free either. If *she* wanted to play games with *him* . . .

'Not a secret, is it?' asked Charles, detecting the carefully calculated tone of mild astonishment in Mark's voice and falling neatly into the trap.

'Well,' Mark drawled, reinforcing the air of mystery. 'Not as such, I suppose. Just that we don't normally discuss, er, such matters with other people.'

'Oh?' Charles was puzzled now. What could be so delicate about an anniversary? He knew perfectly well that Mark and Melanie weren't married, but so few couples were these days. 'Didn't mean to intrude, old chap,' he said. 'Just assumed it was a normal, er, anniversary. You know. Your, er, getting-together, or whatever.'

'Oh, no,' explained Mark helpfully. 'That's in March.' Then he leant his head towards Charles and added in a low man-to-man sort of voice. 'It's just that we have lots of anniversaries of a more intimate nature. You know. Between the sheets? First time this way, first time that. Eh? So sentimental, aren't they, women?'

Charles turned a deep red, and Mark squinted over his shoulder to give Melanie a triumphant that'll-teach-you leer. Melanie glared back at him. Not funny! she thought, and she felt a little of that fabric rip within her. Not funny at all!

In his embarrassment, Charles forgot his etiquette and headed up the steps ahead of his guests. He recovered himself enough to pause at the top and wait until Melanie was abreast of him. Melanie, feeling herself challenged to try to repair the damage her idiot partner had caused, had followed hot on his heels.

'Beautiful house, Charles,' she said sweetly. 'I'd no idea you lived in such rural splendour.'

'Eh? Oh, the house. Yes.' Charles grasped at the new topic as at a lifeline. 'I mean, no. Er, beautiful, yes, but not mine. Belongs to a very good friend and colleague. Helping me out on the Castadiosa business.' He was calming down now, his face regaining its familiar light tan. 'Look, Mel, old girl,' he whispered, as they walked through a wide atrium towards an open doorway at the far right, 'sorry if I put my foot in it just then.'

Melanie took her opportunity. 'Don't take any notice of what Mark says,' she whispered back. 'He's just trying to make me look foolish. It's his revenge for having his plans disrupted this evening.'

Charles, good-natured soul that he was, reddened again, but this time with shame for having been the cause of a rift between his protégée and her man. Melanie bit her lip at the sight of his discomfiture, but it was too late to retract her words. She was running on automatic pilot. If she'd had the presence of mind she normally prided herself on, she might have found a better way of getting out of the situation than com-pounding her original lie and throwing the onus slap-bang onto her boss's shoulders. As a short-term tactic her move had been quite satisfactory. It both discredited her errant consort and put Charles deeper in her debt so that he'd feel obliged to make all the allowances he could for her. But it was the kind of tactic that was bound to turn against her eventually, and she knew this full well. It was only a matter of time before her chickens came home to roost. She just hoped they'd delay their homecoming until this chaotic weekend was over.

They had reached the open doorway. Inside, Melanie saw the familiar figure of Jeanette, Charles's P.A. She was placing a freshly filled teacup on an occasional table that stood beside a large winged armchair. Melanie saw a pair of legs, clad in off-white sports trousers, extend-ing from the chair, but the rest of its occupant was invisible to her.

'I'm sure I don't need to introduce my good friend and colleague,' said Charles to Melanie, 'the owner of this "beautiful house", as you so aptly called it.'

Then a voice rose up from the winged chair. It ascended to the ornate plaster ceiling and rolled in slow motion towards Melanie like an inverted ocean wave before crashing down about her ears in a deluge that almost swept her off her feet. 'Hello, Melanie,' it said. 'It's nice to see you again after such a long time.'

The words reverberated through her head, mingling with other words in the same voice that had echoed there just minutes before, words like 'relax', and 'I won't hurt you', and 'let your sweet rosebud open for me'. Melanie could hardly tell which words were spoken and which were remembered, but she had no doubt who the speaker was, and no doubt that he, at least, was real. And now he was before her, his hand extended to shake hers, his mouth smiling at her in welcome, his eyes gleaming mischievously. It was Phillip Drew.

6

Castadiosa

'Take a seat, Mel, old girl,' said Charles. They were in the library, just she, Charles and Jeanette. After introductions and cups of tea all round, Charles had proposed that he put Melanie in the picture about the Castadiosa business without delay so that she would know what to expect when their other guests arrived. Phillip and Mark had then gone off to the tennis court for a quick set or two before dusk, leaving Charles to escort his brood into the library.

They took their places around the large rectangular table, Charles and the faithful Jeanette on one side, Melanie facing them on the other. Charles laid it on the line for her in concise clipped sentences. The bidding had, it seemed, been closer than expected. Instead of walking it, Bermont and Cuthbertson had merely landed amongst two or three other front runners. Castadiosa had thought it necessary to postpone their final decision while they conducted further negotiations with the surviving bidders. Since two of the Castadiosa top brass were already in the country on other business, Charles and Phillip had arranged to meet them to play golf that morning, and had got the news directly from the horse's mouth. The other bidders were to be informed on Monday.

Señor Ernesto de Léon and Señora Arancha Martinez – for those were their names – would be returning to

Barcelona tomorrow. After some expert arm-twisting by Phillip, they'd agreed to come to dinner this evening to discuss their decision. They'd let it be understood that they would make some sort of proposal to Bermont and Cuthbertson, but if, as Phillip had speculated, this would be to offer them less than the full contract, it would not be accepted. It was to be all or nothing. That was where Melanie came in. He, Charles, would be depending on her to convince them that Bermont and Cuthbertson was the right business partner for Castadiosa. It wouldn't be easy, but he had faith in her. At any rate, if she couldn't do it, nobody could.

Melanie digested this as best she could. She was still at sixes and sevens after the shock – on top of everything else – of meeting Phillip Drew again. She'd only managed to stammer a few words to him as they shook hands, but she'd felt like a thief caught red-handed as she did so. She was sure that everyone present could read all the intimate details of their brief affair on her face, and she'd been genuinely surprised, after Phillip had moved on to shake Mark's hand, that the latter seemed not to have noticed a thing. Neither, it seemed, had Charles. Only Jeanette had peered at her through her narrow vixen eyes with anything approaching suspicion.

Mark didn't know about Phillip, of course, and Heaven forbid that he should find out now! She sighed at the risks she was running. The weekend was slipping further and further out of her control. One simple lapse of memory had started an avalanche. She'd left the office on Friday without that accursed note and, as a direct result, she was facing perhaps the greatest challenge of her professional career with all the cards stacked against her. She was in a deep, deep hole, and seemed intent on digging herself in even deeper. This wouldn't do. She had to get her mind into gear before it was too late – if it wasn't too late already.

Technique! That was what she needed. If your brain's gone out to lunch, fall back on technique. Make a list, for example. That's always useful. Those cards that were stacked against her, what were they, exactly? Melanie's analytical instincts began to take over as she enumerated the handicaps that were piling up on top of her.

No. 1 – The Cold War: She and Mark had got themselves into a confrontation that seemed to escalate at every opportunity. It was too much to hope that they could strike a peace accord in the time available, but she had to keep the lid on it at all costs.

No. 2 – The Love Triangle: Phillip Drew had reappeared – a double threat. Not only was there the risk that Mark would find out about their affair – an eventuality that would turn the Cold War incandescent – but her old feelings for Phillip were in danger of re-surfacing. In fact, she could feel them stirring already.

No. 3 – The Tangled Web: Her lies had placed her poor boss in a very awkward position. He believed himself guilty of triggering the Cold War by spoiling her celebration of a fictitious anniversary whose nature and status he was totally confused about. Charles wasn't very good at handling that kind of stress.

She felt better. She'd managed to reduce the overwhelming complexity of her situation to a simple number, the number 3. Only three problems – no, not problems; call them challenges. Only three challenges, then, when you boiled them down. Not so bad after all. 'Consider it done, Charles,' she said.

Charles sighed with relief. It was only then that Melanie really understood how much he was relying on her. He was genuinely worried about the contract, and her apparent confidence was balm to his soul. She'd uttered exactly the right words: 'consider it done'. She wished she could have said them with more sincerity.

'If we'd had more notice we'd have prepared one of the better rooms for you, on the first floor, but none of the ones available has a double bed. We thought you'd appreciate a double bed, especially on your – ahem – anniversary.' Jeanette was showing Melanie the top-floor room she was to share with Mark that night. It was quite large but rather plainly furnished.

'You knew Phillip Drew at college, I understand.'

Melanie merely nodded. She didn't want to encourage conversation on this topic, especially not with Jeanette.

'He has quite a reputation, I understand,' said Jeanette. 'As a teacher, I mean, of course.' There had been enough of a pause between the first sentence and the second to let the various possible interpretations of the word 'reputation' swirl about in the chilly space between the two women.

'Brilliant,' Melanie confirmed as tersely as she thought she could get away with without actually appearing rude. 'Quite brilliant.'

Jeanette was a woman of about forty. She was a little taller than Melanie, and a little fuller of figure. Her hair was light brown and long, but she wore it fastened at the back so that it drooped in silky swathes around her ears. Melanie was always mildly fascinated by that hair, and always found herself fixating on it when she talked to Jeanette about holiday rosters, dates of meetings, or whatever. Perhaps that was because it was indeed rather lovely, but perhaps also she found it more comfortable than looking into the woman's eyes, which always seemed to be searching suspiciously for some tell-tale mark of perfidy. For Jeanette was very protective of her boss. Now, at this critical juncture in the firm's history and his career, she seemed more suspicious and wary than ever. Melanie, after meeting her gaze for barely an instant, focused on those swathes of hair with more than usual intensity.

'The bathroom is through here,' said Jeanette, opening a communicating door. 'It's a little cramped, I'm afraid, but it has all you need. There's even a bidet.'

When the woman had gone, Melanie added another handicap to her list: No. 4 – The Vixen: Eyes like a fox, nose like a ferret, and on the prowl for scandal.

When Jeanette left her to unpack and prepare herself for dinner, Melanie lay down on the bed and stared at the ceiling. There was still more than half an hour before the Castadiosa people arrived, and a further hour until dinner at 8.00. She could afford to relax for a few minutes. She let her mind slip out of gear and drift where it would. She wasn't in the least surprised to find that it drifted in the direction of Phillip Drew. Here they were, in the same house, later to sleep under the same roof.

In the same bed? No, of course not. Their affair had ended long ago. It had been intense and passionate, for her at least, but it was irrevocably over. It had hurt no one, not even Mark, who had known nothing about it and, she fervently hoped, never would. In fact, it had been good for Mark in a way. She'd learned so much from Phillip that, when she returned to Mark at the end of that wonderful term, she'd been able to use her new-found knowledge to help move their relationship forward. Without that, they might not have stayed together this long.

But she wished she'd come alone this evening, then she could have stayed on the first floor just yards away from Phillip. She imagined herself getting out of bed in the dead of night and finding her way to the master bedroom. Inside, there'd be a large four-poster bed, and she'd tiptoe across the floor towards it, then gently push aside its silken drapes and creep in. He'd be there under the thin covers, naked and asleep. She'd slide under the bedclothes and wriggle down in the darkness, her body so insubstantial it would hardly disturb the crisp white linen. She'd feel him stir as she slithered like a ghost all over him, nipping at his nipples until they were rock hard, or licking his stiffening shaft from its root to its tip. Her hands, too, would be busy. They'd stroke his firm inner thighs, or clasp his prick tightly as her tongue played around the little pink eye at its tip until the taste of his pre-ejaculate would tell her he was ready.

And when she was sure he was ready, she would slide on top of him and guide that wonderful prick into her. She would hear how his breathing changed then, and feel how the muscles of his body tensed in response to her almost imperceptible weight. And she would lie still for a little while, enjoying the feel of his body as his arousal grew. And then she would begin to ride him, slowly at first, almost losing him at the top of her stroke but never failing to catch him again as she began her descent, then swooping down until pubic bone met pubic bone and he would fill her, stretch her, push her innards up to her diaphragm. Again and again she would ride him, listening to his gasps, his moans, feeling with him the progress of his ecstasy, now slowing to prevent him coming too soon, then speeding up again to ratchet his climax to new heights. And when she knew the time was right she would throw off the sheets and lift her body into the air as she rode, her hair flying, her pale breasts bouncing against her chest. And then all the world would see her bring him to orgasm, all the faces peering in through the silken folds of the drapes, Jeanette's face, Charles's face, and Craig's, and Kirsty's, and Arlene's, and, yes, even Mark's. They would all see what her love can do for him, all witness the explosive force of his coming as he yells from the bottom of his lungs and shoots his semen into her like molten iron, so much of it that she can't hold it all and it squirts and squelches from her quim, spattering the bed in long streaks, burning where it falls so that the bed is covered with fiery bands and stripes like the rose-red whip marks on her own buck-naked rump.

Melanie opened her eyes, breathing quickly and deeply. She withdrew her hand from her panties and lifted it to her face, savouring the scent of it as she slowly recovered her breath and her pulse subsided to its normal pace. Time to try out that bidet, she thought.

It was well past seven when Melanie made her way down to the drawing room to meet the dinner guests who, having been driven to Huntscroft from their hotel, had arrived just minutes before. Melanie was last to be introduced. Mark, who hadn't found his way to their room after his game of tennis, was already furnished with a cocktail and stood watching the ceremony with a dispassionate eye. Melanie almost didn't recognise him. He looked freshly shaven and groomed, in an informal jacket of the most exquisite lightweight wool, perfectly creased flannel trousers, and an open-necked silk shirt that emphasised his athletic torso. Melanie was amazed. He looked the way he might always have looked if he'd only followed her advice about clothes. She realised immediately that Phillip must have given him the run of his own dressing room and wardrobe. No, worse than that, he must actually have helped Mark with his grooming and dressing. She felt a double pang of jealousy. Phillip had achieved what she'd so far failed to, and Mark had received the kind of attention from Phillip that should have been reserved for her. It just wasn't fair!

Melanie became aware of Jeanette's eyes upon her, scrutinising her face like a big cat judging its leap. She wouldn't show her true feelings, not to that vixen. She gave Mark a smile that had in it all the warmth and admiration of a bride for her groom on their wedding

66

day. Mark almost gave the game away by looking taken aback, but fortunately the vixen couldn't see that, unless she had eyes in the back of her head (which Melanie wasn't prepared to rule out).

'And this is Melanie Brooks,' Charles was saying. 'Melanie looks after our Creative Design Team, the heart and soul of Bermont and Cuthbertson.' She let Ernesto take her hand and peck her drily on each cheek in a compromise between an English handshake and a Spanish *abrazo*. Arancha, when it was her turn, dispensed with the English element entirely. Her two-armed embrace and the moist kisses she planted on Melanie's cheeks were full of warmth and sisterly affection, and Melanie was surprised at how instantly attracted she felt towards the woman.

Ernesto was in his late forties and showing his age in the steely-grey streaks highlighting his temples. But he was a very good-looking man all the same. His eyes were dark and mobile, and the skin of his face, a light, Mediterranean olive, was smooth and supple-looking. Melanie decided that next time she had the opportunity to greet him she would take the initiative and deliver an *abrazo* like the one she'd just received from Arancha.

Arancha, too, was olive-skinned and had black glistening hair. Her eyes, though, were of a much lighter brown, almost hazel, and they looked at you steadily and with warm interest. Her longish face was quite large in proportion to her size, and her mouth and bright red lips were generous. When she smiled or spoke, which was at every opportunity, she displayed teeth like translucent white porcelain. She had the narrow waist so much favoured by Spanish women, but nothing else about her was meagre. Her hips were broad and round, her legs strong, with thighs that stretched the fabric of her narrow skirt, and buttocks that curved out sharply from her pelvis as if trying to escape to lead an independent life of their own. Her breasts matched her

67

buttocks for size and animation. Melanie wondered what they would look like unclothed, or set off by Arlene's leather harness.

Charles and Jeanette dispensed drinks to those not already supplied, and the party chatted casually in twos and threes. Melanie found herself chatting with Arancha, comparing the late summer weather in England with that in Barcelona. Arancha gesticulated incessantly as she spoke, using not just her hands but her entire body to pantomime weather effects or, more abstractly, to express her feelings on the subject. Melanie was conscious of the way her breasts swayed this way and that, sometimes counterbalancing her weight, sometimes threatening her equilibrium. She was fascinated by those breasts, and found it hard to avoid staring at them. She wondered if Arancha would consider it rude if she did.

Dinner was served by an elderly butler in grey and black. The conversation was mostly small talk until the dessert. When at last the subject of the contract was broached, Ernesto took the floor. 'What is Castadiosa?' he asked rhetorically in his heavy Spanish accent, using the present tense as if Castadiosa was already in existence instead of just a high-risk business idea that might succeed but could just as easily flop completely. 'It is a magazine? No. It is a TV channel? No. It is a website? No. It is all these things, and it is also much, much more.'

Melanie realised that this was a well rehearsed pitch, but she listened to it intently. It was her practice always to pay close attention to what the top man says. It might be largely hot air, but it was *his* hot air.

'Castadiosa is the life of every woman – the life she leads in her heart, if not in reality. Castadiosa is all around her. It informs her. It inspires her. It indulges her dreams. Most of all, it liberates her. Sometimes,

Castadiosa is her guide, her mentor. Sometimes she herself is the *casta diosa* – the chaste goddess. She is a goddess because she is strong, she is powerful. She is chaste because she is woman, and woman is pure.'

He paused, but didn't invite comments.

'So, it is a magazine, a TV channel *and* a website, but all unified, all with the same look and feel, the same image, the Castadiosa image. We wanted to find one design company who could bring that image to life, but we have failed. We were too ambitious. Instead, we have found three companies who together can make it real. Three of the best media design houses in Europe. One of them is Bermont and Cuthbertson.'

Charles looked flattered that his firm should be rated so highly. He looked up to hear Ernesto's next words, which were exactly the proposition Phillip had foreseen.

'So let me congratulate you, Charles, on the very high quality of your bid, and let me propose to you that you become one of our most important business partners in the great Castadiosa enterprise. To be precise, I offer you the website, a one-third share of the TV channel, and a consultative role on the magazine. I hope you will accept this offer, and that you will work with us and the other successful bidders to make Castadiosa not only a success but a revolution for the women of Spain.'

Melanie could see from his eyes that Charles wanted to accept, to make do with half a loaf rather than take the risk of finding himself with no bread, but he was taking advice from Phillip. He exchanged a nervous glance with the latter before calmly, and with considerable aplomb, declining the offer. As he explained, it was not Bermont and Cuthbertson's policy to share contracts with other design firms because of the additional risks that entailed and because it conflicted with the profile they were building for the company. He was sorry, but Castadiosa would either have to reconsider or proceed without Bermont and Cuthbertson. Melanie would have given odds that his palms were sweating as he said that.

Both Ernesto and Arancha looked crestfallen. It seemed they hadn't anticipated this response at all. It threw all their carefully thought-out plans into disarray, and Ernesto, at least, was visibly unhappy beneath his professional calm. He tried repeating the offer, as if Charles might have failed to understand it the first time. He got Charles to repeat his reply two or three times, as if he himself might have misheard. When he was quite satisfied that there were no misunderstandings on either side, he went into negotiation mode, hinting that the quoted shares of the contract might be nudged upwards. This had no effect. Charles spoke of problems he'd had in the past when sharing responsibilities with other firms, and argued that his company had all the competencies required to take on the whole show. In his opinion, Castadiosa, an intrinsically risky venture, would be best entrusted to a single firm with the commitment and imagination to see it through. Bermont and Cuthbertson was that firm, he asserted.

Melanie was called upon to play her part. She told of how she'd taken over a Creative Design Team of talented individuals and had fashioned it into a seamless unit of collective genius. She spoke of past glories and of future promise. She was honest about recent failures but reassuring about lessons learned. She vouched for her team's enthusiasm for the challenges of Castadiosa and for her own confidence in their ability to meet those challenges. She spoke fluently in high clear tones, but her mind was only half engaged. She could see Phillip and Mark along the table, watching her, and she wanted one of them to come to her chair and lay his hands on her shoulders to give her strength, or to kiss her neck in tender encouragement. The trouble was, she didn't know which one, and this more than anything distracted her from her task of persuasion. She knew she was

70

failing. Her words tinkled against her own eardrums like cheap plastic cutlery on a tiled kitchen floor. She didn't need to look at Ernesto to know he remained unmoved.

Eventually, the two Spaniards asked to be allowed to confer together in private and were led off to the library by the butler. Melanie took the opportunity to go to the bathroom. She entered a small toilet in a corner of the ground floor and was closing the door behind her when she noticed Arancha observing her from the library doorway. She thought nothing of it.

Melanie relieved her straining bladder as if divesting herself of all the responsibilities of her complicated life. Perhaps that was what it was coming to, she thought. Was her job not on the line after that dismal performance in defence of B&C? Was not her life with Mark hanging in the balance? The clouds that had been gathering since the previous evening seemed high and black now, and ready to break at any moment in an almighty storm that would leave nothing unchanged. Somehow, peeing seemed to make it easier to accept the inevitable. Trouble is, thought Melanie as the torrent dried up, the relief only lasts as long as you're peeing. After that, reality comes back with a bang.

As she dried her hands at the wash basin, Melanie heard a faint knock at the door. She put the towel back on its rail and wondered who could be in so much hurry to use this particular toilet when there was at least one other on the ground floor, not to mention those on the floors above. The knocking came again just as she reached the door and opened it. Outside was Arancha, who immediately pushed her way inside. Melanie, bemused, was about to apologise for keeping this apparently desperate woman from the means of her relief, but Arancha spoke first, whispering conspiratorially.

'I tell Ernesto I come to pee,' she said. 'And is true, I come to pee. But also I come to talk to you.' She closed

71

the door behind them after checking that nobody had seen her go in.

Melanie's curiosity was aroused, along with her business instincts. When someone from the other side seeks you out in private, you know you are dealing either with an ally or with a deadly enemy. Well, it narrows the field a little!

'Ernesto judge what he see on paper,' she said, 'and what people tell him. He read your bid. He hear about other work you do. He make up his mind.'

Melanie nodded. The voluptuous Spanish lady had her full attention.

'Me, I judge what I see with my heart. I look at a person and I ask myself, Is this the right person? Does this person understand what is Castadiosa?' She looked straight at Melanie, taking hold of her upper arm. 'And I look at you. I watch you. I watch the way you talk, your eyes, the way you move. I watch the way you hold your body.' Her eyes lit up as she homed in on her conclusion. 'And especially I notice how you sit down on the hard, hard chair. I see these things and I say myself, I think I understand this beautiful young woman. I think this beautiful young woman is like me.'

She was gripping Melanie's arm quite hard now, and her brown eyes were staring at her unblinkingly. Melanie's face must have shown her puzzlement.

'I show you,' said Arancha. She released her grip and turned her back on Melanie. Then, to the latter's astonishment, she unbuttoned her skirt and lowered it as far as her thighs. Then she pulled up the tail of her blouse. Melanie gave an involuntary gasp. The muscular, olive-coloured buttocks, bare except for a narrow red thong that disappeared between them almost as soon as it left the thin waistband that held it in place, were criss-crossed with pink stripes, some broad, some fine, some deeply coloured and others on the point of disappearing.

Arancha turned her head while keeping her backside in full view. 'You see?' she said.

Melanie saw all right. She wanted to touch too, to run her fingers along those beautiful stripes, but she didn't dare. Instead, she loosened her own skirt and let it fall to the floor, then pushed her panties down at the back as far as necessary. She proudly displayed her own four red bands to the delighted Arancha.

'I knew it!' she squealed. Then, lacking Melanie's inhibitions, she placed her fingers on the topmost stripe and pressed gently, running them along from one buttock to the other. Melanie thrilled to the caress and squirmed with pleasure. Arancha was full of admiration.

'Such beautiful stripes,' she said, pronouncing the word 'e-stripe-es' in the Spanish manner. 'Such beautiful e-stripe-es. But so few?'

Melanie explained that it had happened that very afternoon and had been her first time.

'Your first time!' exclaimed Arancha. 'You were a virgin just today! *Ai Madre*! I wish I'd been there to see it.'

The two women, backsides still exposed, looked at each other and smiled in confederacy. Then Arancha said she had to pee and let her skirt fall completely. Melanie hitched hers up, trying to avoid looking at the thick bush of wiry black hair that spilled out around the edges of the triangle of lace that scarcely even attempted to conceal it. For her part, Arancha just went on talking as she sat down on the loo and hooked the lace brusquely to one side with a finger. She was telling Melanie that they were undoubtedly soul-sisters and that she was sure now that Melanie would understand what Castadiosa was about. Melanie was almost distracted by the musical tinkle of pee into the bowl and the pleasant warm urine smell that accompanied it, but she didn't fail to take in Arancha's final words.

'You see, that is what Castadiosa must be, Melanie,' she said. 'For the Spanish woman at home, or working in an office, or in a shop, Castadiosa must be the stripes on her backside.'

Melanie said she understood, and she almost believed she did. Then she left Arancha to finish her pee in peace and went back to the dining room. The stripes on her backside, she thought. The e-stripe-es on her back-e-side.

Back in the dining room, the mood was glum. Charles looked crestfallen. Jeanette looked eager to pick on a scapegoat and cast the first stone, Mark silently avoided anyone's eyes (especially Melanie's), and Phillip sipped his brandy contemplatively.

When the Spanish guests re-entered, escorted in state by the butler, an electric buzz filled the room. Everyone knew it was make or break. Ernesto had been presented with an ultimatum – the whole contract or nothing – and Ernesto had been visibly unmoved by the arguments.

Ernesto and Arancha took their seats. Ernesto spoke.

'I have said that we failed to find one company to be our design partner in Castadiosa. You want to tell me I am wrong. Maybe I am wrong. But I do not hear anything to *convince* me I am wrong.' Ernesto was as unhappy as he'd been before the recess.

'I offer you nearly 40 percent of the contract. What you say? You say, Thank you very much? You say, We happy to help you make a revolution? No. You say, No way!'

He paused, breathing deeply. You could almost see smoke coming from his nostrils.

'You give me problem!' he continued. 'Me, I say okay. *Adios*! Goodbye! The others, they will not give me problem.' Ernesto's arms were indicating how comprehensively he would have cast Bermont and Cuthbertson to the fates if the decision had been entirely his.

'My Creative Director –' he indicated Arancha with a gesture that was not devoid of contempt, '– say me No!

She say the project is too risky without Bermont and Cuthbertson. She say Bermont and Cuthbertson understand Castadiosa best. She say she put her reputation on the block. We talk. We agree. Bermont and Cuthbertson *plus* her reputation on the block. One more chance.'

Ernesto had finished. Having vented his spleen at being forced to compromise, he seemed totally uninterested in how his decision might be put into practice. It was left to Arancha to arrange the practicalities. Apparently, Ernesto and she and two other members of the Castadiosa board were due to visit the UK again in a week's time. Bermont and Cuthbertson would give them a presentation of their case then. If they could convince all four, the whole contract would be theirs. If not, Castadiosa would go ahead without Bermont and Cuthbertson.

Dates were settled. Phillip offered them the hospitality of Huntscroft for the extent of their stay in the UK and, once it was established that it was without strings, the offer was gratefully accepted. The party then continued in a half-hearted manner until Ernesto announced his desire to return to the hotel. After a protracted leave-taking while they waited for the hotel driver, the two Spaniards departed, to everyone's barely concealed relief.

'Reprieve?' was Charles's first word.

'Temporary,' was Jeanette's. The vixen eyes squinted accusingly at Melanie.

'But you have a powerful force on your side,' interposed Phillip.

They all turned to him with questioning eyes. Phillip calmly sipped his brandy. 'Feminine intuition,' he said. 'Ernesto is the type who goes by the book, but Arancha works by instinct, and she evidently picked up something here tonight that appeals to her very strongly indeed. I don't know what it might be –' he glanced meaningfully at Melanie at this point '– but something about B&C struck a chord with her. Exploit that, and you can win.'

'But what is it?' asked Charles. 'And how do we exploit it?'

There was a long silence. It echoed around the room, reinforcing the hollowness in people's hearts. Then Melanie chose her moment. 'I have an idea,' she said. 'But I'll need a budget.'

That night, Melanie lay in the large double bed alone. Mark had elected to join Phillip in a game of snooker. How long does a game of snooker last? she wondered. It was two hours since she'd taken her leave and retired to her room. She brooded on the challenge ahead of her, and on the failure that had been postponed but not averted. Had she really understood those words of Arancha's? Did she really have an idea – the remotest clue, even – of how to convince them? Whatever had been in her mind when she'd said that had disappeared now, and the vacuum it left was resonant with her fears.

She needed Mark now as never before. Melanie was a strong-minded woman with a reputation amongst her friends and colleagues for pragmatism and clear-sightedness, as well as intelligence and sensitivity, and yet now she would have given anything for Mark to come to her and tell her what to do. She wanted to feel the reassuring masculinity of his arms about her body, to absorb his strength, to follow his instructions, to give herself to his will. She reached out into the empty space beside her and wept.

'Fuck you, Mark!' she muttered into her pillow. 'I need you and you're off somewhere playing snooker with the only other man who could have helped me through this. I wish I'd brought Kirsty with me instead of you. I wish I were with her now. She'd understand. She'd give me the confidence to go out and win this damned contract. She wouldn't leave me to sweat it out all on my own. You're an unfeeling cold-hearted bastard, Mark!'

When Mark eventually came to bed, Melanie was already half asleep.

'All right, Mel?' he whispered.

'Bastard!' she replied.

They slept in the same bed, but a hundred miles apart.

7

The Early Bird

Melanie woke the next morning when the sun crept across the bed to her pillow and tickled her cheek. Its late summer intensity cleared the dream-images from her head almost before her eyes were open. The gods and goddesses – chaste or otherwise – that had vied for her affections throughout the troubled night all vanished like woodsmoke in an autumn wind. The dream-appetites remained, however, and her stirring limbs cried out for human contact. Stretching and yawning, she turned towards the other side of the bed and reached out for the body that could satisfy her longing. It was a shock when she found just empty cooling sheets.

Evidently, the morning sun had reached Mark's pillow before hers, and he was already up. Her disappointment was something physical. She heard water running in the adjoining bathroom and gazed at the closed door, thinking she might tempt him to linger a while when he came out. The bathroom door opened and Mark tiptoed into the bedroom, his ungainly movements conveying an energy he found hard to suppress in the interests of letting his sleeping partner lie. When he saw that she was awake, the latent energy shucked off its shackles with relief.

'Morning, Mel,' he said brightly. 'Lovely morning. Great to be out in the country on a day like this.' He began to get dressed.

Melanie's hopes plummeted. He looked like a man on a prior mission of pleasure that did not involve her, but she owed it both to that yearning in her loins and to their future together to try to delay him, to begin repairing the damage their relationship had sustained in the best way possible, in each other's arms. 'Mmm,' she murmured, parting her thighs languorously, both for the pleasure it gave her and for the provocative shapes it would make with the thin bedcover. 'Still early, though. Slow down and wait for me.'

'Uh-uh,' he countered. 'Got to rush. I'm playing golf with Phillip in half an hour, and I've got to stoke up on bacon and eggs before then.'

A pang of jealousy struck Melanie with a force. He'd spent practically the whole time since their arrival in Phillip's company, and now the new day was starting as the previous one had left off! And again, there was that ambiguity. Was it losing Mark that hurt her most, or missing the opportunity to see Phillip over the breakfast table? She longed to talk to Phillip, to break the ice at least. All she needed was a hint from him that he hadn't forgotten her and that their final-term fling had been at least a little bit special. It would cost him nothing to give her that, but it would do wonders for her.

'Oh!' she said. 'I . . .' She wanted to plead with him, or to protest, but what was the point? 'Have a good game,' she said instead. She turned her head into the pillow and tried to give the impression that she was too drowsy to care what he did. If he'd bothered to look at her, however, he'd have seen a film of moisture in her half-closed eyes.

When he'd gone, she lay as she was for a few minutes. An impulse to let the tears flow rose up in her bosom but fell back again almost immediately. No, she refused to indulge herself in self-pity, not while she could feel the sun on her face, warming her flesh and her spirit. She stroked her backside to arouse that delicious tingle where the lash had left its mark. It felt good. It tingled right through to her belly. It tingled down her thighs and into her feet and toes, then up her spinal cord to her brain, re-kindling the desire she'd woken up with and bringing into being the resolution to satisfy that desire in a fit and proper way, Mark or no Mark.

Melanie followed the scent of fresh coffee and grilled bacon into the dining room. Jeanette was there before her and was making her selection from a buffet spread with all manner of appetising breakfast dishes. Jeanette, in a light-coloured summer dress with a pattern of large bright hibiscus flowers, and with those rich brown swathes of hair hanging almost to her shoulders, was clearly in off-duty mode. Melanie was struck by how different she looked, more relaxed, more attractive even; less vixen, more foxy lady. It was hard to avoid staring at her.

Jeanette greeted Melanie amiably and they chatted as they filled their plates together. Melanie, in need of reassurance after her failure of the previous evening when her hollow words had bounced so unconvincingly off the hard shell of Ernesto's business intellect, felt herself warming to her arch enemy for a moment, until her own intellect – as hard-shelled as any – stepped in with a caution. When a woman like Jeanette seemed at her most friendly, that was the time to be most on your guard. Melanie smiled to herself at the thought. Jeanette, sharp-eyed as ever, noticed.

'Oh, I'm so glad to see you in such good spirits, Melanie,' she gushed. 'Poor Charles is so much counting on you to win this contract. If it were me, I'd be down in the dumps after last night. Quite useless for anything! But I can see you're the type who bounces back straight away, and that's just what the company needs right now, isn't it?'

Patronising cow! thought Melanie.

Then Charles came in and Melanie decided she'd prefer not to listen to Jeanette poisoning his mind against her with her septic sympathy. She pushed aside her half-empty plate and drained her glass of orange juice, then, wishing her boss a good morning and throwing him a few optimistic words to lift his sagging jowls, she announced her intention to take a stroll in the early morning air.

'See you both later,' she called as she disappeared through the dining room door.

The sun was well above the horizon and the sky was clear, but there was still a remnant of mist in the shadows under the trees and Melanie, dressed in shorts and T-shirt, felt the declining chill on the bare skin of her arms and thighs with pleasure. It made her feel better. She was passing a small orchard of low, heavily fruiting apple trees, and the scent of ripe fruit and fermenting windfalls thrilled her nostrils and sharpened her wits. It sharpened her desires, too, reminding her that she had a mission she was determined to fulfil.

Beyond the orchard was a grove of rhododendrons, which she now entered. They were large mature plants, almost as big as trees, their dusky green canopies swooping down to ground level to claim huge volumes of space for themselves, denying it to all other living things. The path weaved in and out of these sombre grottoes and Melanie sampled their musty interiors with a mixture of revulsion and fascination. They had an eerie feel, as if they'd just been vacated an instant before by unknown beings, whether benevolent or malign.

Finding a narrow strip of open ground between bushes, she left the path and followed it for a few yards before ducking under the hanging wreaths of a particularly large bush. Inside was a much larger and darker space than the others; it took her a minute to accustom her eyes to the gloom. Then she moved further in towards the trunk, a knot of gnarled, brown hawsers that seemed to explode from the ground before dividing into elephantine limbs that corkscrewed upwards and outwards like the predatory tentacles of a deep-sea monster before feeling their way back to ground level. As she walked, her feet sank softly into a thick carpet of leathery brown leaves that littered the ground. It seemed so thick and spongy that she could easily have snuggled down in it and disappeared from the face of the earth, never to be seen or heard of again.

She stopped, and all was silent. She was at the heart of the bush. A thick branch bent out from near the base of the trunk to run along at ground level towards the perimeter. It made a convenient seat, and she sat down on it, straddling it with her legs and leaning back into the bole itself. She gazed up into the convoluted tracery of branches that writhed and twisted above her. They reminded her of those sylvan scenes by Burne-Jones which were so erotic and yet had been so popular in the respectable households of Victorian and Edwardian England. She imagined herself as a nymph in one of those scenes, clad only in a diaphanous gown, arms and legs caught by the living vines as by the arms of a lover. She rocked gently on her seat, letting the rough bark press into her. It felt good.

It would be so easy to do it here, to let those gnarled branches grip her and grope her, to submit meekly as those broad bunches of twigs and coarse leaves lashed her bare thighs or forced their way under her T-shirt and into her shorts like rude intruding hands. Resistance would be futile against so powerful a ravisher with so many limbs, so many protuberances of all sizes and shapes, smooth and slender or rough-ribbed and stout. It would be so, so easy.

She stood up, letting the trunk massage her back as she rose. Deftly, she removed her shorts and the scanty white cotton knickers she wore underneath. The cool moist air swirled around her nakedness like the breath of some incorporeal woodland lover, and she closed her eyes in anticipation. She slid down to the branch again and pushed herself into the angle it made with the trunk. Her whipped backside, still deliciously tender, responded with the by now familiar tingle. Oh yes, it would be so easy to do it this way.

And yet she knew she wouldn't, even as she felt her clitoris harden against the coarse bark of the branch. She squirmed and rocked a little more, and it was very nice, but no, it would not do. If the rhododendron bush would not come to life to ravish her, or if that breathy sprite would not manifest itself in flesh and blood, then she would have to seek her satisfaction elsewhere. She sighed, opened her eyes, and looked about her for her shorts and knickers.

Melanie found her shorts straight away, but her knickers were nowhere to be seen. Somehow, she reasoned, they must have got buried in the leaf litter by the movement of her feet. She was on the point of digging amongst the leaves in search of them, but stopped on an impulse. They would probably be too soiled to wear by now and, in any case, she liked the idea of leaving them here as a kind of offering to the spirit of the woods. Indeed, perhaps they had already been spirited away and were even now being sniffed and inspected by a more substantial, more amorous sprite than the one she had just courted in vain. And who knows, maybe her next visit to the grove might provide her with an altogether different experience than this one had? She put on the shorts and walked briskly out of the gloom, squinting against the glare of the sun.

The warm sun cheered her as she continued on her way. It warmed her thighs. It penetrated her T-shirt and tickled her nipples, honing her desire to a hunger that would need to be assuaged very soon. How to assuage it? She still had no idea, but this beautiful September morning wouldn't let her down, she was sure of that.

She was nearing the house again when she came upon a long low outhouse with a flat roof. She followed the path, now paved with flagstones, along the side of the building until it turned at right angles into a wide gravelled yard. Still on the flagstones, she stopped. The building, it seemed, was a row of garages, and in front of one of them was a car. If she'd known even a little about powerful, fast cars she'd have recognised it immediately as a Ferrari Testarossa. She knew more than a little about men, however, so had no difficulty in recognising the man who leant over it, polishing it with a soft wash-leather. It was Craig.

Craig wasn't wearing his dark glasses this time, but his thick wavy hair was unmistakable. He wasn't wearing his chauffeur's uniform either, but the wide straight shoulders and tapering torso looked the same in a T-shirt as they had when buttoned up in blue serge. He hadn't seen her, so Melanie took advantage of the opportunity to study him for a few minutes. She liked the look of him. She liked the vigour he was putting into his task, the evident power of his arm as he rubbed the long scarlet bonnet.

She could tell this was a labour of love for Craig. He really wanted to see that paintwork shine. He really wanted to feel the ache in his muscles and know that he'd given his all. It was plain to see that Craig was one of those men who love cars above anything else, and such men held a particular kind of appeal for Melanie. Under certain circumstances their predictable, uncomplicated passions could be quite refreshing – and very convenient.

She moved off the flagstones and onto the gravel, her trainers crunching the stone chips with a satisfying sound. Craig heard it and looked up. She strode towards him and the car, conscious of her long bare legs and the way her creamy-white thighs jarred and juddered with each footfall. Craig stopped his polishing and straightened up to observe her approach. His face betrayed no emotion as he stood by the car. He might have been a guard, suspicious of anyone getting too close to his treasure, or an exhibitor, holding back his eagerness to show it off.

'Morning, Ms Brooks,' he said. He glanced down at the car as if he was sure she'd come for no other purpose that to view that magnificent beast. 'She's a beauty, isn't she?'

Melanie followed his gaze to the car and looked it up and down. He'd referred to it as 'she', but it didn't look very feminine to her. The aggressive lines of its wedge-shaped body put her in mind of a weapon of war, the narrow radiator grille, a tight-lipped horizontal slit, spoke of the grim desperation of combat, and the rampant stallion on the badge above the grille confirmed its masculine credentials. It wouldn't do to reveal these thoughts to Craig, of course. Where cars are concerned, gender is in the eye of the beholder. 'She's gorgeous,' she said. 'Absolutely gorgeous.'

Craig smiled with pride, and with something else too. He had a devotee's faith in the power of a fast car to weaken a woman's natural defences, and his eyes and ears were tuned by experience to pick up the signs. And something had chimed with him now. The signs were there: the way she said 'gorgeous', the way she stood with her feet a little apart, pelvis thrust forward? He let his tongue run along his lower lip as he watched her admiring his beloved Ferrari.

'Ferrari Testarossa,' he said. 'Perfect marriage of performance and style. A work of art.'

Melanie drew in her breath appreciatively. Then she lifted her head to take in the car's custodian. 'It must be great to work with one of these beauties every day,' she said. 'Best job in the world for a connoisseur.' She let her eyes flit from him to the car and back again.

'I've no complaints,' he said modestly.

'And you get to go places, too,' she added, gently moving the conversation away from the car and onto the driver.

'A-ah. That's where you're wrong,' said Craig, a mischievous look in his eye as he presented her with the paradox.

'No?' she queried. 'You *don't* go places?'

'I don't *go*,' he said. 'I *take*.'

Nice one, thought Melanie. She was definitely warming to this driver and polisher of cars. She let her face register the barest flicker of shock at the audacity of his words, just so that he'd be aware that their double meaning had not been lost on her. Then she cast her eyes provocatively down while the ghost of a smile creased her dimpled cheeks.

'My boss, now, Mr Drew, *he* goes,' Craig went on. He was so encouraged by these further signals that he almost added 'As I expect you already know', but held back. Things were going well, he thought, but this one was a class act, and a false move could easily blow it for him. He wasn't to know that almost nothing he could have said would have blown it this morning, not even a crude reminder to Melanie of the joys she'd once shared with his exalted boss.

'His guests too. People like yourself, ma'am . . .' This last was daring, and a faint sheen of sweat appeared on his forehead.

This was Melanie's cue, but she waited a few seconds watching the gleam on his forehead intensify before taking up the script again.

'You mean if a guest came to you and said they fancied a ride,' she asked innocently, 'just for the hell of it, you'd take them?'

'That depends,' he said.

'Depends on what?'

'On whether Mr Drew had a prior call on their time.'

His explanation made perfect sense. 'And you'd know that, would you?' she probed.

'I would.'

'He'd have left you in no doubt, I suppose?' She was coming to the crux now. The sweat had evaporated from his forehead, but she felt the back of her own neck prickle.

'None whatsoever,' he said.

She took a deep breath. 'So if I were to say to you now that I'd really fancy . . .?'

'I should think that would be perfectly in order, ma'am.'

And there it was. It would be 'perfectly in order'. It was what she'd already known but had resisted acknowledging to herself. Phillip had 'no prior call on her time'. As far as he was concerned she was just another weekend house guest, one of the legion of women he'd once had an affair with but were now just history. Damn him! she thought. Damn him!

Melanie and Craig stood looking at each other across the gleaming scarlet bonnet of the Ferrari. The polishing leather was still in Craig's hand. He tossed it to the other hand, then back, waiting for her next move. There was nothing he could do or say now. It was all down to her.

Melanie smiled and let her tongue play over her lips. She saw the tension drain from Craig's posture. Then she hoisted herself onto the bonnet, unfastening her shorts as she did so. Craig moved around to the front of the car and helped her arrange her legs along its length. He still held the polishing leather as if he was going to give her the same treatment he'd been giving the car when she first saw him, but that was clearly not in his mind. He let it drop to the ground when she pulled her shorts over her buttocks and he saw she was naked underneath.

Craig leant forward and buried his face between her thighs the instant they were exposed. She slid down the bonnet onto his face, her legs closing around his neck.

She felt his tongue pushing against her clitoris, and it was good. Propping herself with one hand, she took hold of the back of his head with the other and pulled him into her, grinding into his face at the same time. In a little while she would feel his cock sliding into that place, but she wasn't ready for that yet. First, she wanted to feel his teeth hard and sharp against the softness of her vulva. She wanted the roughness, the pain of it. She wanted too the bruises on her back and neck from the hard metal of the Ferrari, and on her thighs from the tightening grip of his hands. She heard her shorts, still around her thighs and obstructing their passion, tear loudly as the seams came apart, but she didn't care. She strained with her legs until they tore completely in two, then she spread herself wider to take him deeper in.

By degrees, and without letting up, they changed positions so that Craig lay on the bonnet and she squatted over him, her cunt still grinding into his mouth. He could hardly breathe. Her clitoris, hard now and fully erect, rubbed itself against the stiff cartilage of his nose. She let the feeling rise without check until she came violently, her juices mingling with his saliva to run down his chin and neck onto the pristine enamel. He's going to have some more polishing to do after this, she thought.

She sensed his relief when she finally eased her assault and raised herself from his face. As he lay gasping on the bonnet, she unfastened his trousers and released his engorged penis, lifting it gently to her mouth. His breathing slowed down to something approaching normal, but he didn't move from the bonnet. She licked the fresh pink glans and massaged the shaft until it was good and hard, then she manoeuvred herself over it and eased herself down, enveloping it in her aching vagina. She heard an intake of breath, but wasn't sure if it was his or hers.

Gently, very gently, she leant over his yielding body and kissed first his cheek, then his lips. Around her, the morning was as still and serene as a Corot landscape. Craig looked up at her, his eyes wide as if trying to drink her in, but her eyes were filled only with Ferrari scarlet as she slowly fucked him where he lay.

8

Discovery

Melanie abandoned her shorts as beyond even temporary repair. Fortunately, her T-shirt was long enough to preserve her modesty if she used her hands to prevent it riding up. That would have to do till she got back to her room. Craig, who might have offered her some kind of covering from his own wardrobe but didn't think of it, had the grace nevertheless to direct her to a back entrance that would make an embarrassing encounter less likely.

The back entrance took her past the kitchen and pantry to a door that opened into the main hall via the stairwell. She tiptoed along to the foot of the stairs, hugging the wainscoting. The hall was empty, so all she had to do was hurry up the two flights to her room. She paused in the shelter of the stairs, then chose her moment.

Her foot was on the first step when she heard someone approaching from a room across the hall. A spur of the moment decision was called for. If she pressed on up the stairs, whoever emerged into the hall had only to glance up to see her retreating backside peeking pinkly out from under the T-shirt. Better to hide, but where? She ducked through the nearest open door, the library.

She realised her mistake at once. There were papers arrayed on the large leather-inlaid table as if someone was working there and had just popped out for a moment. That someone, it now became apparent, was returning. She checked that her T-shirt was tugged well down and composed herself as best she could, just in time to turn with a smile of greeting as Jeanette walked in.

Jeanette was startled to see Melanie there. 'Oh!' she said. 'Did you enjoy your walk, Melanie?'

'Yes. Thank you,' said Melanie. She started to edge towards the door as Jeanette crossed to the table. She didn't like the way those gimlet eyes seemed fixed on the hem of her T-shirt.

'Weren't you wearing shorts?' asked Jeanette.

'Er, I'm afraid they got caught on some barbed wire. Torn to shreds.' Melanie laughed as though it was really quite a funny sort of thing to happen. 'I was trying to get to my room without being seen. Ducked in here when I heard you coming.'

'Oh,' said Jeanette with ostentatious sympathy. 'What a shame. I hope you weren't hurt. On the wire, I mean.'

'Oh no,' said Melanie a little too quickly. 'I was lucky, I suppose.'

'Let me help you,' said Jeanette. 'I can shield you from view as we go up the stairs. There's only Charles in the house at the moment, but we wouldn't want to shock him, would we?'

Melanie had no choice but to accept the offer. The two women left the library and headed up the stairs. Jeanette seemed to want to walk a step or two below Melanie, ostensibly to shield her from view, but Melanie tried to keep her at the same level so that she wouldn't see that it wasn't just shorts that were lacking but panties too. The result was a halting, hesitant *pas de deux* as they slowly ascended first one flight then the second.

They reached Melanie's room and she opened her door. 'Thank you so much, Jeanette,' she said. 'I'm quite safe now. And so is Charles.' She laughed nervously.

But Jeanette wasn't ready to be dismissed. She followed Melanie into the room before the latter had even thought it might be necessary to prevent her. 'Let me tell you what *I* think, Melanie,' she hissed, her face suddenly stern, her eyes narrower than ever. 'I think you're a liar. Barbed wire, indeed!' Her nostrils flared and a flush came to her face as she launched into her accusation. 'I happen to know that Mr Drew doesn't allow so much as an inch of barbed wire on the entire estate. You're a liar, Melanie Brooks, a bare-faced liar.'

Melanie was dumbstruck. She put a hand to her mouth, giving Jeanette the chance to lift her T-shirt with a lightning swoop of her long slim hand.

'I thought as much,' she said. She peered down at Melanie's trim dark bush and an exposed pink and white buttock. 'And I suppose those weals are down to the barbed wire, too?' she asked in a pull-the-other-one tone of voice.

Melanie felt like a schoolgirl caught behind the bicycle sheds doing something she shouldn't. She couldn't think of anything to say, but just gazed at her feet, mouth open. Jeanette wasn't letting up.

'And this anniversary of yours. It's a fabrication, isn't it? Isn't it?

'Y-yes,' admitted Melanie in a weak voice.

'Poor Charles,' said Jeanette. 'The poor man is eating himself up with guilt in the belief that he's ruined your anniversary and jeopardised your relationship with Mark. And all the while . . .' Words appeared to fail her for a moment.

'It makes my blood boil!' she went on. 'He doesn't deserve that kind of treatment from a . . . a *slut* like you.'

The epithet sliced through Melanie like a blade. She felt it in her chest, in her tummy, in her groin. She felt trapped and helpless, completely at the mercy of this ferocious woman. She had no idea what was going to happen next, and it was scary. It was very, very scary. But, somehow, it was exciting too. Melanie's entire future seemed to be at stake, and she felt the thrill a gambler must feel when venturing all his possessions on a turn of a card.

'I . . . I can explain . . .' she began.

'You can explain, can you? Well, that's very good, because that's exactly what you're going to do, you slut!' Jeanette was gripping her arm and leading her to the side of the room where there was a simple wooden chair. 'I'm going to get the truth out of you before you do any more damage with your wicked lies.' Jeanette sat on the chair. Melanie stood facing her, feeling her fingers biting into the soft flesh of her upper arm.

'Bend over,' Jeanette ordered.

'What!' exclaimed Melanie. She could scarcely grasp the woman's intention.

'Bend over,' Jeanette repeated. 'You're going to tell me the truth if I have to beat it out of you.'

This was unbelievable! Jeanette, her boss's P.A., intended to take her over her knee and spank her as if she were a child! Melanie fought back an upsurge of resentful defiance. She didn't have to go through with this. If she wanted to, she could pull her arm free and stand up to her adversary, ordering her from her room. But she knew that would be a mistake. Jeanette, who could so easily expose her to the stern disapproval of her rather old-fashioned boss, was choosing instead to tackle her on her own. Going along with her now, she reasoned, would disarm her for the future. Charles would be no less censorious of Jeanette's behaviour than of her own, and Jeanette must realise this as well as she did. It followed that the aftermath of whatever was to befall would inevitably involve some degree of complicity between the two women, and this was bound to be an improvement on the sniping war that had prevailed up to now.

The logic of the situation was, therefore, to do just as Jeanette commanded, but it wasn't logic that sent that familiar buzz through Melanie's abdomen as she prepared to kneel and bend. The fiery look in Jeanette's eyes, the way those silky swathes shaded her gaunt cheek, and the light hairiness of the stockingless thighs, exposed by the hibiscus dress that had ridden halfway up them, sparked the kind of lust she'd felt for Arlene. She lifted her T-shirt and bent across those thighs, feeling their warmth against her belly. She made herself comfortable as she presented her buttocks, naked, vulnerable, and ready for whatever violations her castigator might bestow.

The first smack fell on Melanie's upper thigh, well away from her tattoo of four pink parallel welts. It wasn't very hard, but smarted pleasantly. 'Why did you lie about your anniversary?'

Melanie tried to think of a plausible answer. Another smack descended, this one harder than the first. 'I want the truth,' said Jeanette. Melanie gave her a partial explanation. Jeanette, dissatisfied, probed for more details, and smacked her a third time when she was again too slow to answer. It made Melanie squeal.

'Just tell me the full story,' said Jeanette, 'from the beginning. And you'd better tell me how you got these marks on your behind while you're about it,' she added. 'I know whiplash weals when I see them, so don't give me any nonsense about barbed wire.'

And, piece by piece, Jeanette extracted all the information she wanted from the hapless Melanie. If the answers came too slowly, the smacks became more frequent and harder. As long as Melanie talked, they eased into gentle pats or tender strokes, except at particularly salacious points in the narrative when the smacks came raining down in quick excited flurries. Jeanette was aroused, and Melanie was fully aware of the fact.

'Now tell me whose cum this is?' asked Jeanette when Melanie reached the end of her narrative. She had scooped a gobbet of coagulated semen from Melanie's vulva and was holding it in front of her face. 'Who did you fuck this morning?'

Melanie told her.

'Craig! The driver!' Jeanette was scornful. 'Couldn't you have done better, slut?'

Melanie didn't like to have her taste in men disparaged like this. 'Craig's good,' she insisted. 'He's hung like a stallion and he knows what to do with it.' She told the tale of their encounter, exaggerating it just a little for Jeanette's benefit. She felt the fingers rubbing her pubes as she spoke, spreading Craig's come onto her thighs and belly. Then she was spanked again for being such a slut, but not very hard. A musky salty smell in Melanie's nostrils told her that Jeanette was creaming copiously, but the latter, after easing Melanie to her feet, stood up herself, smoothing her dress and composing her expression into one of unassailable virtue. 'Now, slut,' she said, and how she relished that word, 'you'd better get yourself cleaned up and properly dressed. Your bathroom has a bidet, hasn't it?'

'Indeed,' said Melanie. 'Just the thing to wash all this come out of my pussy. Perhaps you'd be good enough to supervise, Jeanette? Make sure I do a thorough job?'

Jeanette's eyes gleamed. Melanie smiled inwardly; she was beginning to get the measure of Jeanette.

Melanie was in Jeanette's bedroom on the first floor looking through the handful of dresses, skirts, etc. the latter had brought with her to Huntscroft. She chose a dress and tried it on. It was similar in cut and style to the one Jeanette was wearing, being pale green with a print of orange and red freesias. It fitted reasonably well, if a little loosely. Jeanette approved.

Then Melanie sat at the small dressing table while Jeanette attended to her hair, brushing it out and sweeping it back. The end result would have taken second prize to Jeanette's own, but it was pronounced satisfactory. Then the two women stood together in front of the full-length mirror. The resemblance was apparent, if not striking. Melanie felt as she thought an actress must feel when getting into a part. It was strange how much the dress and hairstyle helped. She tried to compose her face to look as much as possible like the older woman, but didn't really get close. Perhaps that was just as well. She tried a more lascivious expression, and that came much more easily.

'I hope this is going to work,' said Melanie.

'So do I,' said Jeanette. She opened the door and they set off downstairs to the drawing room.

After delivering her richly deserved chastisement, Jeanette had had one further stipulation to make to her temporarily submissive colleague. She was very worried, it seemed, about Charles. The 'poor man', as she called him, was driving himself too hard. He worried about everything, too, which made matters much worse. Since his divorce he had almost no private life, and what social life he enjoyed was so bound up with business that it hardly counted. Jeanette had begun to fear for his health.

Melanie, unsure where this was leading, had asked how she could help. She was told that Charles thought very highly of her and that although Jeanette didn't think she herself could influence him, perhaps Melanie might. Further discussion revealed what was really in Jeanette's mind. Charles, it seemed, needed to be 'taken out of himself', and while Jeanette was not the kind of woman who could do this, a beautiful slut like Melanie would have no trouble at all.

Melanie was shocked. But not for long. She had no great desire to seduce Charles – although he was an attractive man in his way – not least because it would risk an entanglement that could only further complicate her already chaotic situation. On the other hand, Jeanette was right, he did seem to be overdoing things. It would certainly do him no harm to let his hair down for a change. But another idea presented itself to Melanie. Although Charles's relationship with his P.A. had always been strictly professional, the fact that there was a mutual attraction was evident from a thousand little looks and gestures. Everyone was aware of this, and speculation was endemic in the office. Only they, it seemed, had not admitted it to themselves. Surely a compromise was possible in this situation?

So Melanie proposed an amendment to Jeanette's plan. She would play the strumpet and get inside Charles's pants, but not on her own account. She would be Jeanette's sluttish alter ego, doing for her what she didn't dare do for herself. Jeanette's mouth opened as she heard the proposition. She didn't answer, but tears appeared in her eyes after a while. Then she kissed Melanie fully on the mouth in gratitude.

And so, two female figures approached the drawing room across the main hall. As the late-morning sunlight descended from the upper windows and passed through the flimsy summer fabric of their dresses, it revealed that they were wearing nothing underneath, nothing at all.

Charles was sitting in one of the thickly upholstered wing chairs reading a document from a pile that lay on the occasional table at his elbow. He looked up when they entered.

'Ah, Jeanette,' he said. He'd been expecting her some time since. 'And Melanie,' he added in a rising tone. He hadn't been expecting her. 'Did you enjoy your walk, Melanie?' He looked at her curiously, aware that there was something unusual about her appearance but not sure what it was.

'Yes, thank you, Charles,' said Melanie. 'It was very pleasant.'

Charles's face started to take on the anguished look she'd seen so often that weekend. 'I'm afraid Mark and Phillip aren't back from golf yet,' he said. 'Phillip rang to say they'd be . . . ahh, hmm . . . lunching at the club. Met some of his business associates. Won't be back until mid afternoon. Er, perhaps four. Er, could be later . . . even.' It was as if he was breaking news of a serious accident to a relative of the victim.

Melanie was hardly surprised. She'd seen so little of Mark since they'd stepped out of the limousine that she'd almost forgotten she'd come with him. With Phillip, however, it was a different matter. She was still smarting at his indifference to her. Had their affair meant so little to him? She flushed in frustration, a manifestation that Charles misinterpreted.

'Hope our company isn't too desperately dull,' he said, his lips twisted in a sympathetic grimace. 'This can't be the way you'd have chosen to spend your anniversary.'

Melanie resisted an impulse to reveal the truth to Charles. Better not to complicate the task in hand. 'Of course it's not dull, Charles. Your company. I've just had a lovely chat with Jeanette, and now we've come to join you. We women get lonely when we're too long away from a man. We start to feel deprived. Isn't that right, Jeanette?'

'Er, indeed,' muttered Jeanette shyly.

'Oh, er, yes, well,' muttered Charles uncomfortably.

Melanie wasn't at all sure how to go about her assignment, how to get the right balance between the provocative and the reassuring, the arousing and the tranquillising. So far she'd only succeeded in making him uncomfortable with the mildest innuendo.

98

Jeanette crossed to the coffee dispenser on the sideboard and poured one for Melanie and for herself. Jeanette handed Melanie hers. To drink it, she propped herself against the arm of Charles's chair, the cloth of her dress tensing against the flesh of her backside, showing its contours and even a tinge of pink through the fine material. Charles's face reddened slightly and his eyes turned towards the window. He had picked up his coffee cup from the occasional table, and it rattled in its saucer.

Melanie sipped appreciatively and only a little ostentatiously. 'Mmm! This is good coffee,' she said. 'So strong. Such a rich flavour.' She emphasised the adjectives, her eyes transferring them from the coffee to Charles himself.

Charles avoided her gaze and reached towards the pile of papers, but Melanie caught his hand before it got to its destination. 'Leave the papers, Charles,' she said. 'This is the weekend, and you should be relaxing, especially after the stresses and strains of yesterday. Anyway, you promised Mark and me a weekend to remember. Well, Mark's having the time of his life with your friend and my ex-tutor, so it's up to you to entertain me, don't you think?' Melanie knew it was cruel to keep re-awakening his misguided sense of guilt, but it was a really handy way of throwing him off kilter.

'Not my forte, I'm afraid,' he muttered. 'Entertaining the ladies, I mean. No gift for it.'

'Nonsense,' said Melanie gently. 'I know I shouldn't say it to my boss, even on a weekend, but you're a very handsome man, Charles. Isn't he, Jeanette? Isn't he a lovely man?'

Jeanette stumbled over her words as she agreed. 'Oh, er, yes,' she said. 'I've always considered . . . I mean . . . Yes, very love- . . . er, handsome.'

Charles looked from one to the other, unable to comprehend what was happening. He had a vague sense of valuable professional relationships in jeopardy, of future embarrassments, of personal problems disrupting the smooth flow of his business life. On the other hand, there was something compelling about their soft words, their smiles. It was as if they were unlocking something inside him that he'd forgotten was there. He wanted to put a stop to this before he succumbed completely, but Melanie was holding his hand in both of hers now, and he didn't want her to let it go for the moment. He sat silently, breathing in the gentle perfumes of the two female bodies, absorbing the warmth that radiated from them.

'Oh, er,' he coughed. 'Nice of you to say that.' In his book, it was the man who paid the compliments to the ladies, not the other way about, but that just seemed to add to the poignancy of the situation. He was softening inside, and he was aware of it.

'Why don't we, er . . . Why don't we, er . . .' He was desperately trying to think of a way to redeem the situation. 'Er, why don't we all go for a walk?' he blurted.

'But Jeanette and I aren't dressed for the outdoors, are we, Jeanette?' Melanie straightened her body inside the loose-fitting dress. Now it was the turn of her breasts to feel the tension of the cloth against them. Charles nearly knocked his cup and saucer from the arm of his chair as her nipples pricked forward under the freesia print and imposed themselves on his consciousness.

'You see,' she continued, showing off the blooms on her bosom, 'we're a couple of hot-house flowers. We need plenty of care and attention.'

Charles took his hand away from her light grasp. For a moment, he thought it would reach up of its own volition and touch those blossoms, but it didn't. 'Look, Melanie,' he said seriously. 'I know you must be upset about, about . . .' he couldn't bring himself to re-open the wound '. . . and Jeanette and I are prepared to make

100

allowances,' he glanced at Jeanette for corroboration, 'but please have a care. This kind of talk. Not used to it . . . old girl.'

The appended 'old girl' was intended to convey all the sympathy and understanding he was capable of, and forgiveness, too, if she'd only ease off the pressure. Melanie looked at Jeanette, whose eyes were wide and glistening as she returned Melanie's gaze. Melanie heard her silent plea not to give up, not to let him off the hook.

'That's a pity, Charles,' she said. 'A man like you has so much to give to women like us, to Jeanette and me.' She stroked his cheek. He winced and turned imploring eyes to Jeanette, hoping for the support he so often relied on from his loyal, irascible, formidable P.A., but he saw in her eyes only a more timid version of whatever it was he saw in Melanie's. He knew then that he was lost. Nevertheless, he held Jeanette's gaze as if it were a lifeline.

Melanie saw that they were winning. She gestured Jeanette to come closer, and made room for her at the foot of the chair.

'Jeanette is so worried about you, Charles,' she said. 'She thinks you work too hard, and I agree.' She massaged his neck so gently he seemed unaware she was doing it. 'We don't want our favourite boss getting ill, do we?' whispered Melanie. 'And such a lovely boss, at that.' Jeanette took his hand in hers while Melanie leant into the armchair so that her lightly covered breasts were close to his face. He was breathing deeply. His eyes were moist and dull.

'Let me loosen your shirt so you can relax,' said Melanie. His short-sleeved sports shirt was already open at the neck, but there was no harm in undoing another button or two. 'Such a manly chest,' Melanie went on, 'So strong.' She put her hand into his shirt and stroked his pecs, letting her fingers play over the nipples.

101

'What? . . . What? . . .' he started to say.

'Sssh,' whispered Melanie. 'Just relax, dear Charles. You'll feel so much better if you relax. Jeanette and I will make you feel so, so much better.'

Melanie reached for his fly with her other hand and gently undid the top button before unzipping it. His sigh told her the release of pressure was appreciated. She continued her stroking, enjoying the hardness of his nipples. She glanced at Jeanette, who was still holding his hand in both of hers, but the latter didn't understand the signal, so Melanie reached into his fly and brought his half-erect prick out of its inner wrapping. Charles saw his exposed cock and suddenly became alert, as if awakening from a hypnotic trance. Melanie had to regain the initiative immediately.

'Now, Charles,' she said, her voice firm and authoritative. 'Don't resist. We know what's good for you, and we're going to make sure you get it.' She held her hand against his chest in a gesture of restraint. When she was sure he wouldn't make any sudden move, she stood up and pulled her dress over her head in a single sweep. She felt her breasts bounce back onto her chest and knew the sight of them, with their firm erect nipples, had excited him. His gasp confirmed it. She brought her breast to his face. 'Do you like my tits, Charles? I want you to play with them. Like this.' She plucked at her nipples, and rolled them and squeezed them with her fingers. It was vital she get him to do the same, right now. He hesitated. 'Take them, Charles. I so want to feel your strong fingers squeezing my lovely nipples. Go on, Charles.'

It took Jeanette, in a temporary show of sluttishness, to clinch the matter. 'Go on, Charles,' she said. 'Suck her nipples. They taste of strawberries.' Charles obeyed and opened his mouth as Melanie pressed her right breast forward.

Despite his previous hesitancy, Charles didn't hold back once the barriers were down. He sucked vigorously at Melanie's nipple, working it with his tongue so that it became hard as a rock. He grasped at her breasts with both his hands as he sucked. He was so strong, Melanie was afraid he might twist them right off. She knew he still needed careful handling, however.

'Oh, Charles,' she murmured. 'Wonderful, wonderful Charles.' She gestured with her eyes to Jeanette. Again, Jeanette failed to understand, so Melanie had to mouth the message 'suck his cock'. Jeanette's lip-reading was up to scratch, and she went down on his lap, taking his now firmly erect cock into her mouth. Charles groaned loudly.

'You see, Charles,' said Melanie. 'Jeanette thinks you're wonderful too. She's wanted you for so long. She'll swallow you whole, if you let her.'

Charles released Melanie's breasts and reached for Jeanette's head. He put one huge hand on the back of her neck and looked into her eyes as she sucked and licked his long shaft. 'Jeanette . . . old girl,' he muttered between groans. 'I . . . I just never knew.'

Since Jeanette wasn't in a position to speak for herself, and wouldn't have known what to say in any case, Melanie did the talking for her. 'She's longed for you, Charles. She's creamed herself thinking of how good you'd feel inside her. She's creaming herself now as she sucks your gorgeous cock. She wants you to lick the cream from her slit, then fuck her, Charles, fuck her for all the times you could have fucked her before but didn't.'

Jeanette did not deny this. She let his prick slither from her mouth and rose from her kneeling position and moved forward to take his yielding head in her hands and kiss him on the lips. As they kissed, Melanie took a grip of Charles's trousers and pulled them off. She did the same with his underpants. Then she took hold of Charles's prick and guided it under Jeanette's dress to the bush of light brown hair. She parted the moist labia with her fingers and directed the prick into place. Jeanette's body sank on cue and the shaft disappeared into the tender hairy folds.

When Melanie left the room shortly afterwards, having recovered her borrowed dress from the floor and put it on, she was smiling to herself. She felt truly happy for the first time since her arrival at Huntscroft.

9

Home is Where the Heart is

Back in the lonely room at the top of the house, Melanie's mood took a deflationary turn. Her satisfaction at having helped Jeanette and Charles find each other at last was matched by the realisation that now there was no one left for her. Huntscroft, as far as she was concerned, might as well be the ice floe she had taunted Mark with in the car, except that not even Mark was present to share it with her. After a quick shower, she changed back to her own clothes, made a telephone call on her mobile, then picked up the house phone and pressed the button labelled 'driver'.

'Hi, Craig,' she said. 'What if I were to tell you I'm ready for another ride?'

Craig's answer was brief.

'No, definitely not the Ferrari again,' she said, smiling. 'And not the limousine, either. Something plain and functional this time.' They exchanged a few more words and the arrangement was made.

Ten minutes later, her overnight bag in her hand, Melanie descended the stairs and crossed the hall. The drawing room door was closed, just as she'd left it. The house seemed deserted. Craig was waiting outside, leaning on the bonnet of a silver-grey BMW that had to be the top-of-the-range in its class.

'Is that the best you could do?' she asked as she handed him the bag to put in the boot.

''Fraid so,' he said. 'But to make up for it I didn't bother with the uniform.' He was, in fact, dressed in a sports shirt and slacks.

She eyed him up and down. 'That looks functional, all right,' she said. 'But I don't think you could look plain if you tried.'

Craig beamed. 'Front or back?' he asked.

'My, you're certainly one for the *doubles entendres*, aren't you, Craig?' she teased. 'Will I be safe in the front seat with you?'

'As houses, ma'am,' he said. He meant it, too. She'd let him know if she wanted it again. No point in alienating her. No point at all.

Melanie got in and they veered off across the clean white gravel to the long driveway. Melanie peered over her shoulder as the woods closed around the diminishing facade of Huntscroft. Just at that precise moment, she didn't care if she never saw it again.

After only thirty-five minutes on near-empty roads, the BMW glided to a halt. Melanie turned to Craig and thanked him for a pleasant, safe ride into town. She also planted a little kiss on his cheek by way of thanks for the rather more exciting ride to quite another destination he'd given her that morning. Then she got out of the car and stood on the kerb while he fetched her bag from the boot.

'If anyone asks, you dropped me at my house, okay?' A generous tip began its journey from Melanie's handbag to Craig's pocket, but it didn't even see the light of day.

'Not necessary, ma'am,' he said, waving her aside. 'Pleasure to be of service to you.' He got back into the driver's seat and closed the door. It suited him to leave her feeling indebted. He had an idea that he'd be seeing more of Ms Melanie Brooks.

* * *

Melanie rang the top bell of the stack. The buzzer sounded almost immediately and she pushed open the door. As she walked up the stairs she could see a welcoming face peering over the stairwell from the very top. She smiled up at Kirsty, and her heart was smiling too.

There was an array of things to eat on the table in the tiny kitchen. They were mostly out of packets via the microwave, but it was already 1.30 and Melanie hadn't eaten since breakfast. She ate ravenously and with appreciation for her friend's thoughtfulness. Kirsty too was hungry, having postponed her own lunch when she'd got Melanie's phone call.

They sat along adjacent edges of the table, chatting as they ate and exchanging light fleeting touches. Melanie was nervous. On the previous day, she'd come back to the flat after her encounter on the stairs with Arlene feeling a kind of unsteady, uncertain lust for the hitherto un-sampled flesh of another woman. That had been easy to deal with. Today, it was different. Today, it was the warmth of Kirsty's affection for her that she was most aware of and, next to that, the warmth she felt for Kirsty in return. And that was much harder to deal with.

Kirsty seemed to know how Melanie felt because she did nothing to precipitate the situation. They'd been together for half an hour, and they hadn't even kissed. In fact, Kirsty seemed to be enjoying her friend's hesitancy, as if reading into it nothing but positive signs for herself. And perhaps she was right. Apparently deserted by Mark, evidently ignored by Phillip, and practically frozen out by the haughty Huntscroft, Melanie had found a welcome here in Kirsty's cramped unlovely kitchen. She felt that, should she choose to do so, she could stay forever, basking in the glow of her love. And that would be such a radical step to take, wouldn't it? No wonder she was nervous.

The warm food and hot coffee revived and calmed her. She told Kirsty about Ernesto and Arancha, and about the reprieve B&C had been granted for the Castadiosa contract. She told her about Phillip Drew, her former tutor, and his sumptuous country residence, though without mentioning the affair she'd had with him in the dim and distant past. She told her too how Phillip had promptly commandeered Mark, so that she'd barely had any time with either of them the whole weekend. In all, she told her most of the things that mattered and several that didn't, but she kept quiet about Craig, and about Jeanette and Charles.

When they'd finished their lunch, they went to Kirsty's bedroom. It was the first time Melanie had entered it. She was surprised; if the sitting room was functional and cold, the bedroom was as cosy as a womb. It was decorated in subdued warm pinks and ochres with subtle hints of the deeper more sensual tones of mauve and purple. It seemed to calm Melanie's mind while fanning the already glowing coals of her desire. Like the sitting room, its walls were well bedecked with drawings, though here they were arranged with evident care, and many of them were framed in coloured card or stained wood. Their subject matter was different too, not designs but portraits and full-figure studies. All were of women, some young, some of middle age.

On one wall, there was a cluster of portraits of a woman Melanie recognised. It was herself. If she'd harboured doubts about Kirsty's feelings for her before, those portraits would have put an end to them. They were executed with such feeling that the involvement of artist with subject could not have been questioned. Melanie looked at them, then at Kirsty. No words were exchanged, but they kissed for the first time that day.

They undressed like old lovers, each removing her own clothes without ostentation and folding them neatly or hanging them out of harm's way. Then they got into the bed, whose sheets – freshly changed for the occasion – smelt deliciously of summer flowers and were soft and cool on their skins. They lay facing each other, covered by a single sheet that seemed more to heighten their nakedness than mask it. Melanie studied the soft contours of Kirsty's face and neck and breasts. She wanted to give something precious to this lovely young thing who was offering her so much. She was still aware of the dangers, but her heart was so full she didn't care. The moment made its own demands and wouldn't be satisfied with less.

Melanie slid her hand between Kirsty's neck and the pillow, drawing her face slowly towards her own. She put her lips to Kirsty's and let them play to and fro across them before easing them apart with the tip of her tongue. Not a kiss as such. Nothing so energetic. More a caress, gentle and slow, that could be made to last a minute, an hour, a whole day even, without risk of anticlimax. Kirsty sighed softly as she gave herself to it.

Mouth to mouth, they intoxicated each other in slow motion. For a long time, only their mouths and the points of their breasts were in contact, but it was as if they were melting into each other's bodies. Later, Melanie let her other hand trace the contours of Kirsty's flanks until it found her hip, her thigh. The thigh parted from its neighbour, allowing the hand to slip between. With her fingers Melanie probed between the soft wet labia and pushed slowly into Kirsty's vagina. Kirsty sighed deeply. Her pelvis shuddered, then pushed down onto the fingers. Melanie's thumb burrowed upwards under the soft folds of flesh to find the sweet bud of Kirsty's clitoris, and stayed there palping gently as the bud hardened and expanded under it.

After that, it wasn't necessary to move her fingers at all, just to hold them firmly where they were and flex or relax her muscles from time to time, for Melanie was making love mainly with her lips. She ran them lightly along Kirsty's own, nipping at them gently, or blowing softly at the corners of her passive mouth. Sometimes Melanie's tongue would reach in to find its counterpart and stroke its tip, its underside. Melanie knew that Kirsty would barely be able to distinguish between the sensations in her mouth and in her pussy, and she felt a pang of lust for the taste of that pussy in her own mouth, but her lust was irrelevant now. All that mattered was to give to Kirsty what she was so avidly taking, and the giving of it was so, so sweet. Kirsty's eyes were closed now, and her body was beginning to tremble. Melanie fed that tremble without cease as it rose and subsided, rose and subsided in a series of waves like an offshore swell after a storm.

Melanie lost count of the peaks and troughs as the tranquil turbulence played itself out over untracked time. Although the giver, it felt to Melanie as if those soft orgasms belonged as much to her as to Kirsty, as if they were sharing her gift as they had shared the lunch Kirsty had prepared for her, and the bed whose sheets she had changed and perfumed. And at that moment Melanie could think of nothing that could possibly be better than this, being here sharing these things with Kirsty.

Afterwards, Kirsty slept in Melanie's arms. It gave Melanie time to think. Too much time. What she had just experienced was love. There was no doubt about it. She had soaked up Kirsty's love as a marooned and desiccated eel soaks up the rain, and she had reflected that love straight back to Kirsty, who had herself absorbed and amplified it, so that the cycle of love had grown between them until it had filled the universe.

But a rehydrated eel usually goes straight back into the river. Was the same true of Melanie? Was she here just to fill the vacuum created by Huntscroft before resuming her previous life? Only thirty hours before, she was Mark's lover, and he was hers. They had belonged together and didn't question it. The idea that she could feel anything comparable for a woman, or that a woman could be in love with her, hadn't even entered her head. How could things have changed so much in so short a time? It seemed impossible.

And yet, it had been wonderful just then. It had been wonderful with Mark, of course. It had been wonderful with Phillip, too – oh, so very wonderful. This wasn't more wonderful, nor less, but very, very different. Was she going to have to choose which kind of wonderful to settle for?

Did she even have a choice? Could she return to the *status quo ante* now, even if she wanted to? Was Mark still her man, or had he given her up for snooker and golf and who-knows-what with Phillip? Oh dear! she thought. It seems she had once again solved a short-term problem by creating a long-term one. And the long-term problem was now waking up. Kirsty opened her eyes, and those eyes were filled with adoration.

'That was wonderful, Mel,' said Kirsty. She smiled like a contented cat. 'You know, it's never been as good as that for me before, not with anyone.'

Melanie winced inwardly. She didn't want to hear that, even though she was flattered. She was far from ready for the kind of conversation she saw presaged in Kirsty's earnest adoring expression. She pecked Kirsty on the nose. 'It was great for me too, kid,' she said.

'But you didn't come!' said Kirsty. 'Tell me what you want, Mel. Let me do it for you now.'

'I didn't need to, Kirsty love. You came for both of us. It really was wonderful, honest.' She kissed Kirsty again, eliciting a sigh that was almost threatening. 'But I'll tell you what you can do if you want to make me happy,' she said.

'What?' asked Kirsty eagerly.

'You can tell me what you think about Castadiosa.'

* * *

111

Melanie, Kirsty and Arlene were seated on beanbags in Kirsty's chilly sitting room. Plumes of steam rose from their coffee mugs. Melanie could almost imagine plumes of steam rising from their skulls, too, such was the intensity of their conversation. They were talking about Castadiosa.

It had been Kirsty's idea to involve Arlene. After hearing Arancha's cryptic final remark to Melanie, Kirsty had thought it natural to call in the expert on 'e-stripe-es' and 'back-e-sides'. Melanie had raised no objection.

'I guess we're talking virtual stripes here,' said Arlene. 'Ain't no world-wide-web been invented that could transmit the kind of thing I can do with my flexible friend, unless your Spanish housewife's in the habit of sticking her ass in the mains socket.'

'I think the word is "metaphorical", Arlene,' said Kirsty. 'We've got to stripe her bum metaphorically.'

'Tough call either way,' said Arlene. 'Show me a real ass, now, and I'll put some mighty fine stripes on it, ain't that right, Melanie?' Melanie nodded vigorously. 'But metaphorical is tough.' Arlene was accepting the challenge. 'We gotta look behind the stripes themselves. Stripes wake you up. They make your mind turn over new pages. They change your life. We gotta do the same thing but without the aid of Arlene's sinuous sidekick.'

'Okay, but we still have to give her a jolt of some kind, don't you think?' Kirsty was deep in thought. 'We've got to deliver some kind of shock, even if it isn't through the mains socket. We've got to awaken her imagination. Show her that there's more to life than her routine. More to life *in* her routine than she thinks.'

'You mean like itemise the household objects she can bring herself off with?' asked Arlene.

'No!' protested Kirsty, shocked by her friend's crudeness. 'Okay, yes,' she conceded after a moment's pause.

'In a way. What I mean is, we've got to show her the possibilities that surround her. We've got to make the familiar strange and erotic, show her channels for her sexual energy she didn't know existed.'

'I catch your drift, Kirsty my love,' said Arlene. 'Disassociation and re-association. Take a familiar object. Snap off all the dead customs and habits bristling from it and you're left with something smooth enough to shag a nun with. Snap! Snap! That's where the shock comes in. Show her the essence of the thing. Then open up her imagination to put it in a new context, a context of her choosing, without censure, without restraint. She's in control. She's the goddess. If it's good enough for her, it's good.'

'That's it,' said Kirsty. 'We've got to give her the world and trust her to fashion it as her instincts tell her to. But we'll have to convince her first that the world is hers to fashion. It won't be easy. We'll have to find a way to tap into her psyche.'

Melanie was fascinated by their talk. She wanted to contribute, but this kind of brainstorming wasn't her forte. The kind she was good at was all about management procedures – how to increase the efficiency of this process or that, how to cut costs, how to maximise the return for a given expenditure. This was different. This was about changing the world. This was about raising the consciousness of half the population of, in the first instance, Catalonia.

But, fascinating though it was, there was something not quite right about it. There was something they were overlooking in their enthusiasm. She cleared her throat.

'Great stuff, girls,' she said, 'but aren't you putting the cart before the horse?'

They stared at her expectantly.

'Before we sell Castadiosa to the women of Spain, we've got to sell Bermont and Cuthbertson to Castadiosa.'

There was silence for several minutes. Heads were scratched, glances were exchanged. Then all three started speaking at once.

It was almost three o'clock in the morning when three exhausted women flopped fully dressed onto Kirsty's bed, leaving a mound of plates, coffee mugs, snack containers and wine glasses on the sitting room carpet. On the sofa was another mound, of scribbled notes and sketches on crumpled sheets of paper. It was the plan of campaign that would win the contract for Bermont and Cuthbertson.

For Melanie, it was also the plot of the vivid dreams that rattled through her brain as she lay entwined amongst the arms, legs and gently heaving torsos of her lover and her friend. Not surprising, this, since it was Melanie who would carry the responsibility for the success or failure of that campaign. But the dreams were not the anxiety-filled torments that you might expect, because Melanie had known, when the last sheet of paper was laid on the pile, that the plan was a brilliant one. Kirsty and Arlene – with significant contributions from Melanie herself, she was proud to recall – had pieced together a scenario guaranteed to blow away Ernesto's doubts and save Arancha's reputation. It was going to be good. It was going to be exciting. And Melanie was so looking forward to it that she couldn't stop running it through in her mind, even as she slept.

She was still playing it through early the next morning as she washed enough mugs and plates for a cursory breakfast. When the coffee aroma began feeling its way through the flat, she was joined by Arlene, who rubbed her eyes in the artificial light as if she couldn't believe she could be up so early.

'Gimme summa that coffee,' she muttered. Melanie poured her a mugful and passed her the sugar and milk.

'Some night last night, huh?' said Arlene after a few gulps. 'I feel like I been at an orgy, and I never even took off my pants!' Then her voice dropped an octave as she vented what was on her mind. 'Listen, Mel,' she said, 'I guess you know how Kirsty feels about you, don't you?'

Melanie nodded.

'I mean she's really in love with you. I ain't never seen her like that before, and I've seen her through an affair or two, I can tell you!'

Melanie nodded again. She'd been afraid this was so.

'She's a great kid, Mel,' Arlene went on. 'I know you got other irons in the fire, and I guess you've got some serious sorting out to do, but don't hurt her. Understand? Kirsty's my friend, and I won't see her hurt.'

It was almost a threat, but Melanie didn't take offence. She felt the same. She didn't want to see Kirsty hurt, and she certainly didn't want to be the cause of any hurt to her. How to avoid it, though? That was the problem.

'I won't hurt her, Arlene,' she said. 'I promise you that.'

Arlene smiled and put her arm around Melanie's shoulder. It made Melanie feel guilty. Why did she keep doing this sort of thing, promising things she didn't know how to deliver?

10

Starting the Week

Back in her own home, Melanie showered and changed. She'd left Arlene tidying the flat and Kirsty sleeping like a child. They would make their appearance in the office later in the day. Melanie would get there early to prepare the ground, but first she had to sharpen her sleep-deprived wits and smarten herself up. A shower and another cup of coffee worked wonders. A smart pinstripe trouser suit and a touch of make-up finished the job. Melanie was the Creative Design Team Manager again.

The red light on the answering machine had been blinking at her since she'd come in, but she'd successfully ignored it up to now. It would be Mark, she guessed, explaining why he hadn't come home the night before. She'd decided, as soon as she'd established the fact of his absence in the cold unwelcoming house they shared, that she didn't really want to know. It had made her angry, his absence, even though she'd been absent herself. But, ready now to set off for work, she knew she had to hear the message. It probably wouldn't improve her mood, but then, neither would continued ignorance. She pressed the button on the machine and tried not to listen too attentively to the fractured digital monologue.

'Hi, Mel. Sorry you'd gone when we got back. You're missing a great party. We met a couple of Phillip's friends at the golf club and they came back with us. Great guys. Could be some business in it for me, too.'

There was a pause and a crackling sound, then Mark's voice again.

'Ah-um, I won't be back tonight, if that's all right with you. Bit late for a long drive. I'll go straight to the office tomorrow and see you in the evening. By the way, hope you're not feeling bad about last night. You did your best. Nobody blames you. Could still turn out okay, don't you think?'

The machine bleeped three times and fell silent.

'Bastard!' said Melanie aloud. ' "You did your best",' she mimicked, ' "Nobody blames you." Patronising bastard!'

Melanie continued to curse her partner as she left the house and got the car out of the garage. It wasn't until she sat at the wheel, ready to roll down the short drive to the quiet tree-lined roadway, that she let her true emotions have their way with her. She rested her forehead on the wheel and burst into tears. How could this be happening? Mark was her man. They'd been together for more than three years, as happy as anyone could wish. They liked the same food, the same TV programmes, they laughed at the same things, they both loved sex and knew how to excite and satisfy each other. Hell! She'd have said they were 'compatible' if that didn't make it sound so boring. And now it was all falling to bits, practically without warning.

It's Phillip, she thought. Phillip had taken him up as soon as they'd arrived at Huntscroft and Mark had forgotten Melanie from that very moment. If only she'd gone there alone. She would have revived that distant

117

affair, just for one short weekend. She would have enjoyed once again Phillip's incomparable love-making, then returned home to Mark, renewed and invigorated. He'd have known nothing about it. No harm done. Instead, Phillip had seduced Mark away from her, and there was nothing to indicate that she'd ever get him back. How had he done it? With tennis, golf, snooker? Or was there more to it than that?

She dried her eyes and repaired her make-up, cheering herself with the thought of the exciting project she was embarking on with Kirsty and the rest of her team. Ah, Kirsty. Perhaps Kirsty and she were an item now? Could that be? Could she accustom herself to life with Kirsty? It would be no hardship, after all. She thought of Kirsty's soft skin, her graceful limbs, her feminine intelligence and creative intellect. No hardship at all.

Jeanette smiled an uncharacteristically welcoming smile as Melanie put her head around the door of Charles's outer office. 'Melanie, dear!' she gushed. 'Charles was hoping you'd be in early. We've all got a lot to do, haven't we? And we're all depending on you.'

Jeanette got up from her desk as Melanie approached. In a quiet voice, she added 'Thank you so much for what you did yesterday.' She took Melanie by both wrists and kissed her lightly on the cheek. 'You were wonderful. And Charles feels the same as I do, so please excuse him if he appears a little awkward with you when you go in. It'll just be embarrassment. Men can be so silly, can't they?'

Melanie returned the kiss. 'I'm so happy for you, Jeanette,' she said. 'And for Charles, too, of course.' They communed silently for a few seconds, then Melanie crossed to the communicating door and tapped gently on it.

Charles looked up from his desk as she entered, and turned bright red. 'Ah, er, Melanie,' he stammered.

'Glad you could come . . . I mean, get here so early. Er . . .'

Melanie decided on positive action. She went around the desk to his side and put her hand on his broad shoulder. 'I was just saying to Jeanette how happy I am for you both,' she said, then kissed him on the cheek. It seemed to put him at ease.

'Thank you,' he said, his colour subsiding. He wanted to thank her in more specific terms for what she'd done, but that was beyond his powers. 'Thank you,' he said again.

To business. 'You agreed on Saturday that I could have a budget for the campaign,' she reminded him. 'Here's what I need.' She took a sheet of paper from the folder she was carrying and presented it to her boss. Charles looked at it and whistled. She knew he'd do that. He always did. But this time he had good reason.

'It's a lot, I know,' she said, 'but it'll be worth it.'

Charles frowned as he struggled to see where all the money was going to go. 'You'll have to talk me through it, Mel,' he said.

Melanie explained the plan, pacing the room as she spoke and stressing its innovative aspects with vivid language and combative hand gestures. By the time she'd finished, Charles had fully understood that this would be no ordinary presentation with lists and graphs on overhead projector slides. He could see in his mind's eye the images she'd tried to convey with her words. Some of them brought the colour to his cheeks once again, but he was a far less prudish man today than he'd been a couple of days ago, and he had to admit he rather liked the whole thing. If that didn't sell B&C to the Castadiosa crew, then nothing would!

Melanie sat down. Charles continued scrutinising the budget for a few minutes as if there were still a possibility he'd reject it. 'This item here,' he said. 'Technical Consultancy, A. deV. What's that, exactly?'

119

Melanie told him how the plan had been generated and the part Arlene deVere had already played. She hadn't obtained authorisation to bring an outsider into the proceedings, but she didn't expect a reprimand under the circumstances. In the event, a raised eyebrow was all she got.

'Okay,' said Charles. 'It'll put me out on a limb with Cuthbertson, but I think it's worth the risk. If we don't win the contract, there'll be more than a limb at stake anyway. I'll arrange for you to have access to Huntscroft from next Saturday morning until after the presentation on Monday. If there's anything else you need from me, just let Jeanette know.'

That was it. Charles had listened, digested, decided and, like the professional he was, taken on full responsibility for the outcome. He was a good boss, all things considered.

When Melanie got back to her office, the only vacant desk in the studio beyond the glass partition was Kirsty's. Five eager faces turned towards her as they got wind of her arrival. They all knew how important the contract was, and they'd all played some part in the original bid. Would they be disappointed that it hadn't yet been awarded? Certainly. Would they be disheartened at the thought of another week of hard work? Not if she could help it. Positive thinking, that's what was needed. Good news, not bad. Melanie opened the door and entered the studio.

In the event, they took it rather well, until the moment when Melanie waved the untidy sheaf of notes and sketches at them and told them, 'Sorry, boys, we've already got a campaign plan,' thereby stopping in its tracks the brainstorming session they were already working themselves up to.

'Did *they* give you that?' asked Steve incredulously. He meant Castadiosa. The idea that a client should specify content in such detail was anathema to them all. A protest loomed, but Melanie could easily head it off. 'No,' she assured them. 'The client wants to be wowed.'

'Fine, but where did this plan come from, then?'

'The thing is,' Melanie temporised, 'this job presents some special challenges. One is the timescale. We've only got a week, so there isn't time to go through the usual loops. Another is the style. It's got to be feminine.'

Faces turned towards each other as if to ask, What's so challenging about that?

'I'm not talking busty bare-arsed blondes on car bonnets here, boys. I'm talking feminine with a capital F. Some things need a woman's touch.'

They groaned as one man. The suggestion that they couldn't design to a feminine viewpoint was an insult to the versatility they prided themselves on. It was Dean who voiced the general indignation. 'Busty bare-arsed blondes!' he mocked. 'Is that all you think we're good for! We were designing for a female target when you were still selling holidays on Costa Blanca building sites! Bloody cheek, I call it! What about that tampon campaign we did three years ago? What about all the kitchen campaigns we've been involved in? And just take Adrian, for example. Practically grew up in panty liners, he did!' Dean could be relied upon to throw in a dig at Adrian.

'I could still get you a supply at cost, Dean,' Adrian responded. 'That's if you think you've grown out of nappies.'

Melanie let the storm rage for a few minutes. 'You know I didn't mean it like that, boys,' she intervened at last. 'You're the best in the business, and everybody knows it. But when I met two of the top Castadiosa people at the weekend, it was clear to me that we'd need to hit them with something really spectacular that went right to the heart of the Castadiosa concept. And what is that concept exactly? Well, they made me realise that

121

none of us at B&C knew what it was. We'd done a great bid, but we didn't really understand what we were bidding into.'

The silence that greeted this told Melanie that she'd struck a chord.

'To cut a long story short,' she continued, 'I picked up a clue from those people. I took that clue to some people who I thought might understand it better than me. They did. Then we put our heads together and came up with this plan. I'm going to let you study it for the rest of the morning. If you aren't impressed, I'll go down on my knees and beg your forgiveness for my lack of faith in your underrated talents. However, if you *are* impressed, I'll expect you to put those talents to work to wow the client and win us the Castadiosa contract next Monday. It all depends on you, now.'

Melanie put the sheaf of notes on Dean's desk and they gathered round. She still hadn't told them who her collaborators had been and she wasn't looking forward to them finding out. Kirsty was, after all, the junior member of the team. They'd be impressed with Arlene, though. That was for sure.

Driving home at the end of a long day, Melanie felt pleased with herself. The team had readily approved the campaign plan and lost no time in mobilising their respective talents to the task of bringing it to life. By the time the studio had emptied for the night, the entire presentation had been story-boarded, the major design variables had been determined, and most of the resources had been booked for the week ahead.

Kirsty and Arlene had shown up together just after lunch. Melanie had solved the delicate problem concerning Kirsty's leading role in the plan, and the acceptability of that to her male colleagues, in the simplest, most obvious way; she had delegated it. It had been a risk, but one worth taking. Taking Kirsty aside, she'd asked her to oversee the whole campaign. Kirsty had eagerly agreed. Then she'd asked her to inform the others. Kirsty had demurred.

'I could tell them myself,' she'd said, 'but that wouldn't make it any easier for you. On the contrary, it'd leave them feeling they can come to me behind your back if there's something they don't like. If you just go out there and tell them you're running the show, they'll have to accept it. You have the advantage that they already love the campaign plan, but they don't yet know it's mainly your brainchild. You'd better make that crystal clear to them first, or they'll go off like a rocket.'

Kirsty had gulped several times, then accepted the challenge.

'Good girl,' Melanie had said. 'Best thing I ever did was taking you on.' Then they kissed fleetingly and sweetly, having first made sure no one was looking.

And it had worked. Kirsty had taken her courage in both hands and gone out there to harness the fiery stallion that was the Creative Design Team. They'd puffed and stamped for a while, but Kirsty stuck to her guns and they soon settled down. Arlene's presence had helped. Without speaking, she'd shown her support for her friend by standing alongside her, projecting her intimidating breasts at the baying male crowd. After that, it hadn't taken them long to realise where their best interests lay.

So, definitely a good day, then. And yet, Melanie was starting to get fretful again. The further she got from the office and the closer to home, the more fretful she became. What was waiting for her there? A reconciliation? A blazing row? The continuation of this tiresome cold war?

None of these any good to her just now. Reconciliation with Mark would destroy Kirsty, the campaign, the contract, and her career with Bermont and Cuthbertson. A row was no more attractive an option, either. At this stage, it would probably be terminal, and Melanie wasn't ready to end what had, up until a few days ago, been such a satisfactory relationship. Maybe she was falling in love with Kirsty. Maybe she was finding a new path in life as a woman amongst women, a convert to the soft satisfactions of lesbian love. Maybe, but she wasn't sure yet. She couldn't risk breaking with Mark and burning her boats, perhaps pushing her into a life she would not, in the event, be able to sustain. And the third alternative? To rub uneasily along with him until the Castadiosa business was resolved? That would not only be hell to endure, it was probably also an impossibility. No, it would either go one way or the other. She could practically smell the burning boats already, and it was a very acrid smell.

Sometimes, when you think you've covered all the angles, life throws you a curveball that you didn't anticipate. Mostly, the surprise is an unpleasant one. But just occasionally it's something you thank your lucky stars for, something that makes you believe you might have a fairy godmother after all. And so it was for Melanie when she arrived home.

The place was dark, cold and empty. There was no Mark, only a note on the kitchen table:

Dear Mel,
Great news! Those friends of Phillip's need a man of my talents to help them out of a jam they've got themselves into. Ultra urgent! No time to waste! So, I'm going north for a few days. Maybe a week or more. Short notice, or what! Sorry to spring this on you, but the pay's fantastic. Too good to turn down. By the time you get this note, I'll be on my way. I'll let you know where I am when I get there.
Good luck with the bid.
Mark.

But Melanie's first reaction was rage. ' "Good luck with the bid",' she spluttered. 'Fat lot you care!' How could he go off and leave her at a time like this? How could he not appreciate the strain she was under, her need for his support?

But exultation was not far beneath the surface and it came welling quickly up with the realisation that the reckoning, the crunch point in this chronicle of lust and lies, was hereby, and for as long – probably – as she needed it to be, postponed. She picked up the phone and dialled Kirsty's number. She'd planned to return to Kirsty's flat after 'sorting things out' with Mark, but Kirsty's flat was chilly and squalid by her standards. She didn't know how long she could have tolerated it, and now she didn't have to. 'How would you like to move in here for a while, Kirsty?' she asked.

11

The Wood Sprite

It was mid-week, and Melanie, Kirsty and Mike Heppenstall were on their way to Huntscroft in a small van. Mike was driving, and it was he also who would be operating the expensive video recording equipment that filled the back of the vehicle.

Kirsty, who was spending her time checking a screenplay and removing stray threads from a garment of pale lilac chiffon and silk, would be the sole performer in the mini-drama they were going to record. Melanie was there to make sure they found exactly the right location and to lend moral support to the reluctant Kirsty, who wasn't very keen to go in front of the camera.

When they arrived at Huntscroft, Melanie got out and rang the bell. She'd been told that Phillip and his butler were not in residence, but that they only needed to notify the household staff of their arrival, then just get on with the filming. The door was answered by a girl of about nineteen. She had long dark hair and large, deep-set black eyes set in a squarish face. Her skin was pale and translucent. She was dressed in dark shades of grey with touches of white; not quite a uniform, but near enough to identify her as staff. Melanie started to give her the redundant message – namely, that they had arrived – but her voice faded out before she could complete her sentence. An idea was forming in her mind.

'Excuse me,' she said. 'Could you just wait there a moment? I need to check something with my colleague.' She went back to the van. Kirsty was staring at the girl, and Melanie guessed that the same idea had come to her. There was no need to spell it out. 'What do you think?' asked Melanie.

'Perfect,' replied Kirsty. 'Just perfect.'

Melanie returned to the girl, who waited obediently at the door.

'What's your name?' she asked.

'Magda,' replied the girl, a faint accent betraying an origin somewhere to the east of Vienna.

'Well, Magda,' said Melanie. 'How would you like to be in a movie?'

The shooting went successfully, even if the change of plan had meant a significant delay. Melanie had led them to the precise rhododendron bush she had briefly sojourned under during her morning walk, and Mike had set up the equipment within its shade. The role of wood nymph that had originally been Kirsty's was taken by Magda, who showed considerable intelligence in grasping its essence, and remarkable acting talent in carrying it out. She also looked stunning in the flimsy lilac shift. Kirsty, in particular, was enthusiastic. She'd argued for a brunette wood nymph from the start, and had only agreed to do it because there was no one else available. To have hired an actress would have meant postponing the filming until Friday, and that would have been tempting fate. As it was, fate had intervened on their side and delivered them Magda, the very embodiment, they all said, of the Nymph of the Rhododendron.

For Kirsty, it was an opportunity to show her skills as director. She it was who decided where the camera would go, and the lighting. She fussed around their new-found star, adjusting the shift with a few lightning tucks to fit Magda's more gracile figure, applying the anti-glare face powder and lip paint, and all the while preening her with appreciative remarks and gentle strokes to encourage her and keep up her spirits under the heat of the arc lamps. Mike Heppenstall, many of whose responsibilities she was usurping, was effectively demoted to technician, plugging in cables and manhandling tripods and lamps, all to Kirsty's precise instructions.

Melanie was delighted to see her lover take charge so effectively. She'd had misgivings about bringing Mike, who seemed uninspired by the whole Castadiosa affair. Now she was glad, since none of the others would have accepted relegation like this without at least bitching, balking, or walking off the set. If anything, Mike seemed relieved.

After the shooting, Kirsty escorted Magda back to the house to change out of her costume. Melanie stayed with Mike in the rhododendron bush to help dismantle the equipment. She started packing the camera in its padded, reinforced travelling case at the perimeter of the bush while Mike went into the centre to dismantle one of the flood lights. She could see him out of the corner of her eye and noticed him bend down and pick something up from the leaf litter. She turned to look.

Mike was standing there with a piece of white cloth in his hands. He seemed not to know what it was, but Melanie recognised her lost knickers instantly. She expected him to throw them to the ground in disgust as soon as he worked out what they were. She wouldn't have been offended. After all, they had been mouldering in the leaf-litter for days. But he didn't do that. Thinking himself unobserved, he quietly stuffed them into his pocket.

Melanie was astonished. Continuing with her task as if she'd never stopped to look, she marvelled inwardly at the sight she'd just witnessed. Mike Heppenstall! Poor lonely, unhappy Mike Heppenstall! What could he possibly want with a dirty discarded pair of knickers?

Her imagination began to play through the lurid possibilities. Did he collect them? Did he tour lovers' lanes on his weekends off and pluck them out of the brambles? Did he steal them from spin dryers in launderettes? Or perhaps he bought them from department stores and boutiques? Perhaps he was one of those men who pester shop girls, asking them with averted eyes which particular crotchless concoction they think his wife – who just happens to look a lot like you, Miss – might like as a birthday present, or querying whether the comfort of a broad gusset outweighed the convenience of a detachable flap, making them feel so uncomfortable that they give the pre-arranged signal that brings the security man to hover in the background as he pays for the item and leaves in a hurry. 'I had one of those pervy types in this afternoon,' the girl would tell her colleagues at tea break. 'Real creepy, he was. Felt like I needed a shower afterwards. Know what I mean?' And they would all know exactly what she meant.

And what would he do with this grubby undergarment when he got it home? Would he sit with it spread out on his unzipped lap, conjuring up in his mind the most lurid scenarios to account for its presence there under the bush? Would he imagine an innocent young virgin, snatched from the path, dragged into the bush and taken by force? Or would he picture a sly nubile temptress, brazenly flaunting her curves at a passing monk, luring him from the path of righteousness, testing his faith against his lust and proving it the weaker?

Or perhaps he would put them on? Perhaps he would tuck his genitals between his legs and pull the panties up tight, so that it looks as if he has nothing underneath but pussy? Would he put on a suspender belt and fishnet stockings, too? A padded bra? A dress? Make-up, even?

Would he then stand in front of a mirror to admire the effect? And then what? Would he suddenly pull out his erect penis from under the skirt, shattering the illusion with a delicious orgasm-inducing shock? Or would he weep salt tears for the woman he might have been, the woman that no amount of make-up, or frilly underwear or false bosom can turn him into?

Poor lonely Mike, she thought. He would be first on her list for redundancy if they didn't win this contract. Even if they did win it – and she was confident, now, that they would – he'd have to buck up if he wanted to keep his job. What should she do?

Something else then tugged at Melanie's memory. Hadn't she abandoned those panties as an offering to the spirits of the wood in the hope they might make up, on her next visit, for their failure to satisfy her on her first? Indeed, she had. And now – Oh, Heavens! – that offering had been picked up and pocketed by none other than Mike Heppenstall!

Melanie would never admit to being superstitious. If she read her horoscope most days, it was for entertainment only. If she sometimes felt a thrill in a place like this, as she had that Sunday morning, it was just an indulgence of her fertile fantasy. She didn't believe in wood spirits, or sprites, or nymphs. Of course she didn't. Especially not now. The natural light of a grey September afternoon completely robbed this grotto of the romance she'd found here that misty sunny dawn and, although their floodlamps had turned it temporarily into a kind of fairyland, those lights were cold now, and the place was just dull and damp and gloomy.

And yet – there was no getting away from it – she had left an offering, and that offering had just been accepted. That man, Mike, quietly reeling cable into a can, had picked up her knickers and put them into his pocket. It had to mean something. Hadn't it?

They had finished their work. The crates and cases were packed and ready to be carried back to the van. It would take two or three trips, but it wasn't far, and there was no hurry. Melanie picked up two of the smaller cases, one in each hand. Mike shouldered the largest case and took a small one in his free hand. Melanie led the way out through the overhanging canopy towards the open air, but she stopped before she got there. Something was holding her back.

Mike almost knocked her over. The large case teetered on his shoulder as he staggered to a halt behind her. She heard him curse under his breath as he struggled to retain his load.

'Sorry, Mike,' she said, turning around to face him. 'I don't know why I did that.'

'Gee, Mel!' he stammered, his face red. 'You almost got this on your head! And I've almost ruptured myself saving you!' He was still shuffling and twisting to keep the crate steady on his shoulder.

'Put it down, Mike,' she said.

'What?'

'Put it down for a minute. Please.'

Mike carefully lowered the crate until it rested safely on the ground. He straightened, flushed from the unexpected exertion. 'What's the problem, Mel?' he said.

'Do you believe in wood sprites, Mike?' she asked.

Mike grimaced. 'Wood sprites!' he blasted. 'Wood sprites! You practically knacker me just to ask me if I believe in wood sprites! Well, no I don't, as a matter of fact. So can we just get on with it now?'

'No, of course you don't, Mike,' she said. 'I don't believe in them either.'

He glared at her. 'That's settled, then,' he said, and made to pick up the crate again.

'No, Mike,' she said. 'Don't pick it up just yet. Don't ask me why, but there's something we've got to do before we get out of here.'

'What?' he asked. 'Have we got to placate the wood sprites, or something? The ones you don't believe in, I don't believe in, nobody believes in. You know, *those* wood sprites?'

'Don't laugh at me, Mike. It's got nothing to do with wood sprites. Not directly, anyway.'

Mike was beginning to lose his temper, but she was his boss, and you had to make allowances for your boss, hadn't you. 'Okay,' he said. 'But I wish you'd tell me what the problem is. If we get a move on we can be back in town by 4.30 and I can at least tidy my desk before it's time to go home.'

'Problem?' she said. 'There's no problem, Mike. Except that I'm here again and there isn't a wood sprite in sight. No problem, except that this gnarled old rhododendron, even though it creaks and wheezes in the wind like a bronchial old man, will never do what a man might do to please a woman, to satisfy her. So although we could get a move on, as you say, and get back to town by 4.30, we would be leaving something undone if we did. We would be leaving a spirit, a *casta diosa*, if you like, unfulfilled. We wouldn't want to do that, would we, Mike? That wouldn't be right, would it?'

Mike stood aghast. What was she talking about? It sounded suggestive, but it didn't sound like the Melanie he knew. He was starting to worry.

'So it's up to you, Mike,' she went on. 'Do you want the spirits of the wood on your side, the *castas diosas*? Or do you want to rebuff them? Do you want to keep the chains you've bound yourself with, or do you want to break them? If you want to break the chains, Mike, now is the moment. Do it now, Mike, or they'll bind you forever.'

This was definitely getting serious. What had got into her! It must be overwork. This Castadiosa business must have stressed her out. Best tread carefully. 'Look, Mel,' he began. 'I know it's been tough, and that scene we just shot was getting to me as well. It's amazing what lighting and a wind machine can do, isn't it? Makes this old bush almost come to life. Spooky! But just take a step out there, out from these old branches. Tell you what, let's both take a step out.'

He took her arm and guided her through the drooping canopy into the pale autumn light. She blinked, and looked at him. Why had he done that? Why had he broken the spell? Was he crazy!

Mike left her standing there as he went back into the grotto and began carrying all the packages out onto the grass. He wasn't going to risk her going in there again. When he'd done, he passed her the two small cases she'd originally taken up and proceeded to lift the biggest crate again. When the weight was safely balanced on his manly shoulder, he winked at her and said, in reassuring tones, 'Don't worry, Mel. It just didn't happen. Okay?'

Later, when the van was packed and they were ready to leave, she saw him drop something into one of the bins at the side of the house.

'Just some litter I found under the rhododendron,' he explained. 'I can't stand to see litter in the countryside.'

Poor, poor Mike, thought Melanie.

12

Female Friends

Melanie and Arlene were sipping red wine in Melanie's kitchen. Arlene had accepted an invitation to dine and spend the evening with her and Kirsty at home, an invitation she had herself blatantly solicited. Kirsty was taking a nap upstairs, having been exhausted by the day's shooting in the unaccustomed country air, so Arlene had Melanie to herself for a while. The latter braced herself for a probing conversation about her affair with Kirsty and sought to postpone it with diversionary talk. Melanie was curious to know if Kirsty had ever submitted to the Chamber of Correction.

'Sure,' said Arlene. 'She just loves it. She even helped me design it when I first moved into that flat.' Then, seeing a look of puzzlement creep over Melanie's face, she went on, 'You're wondering why her bottom's as white as the driven snow?' Arlene's face softened as she started to explain. 'Well, just picture it, Melanie hon. You've got that cute little butt spread out on your block. That pale skin, like alabaster. Those soft round cheeks like peaches carved from marble. What you gonna do? Raise a welt on it? I don't think so!'

Melanie smiled at the unexpected streak of sentimentality her friend was disclosing.

'Oh, you may think you're gonna do it. She may want you to do it. But you pick up Mr Whiplash and you hear him pleading with you. He's saying "Don't make me do it. Please don't make me do it. Let me twine myself around those tender thighs. Let me caress that downy flesh, tickle and tease that sweet little butt-hole, but please don't ask me to despoil that pristine whiteness with so much as a fleck." And you know you can't do it. You just ain't got the heart.'

'You didn't scruple in my case,' said Melanie dolefully.

'Ah! Different strokes for different folks,' explained Arlene. 'Mr Whiplash was so keen to get at your gorgeous ass he was practically leaping out of my hand. You see, Kirsty's ass is so lovely it almost makes me weep. Yours is so sexy, it almost makes me cream myself. And it gets even sexier when it's got a few raw red smarting streaks across it. So don't hesitate. Next time you feel in the mood, just call on Auntie Arlene. Number 4. Remember?'

Melanie thanked her for the compliment and said she was unlikely to forget.

Arlene took a sip of her wine and looked sternly at Melanie. The interrogation was about to begin, and Melanie couldn't postpone it any longer.

'Tell me, Mel,' Arlene began, 'how's things between you and Kirsty?'

'Fine,' said Melanie.

Arlene gave her a sceptical look. 'Sure,' she said. 'But don't worry, I'm not going to pry. I'm just going to remind you of your promise to me that you won't hurt her. I'm holding you to that.'

Melanie nodded her acknowledgement of her obligations. If she'd hoped this would satisfy Arlene, she was quickly disappointed.

'Now, I can't decide your life for you,' Arlene went on, 'and I don't think even you are sure yet which way your cookie is gonna crumble. So I'm not waving no shotgun at you. But you're getting yourself in pretty damned deep with Kirsty, and the deeper you get in, the harder it'll be to get yourself out if you come down heads instead of tails. You've managed to get rid of your man for a while, and that's very convenient, but you'll have to face up to him before long. You'll have to make your choice.'

Melanie didn't like being lectured at in this way, especially since she knew that everything Arlene said was true. Nothing was resolved. She'd managed to postpone a resolution, but only until the Castadiosa contract was settled one way or the other, and that was only days away now.

Was that all it was about? Had she got herself entangled with Kirsty simply for the sake of the contract and her career? Or did she really love her? Would her rift with Mark quietly settle into permanency, or would she ache for him in body and soul again once this whirlwind week was over? She simply didn't know and, what was worse, she didn't want to know either. Not yet. It wasn't convenient.

'I'm your friend,' Arlene was saying, 'and I'll help all I can. But I'm Kirsty's friend first, and I just couldn't bear to see her get hurt. Just remember that.'

Not for the first time, Melanie dreaded to think what Arlene's righteous wrath might be like. It wouldn't be pleasant, she was sure of that much.

Melanie must have looked very glum indeed, because Arlene now got up from her chair and came round to her side. She put her arm around her shoulder and gave her a hug that was clearly meant to be inspiriting.

'Cheer up,' she said. 'I didn't come around here to give you a bad time. I came for some supper and some fun. Fun first. There's sounds coming from upstairs telling me Kirsty's got that lovely big Jacuzzi of yours going. It was built for two people, but it oughta hold three no problem, don't you think?'

Melanie looked up with lugubrious eyes. She was feeling a little battered and just wanted to be left alone, but she didn't have the strength, just at that moment, to resist. She allowed herself to be eased up from her chair and led towards the stairs. Before they started to climb them, Arlene, standing behind her, put both arms about Melanie's waist and whispered in her ear.

'You know, honey,' she said. 'Some things work out fine, and some things work out not so fine. But in either case there's good times to be had along the way. And you're about to have the time of your life.'

Then they proceeded up the stairs.

Fun, Arlene had called it, and fun it was. Three women letting their hair down, soaking together in the big round tub, exposing their grateful skins to the invigorating jets of the Jacuzzi. Melanie's depression of a few minutes before was quickly lifted as the tension and stiffness evaporated from her muscles and joints. So she had a few problems to sort out? So what? Wasn't that what her life was about, anyway? Problems, and solving them, were her livelihood, her meat and drink. No sense letting them get her down. She would find a way out. She always did. Meanwhile, just relax and enjoy.

And there was much to enjoy. The Jacuzzi, ample in size for her and Mark on a Sunday morning, was less accommodating for three, but the tangling of limbs and bodies was part of their pleasure. Three female bodies, all built to the same general plan, but each offering its unique delights to the other two. Arlene's were conspicuous enough: those magnificent breasts with their wine-dark nipples, so sensitive to the touch of a woman's lips that their owner could get off on that alone, and that brutal flash of crimson when she spread her labia; shocking as a knife wound, alluring as steak tartare to a hungry diner.

More subtle were Kirsty's, her blonde beauty less dramatic, its effect more cumulative as you contemplated the soft curves of her youthful body and stroked the smooth velvet of her downy skin. Hers was the sort of beauty you could watch and appreciate without arousal as she soaped herself or ducked and splashed in the warm sparkling water, until you found yourself so intoxicated you couldn't avert your gaze from the neat round breasts, the marble thighs and buttocks. And then you were lost. You'd have to touch those slender limbs, to feel the sensuality that animated them. You'd have to let your fingers play along their contours, picking up an electric charge that turned your tummy to jelly. Then your lips would long to taste the sweetness of her skin, the tang of her small pink nipples, the honey of her vulva, dainty as a porcelain rose. And then her neat little bum-hole, clean as a cat's, would wink at you, making you salivate afresh, and your tongue would not rest until it was probing and licking, coaxing the resilient sphincter into soft compliance, then sinking through to the mellow plush beyond as she quivered to a climax in your arms.

And Melanie too, of course, brought her own sweet-meats to this feast of flesh. Her breasts, if lacking the drama of Arlene's or the ideal rotundity of Kirsty's, were shapely and full. Her belly curved voluptuously down to her delta where the innocent swatch of dark hair caught the eye and held it as she lathered her smooth strong thighs, or wriggled to admit a stream of bubbles to just the right place, just the exact spot that would heighten her mood and bring a contented smile to her face. Her curves had their own appeal for her two friends, who didn't fail to show their appreciation with tender caresses and moist kisses. But for them, those kisses and caresses were just a prelude to the main dish, just an appetiser, or perhaps a sop to coax her into repose, to loosen the muscles of those thighs until they relaxed their guard over the treasure they really sought, her unique contribution to the feast, her wonderful clitoris. It nestled deep in the rippling folds of her minor labia, themselves lavish and beautiful to behold, but, once persuaded to emerge, it impressed and captivated the treasure-seeker with its audacity, its eager lust for the attention of fingers or lips or tongue. It would start forth from its hiding place so quickly and to such an amplitude that it took their breath away. It would harden between their lips until it might have been a finger or a toe they were sucking. Except that no finger or toe could taste as sweet. No finger or toe could make its owner writhe and twist so that you had to clasp her tight to hang on. Nor could a mere digit induce such intense ecstasy, nor reward the treasure-hunter with such a flush of liquid honey that it took several minutes to lap it up. 'I love your clit, Mel,' Kirsty would say with a faraway look in her eyes, 'I really love your clit'. 'You do terrific shrimp-in-a-basket, hon,' would be Arlene's less romantic endorsement. And Melanie would beam with pride and spread her legs all the wider.

And so the three gambolled and cavorted in the bubbling hot spring of the Jacuzzi until hunger drew them back to the kitchen and a supper of pizza and wine. There, they drank to the charms of the female body, to its infinite variety. They drank to their eternal friendship and a love they would share freely and forever. And they drank to the success of their campaign for the Castadiosa contract.

That night, when she was alone again with Kirsty, Melanie was reminded of Arlene's words of warning by her lover's sighs and protestations of devotion. 'You're getting yourself in pretty damned deep,' Arlene had said. Indeed she was, but could she do anything other than dig in even deeper? When Kirsty said 'I love you, Mel,' what could she reply except 'I love you too, Kirsty'? When Kirsty swore that her love was getting stronger with every passing day, what could Melanie say except that it was the same for her too? And when

Kirsty told her how she'd never experienced the kind of orgasms Melanie gave her, how could she desist from kissing her and promising her a never-ending supply?

And on this night there was a new complication for Melanie to consider. They had been discussing Magda and how lucky they'd been to find her, when Kirsty suddenly asked if Melanie thought her very beautiful. Melanie said that she did, but that she thought Kirsty more so. Then Kirsty, who had been alone with Magda after the shooting and had evidently conversed intimately with her, said that she, Magda, had told her she considered Melanie very beautiful and that Kirsty was very lucky to have such a lover.

'You told her about us!' exclaimed Melanie.

'She guessed,' Kirsty explained. 'It's not so surprising. I'm sure I go about all the time with the words "I love Melanie" written on my face for anyone with eyes to read them.'

Melanie kissed her. Then Kirsty became very serious. 'You won't go and fall in love with her, will you?' she whimpered.

'Don't be silly,' said Melanie.

'Promise you won't,' insisted Kirsty.

'Of course I won't fall in love with Magda. Whatever gave you such an idea?'

'I think she might have fallen in love with you,' replied Kirsty. 'It was the way she talked about you this afternoon.'

'I'm sure you're imagining things,' said Melanie, giving the girl a reassuring hug and kiss. But she sighed inwardly with growing despair. Jealousy! she thought. That's all I need!

13

Huntscroft Revisited

Saturday morning found the Creative Design Team in a convoy of two pantechnicons and a minibus *en route* for Huntscroft. Melanie and Arlene had arrived early. After a brief stop in the forecourt for the two women to unload their personal luggage and inform Magda of their arrival, they drove around to the garages at the side.

Craig was expecting them. 'Good morning, Ms Brooks,' he said. His eyes glistened as he watched Melanie get out from the driver's side, then flashed excitedly as Arlene appeared from the other side. 'And good morning to you . . .' he began.

'Arlene,' said Arlene. 'And you must be Craig. Melanie didn't tell me you were quite such a hunk.'

'You should see his Testarossa!' chipped in Melanie.

'I should be so lucky!' added Arlene.

'There's a Silver Cloud as well,' said Craig, ready for any game these two lovelies wanted to play. 'A transport of delight for ladies who appreciate a smooth ride.'

'Smooth?' taunted Arlene. 'Isn't that what they say you have to take the rough with? But hey! Tell me Craig, are those lovely muscles just for show? We've got a couple of vans coming in half an hour and we could use a little help.'

Craig agreed to meet the vans when they arrived. Melanie tossed him her keys and she and Arlene set off on foot back to the house while he parked the car under cover. Magda was waiting for them in the drawing room with a large pot of fresh coffee. She wore the same dark greys she'd worn earlier in the week, before her transformation into the Nymph of the Rhododendron. They sat down to discuss the arrangements.

The quiet of late summer in the country was, if not rudely shattered, at least comprehensively undermined by the rumble of trolleys, the shouted instructions, and the general bustle and bump that accompanied the unloading of the wagons. Craig, whose mental image of 'a couple of vans' hadn't quite done justice to the scale of the operation, demonstrated nevertheless that his muscles weren't just for show and was usually to be found supporting an end of one or other of the many large containers that had to be manoeuvred with care into the library. At the other end would be Adrian, whose conspicuous admiration of Craig threatened to embarrass its object.

Also present was Victoria, Tony's long-term partner, who had insisted on accompanying her man in preference to spending the weekend alone. The two of them took on the task of unpacking the cases in the library, and they were never more than a few metres apart. Dean joined them. He eyed Craig malevolently every time he and Adrian appeared in the library with a new case. This added to Craig's discomfiture, and he was visibly relieved when the vans were empty and he could reasonably make his excuses and leave.

With Kirsty firmly in charge, Melanie and Arlene were free to review the catering provisions and the allocation of bedrooms with their hostess. Magda first showed them to the kitchen, where two women from a local catering firm were arranging thin sandwiches, salads, and small savoury pastries onto trays.

'They'll be hungry as hawks after all that work,' commented one of the women. 'If it was up to me it'd be pie and chips all round. And mushy peas, too. My old man would have a fit if you offered him stuff like this after a morning's humping.'

'Come off it, Marje,' said the other one. 'When was the last time you got a morning's humping out of your old man?' They burst into gales of coarse laughter.

'Well, I ain't saying nothing, Dulce,' said Marje when she'd recovered, 'but he was just remarking the other day how he's practically forgotten what my mushy peas taste like.' They guffawed some more.

Melanie and Arlene exchanged amused glances, then left the kitchen to follow Magda's sylph-like form up the stairs. The first floor bedrooms, Magda explained, were reserved for Mr Bermont and the Castadiosa executives who were due to arrive on Monday. The upper floor, to which the trio now proceeded, would accommodate Melanie and her team, as long as some people were willing to share. For example, Magda hoped it would be acceptable for Kirsty to share with Miss deVere. They entered a room with two single beds in it.

'Kirsty will share with me,' said Melanie firmly. 'And we'd like the room I had before, if you don't mind.'

Magda's pale face flushed perceptibly. 'Yes, of course,' she said quickly. 'I thought, as the senior person, you would prefer a single room. I do apologise.'

It sounded a perfectly natural assumption for her to have made, but Melanie thought she caught something in her eyes as she spoke, a hint of sadness that went beyond professional regret for her mistake. If so, it was gone in an instant, but not before Melanie recalled the fear Kirsty had confessed to her a few nights ago, a fear she'd dismissed then as Kirsty's imagination. Could there be something in it after all? Had Magda deliberately tried to separate them for that reason? Melanie looked into those deep dark eyes, but Magda had regained her poise and was already moving on to the next bedroom, a single, which, given the change of plan, Miss deVere would occupy alone.

Miss deVere expressed her sense of honour at being granted a room to herself, hoped very much she wouldn't be inconveniencing anyone else, and volunteered her willingness to double up – with Magda herself, for example – if it would make things easier. Magda assured her that this would not be necessary and that in any case the staff had their own accommodation elsewhere on the estate. 'Pity,' said Arlene under her breath, then later, when she and Melanie were alone again and on their way to review progress in the library, 'Nice chick, but is she always so stuffy?'

'She wasn't stuffy when we shot the wood nymph sequence on Wednesday,' said Melanie. 'Perhaps that's a tribute to Kirsty's talent as a director.'

They entered the library to see the talented director in action once more, assigning tasks, inspecting equipment, checking plans and blueprints. When she saw them, Kirsty looked at her watch and called the lunch break. The sudden change from hubbub to comparative silence was like the parting of the waters of the Red Sea. Kirsty smiled proudly across to Melanie. You see what power I have, she seemed to be saying, what control!

The buffet was served in the drawing room. The workers passed along the table with their plates, selecting delicately spiced samosas, filo pouches, and sandwiches of smoked salmon with mayonnaise, or pastrami and horseradish purée. Marje and Dulcie were in attendance, pouring coffee and tea and fruit juice. Marje, whose sense of the proprieties of her trade had clearly been deeply offended, canvassed the customers' views on the provender. 'I bet you'd rather have a nice hot dish instead of these knick-knacks,' she'd suggest to one, or, to another, 'Nice plate of steak and kidney pie's what you need, young man, after all that work.' She was surprised to find that her views were not generally shared by the company, but she knew what was right, and when Adrian appeared before her she was sure he, if no one else, would be on her side.

'That stuff's no good to a growing lad like you,' she said admiringly. 'Pie and chips, you want.' She glanced aside to her friend. 'And mushy peas.' They collapsed into laughter as if mushy peas were the funniest thing in the world. 'Do you like mushy peas, love?' asked Marje through her giggles.

'I like anything mushy,' said Adrian, who didn't understand the joke but wasn't going to let that get in the way of a good laugh.

'Ooh! Hark at him!' said Dulcie.

'I do a lovely mushy peas, I do,' said Marje. 'My old man always said I did a lovely mushy peas –' she glanced at her friend again as she began the inevitable rider '– except he hasn't had any for years!' The two collapsed again.

'If I were your old man,' said Adrian, 'I'd insist on having it every day.'

'If *you* were my old man,' spluttered Marje, 'you wouldn't have to.'

They were completely helpless now. Melanie found herself taking a professional interest. Here were two women expressing their deepest desires and frustrations in what was probably the only way they felt able: innuendo and rude laughter. What could Castadiosa do for them? Could it restore their respect for their sexuality? Could it replace self-mockery with pride? Would society collapse if women like these re-asserted themselves as sexual beings? Melanie and Arlene exchanged meaningful looks.

'These two going to be with us all weekend?' asked Arlene.

'Probably,' said Melanie. 'We've got the same catering company right through. Plumtree Provisions. You're thinking what I'm thinking, aren't you?'

'I reckon I am,' said Arlene.

After lunch, when everyone was back at work, Melanie took an opportunity to slip away and climb the staircase unseen. She tiptoed along the first floor passage, tapping gently at the doors and, receiving no answer, opening them. In each room she looked quickly around, then silently retreated, closing the door after her.

Finally, she reached a door at the end of the passage. She opened it gingerly. This had to be it. This had to be the master bedroom. It was larger than the others and, although it felt cool and empty, it spoke, in the style and quality of its contents and décor, of the taste of an individual, of being an intimate part of someone's life.

She went inside and quietly closed the door behind her. The bed was furnished with sheets and bedclothes as though it might be slept in one of these nights. It wasn't the four-poster of her fantasies, but it was large and heavy, with a high, carved mahogany headboard depicting plump dolphins on a lattice of stylised ocean waves. Yes, this had to be where Phillip slept when he was at home.

There were two doors leading off from the room, and Melanie opened each in turn. One gave entry to a small, sparsely equipped bathroom. The other opened into a dressing room. It was quite large and contained enough wardrobes and chests of drawers for an entire family. Phillip, she knew, loved fine clothes. She opened a wardrobe. Inside, there were dozens of beautiful shirts hanging in groups on two levels, sorted by material and colour. She put her face to a rack of silks and breathed in deeply. Eventually, she closed the wardrobe and turned to re-enter the main bed chamber.

'Can I help you?'

Startled, Melanie spun around sharply, her heart in her mouth. The bedroom door was open and a grey-clad figure stood there. 'Oh! I . . .' began Melanie, but there was nothing she could say.

'You were his lover, weren't you?' said Magda, closing the door and moving into the room. 'Mr Drew's, I mean.'

Melanie watched her approach the bed and sit on it. 'Did he tell you that?' she asked.

'No,' said Magda. 'They were talking about you on Sunday evening. I was on duty then. They are depending on you, you know, Mr Bermont and Miss Jeanette. Mr Drew spoke very well of you. I could tell his interest was personal. And now, I find you in his room.'

'I guess it's pretty obvious, then,' said Melanie.

'He is a beautiful man,' said Magda. 'It must be hard to put aside a man like that when once you have tasted the pleasures he can give you, when it is time to move on.'

'Yes,' said Melanie. She was sure this girl understood her presence here and forgave it. Perhaps she too had enjoyed those same pleasures. Perhaps she'd come here now on the same mission as Melanie. Melanie looked into her eyes and saw a play of emotions in them that did not contradict her speculations. She sat on the bed next to Magda.

'You are a very lucky woman,' said Magda sadly. 'You have experienced the joys of love, even if some of them cannot last. But I must put aside my love without having tasted its pleasures, its joys.'

Melanie had been thinking how lucky Magda was to work in Phillip's house, to be able to go to his bedroom whenever she wanted, to feel the residual warmth of his body on the sheets, to smell his smell in his discarded clothes. But now she saw how painful it must be for her to be so much in his proximity without even the memory of his touch to sustain her.

147

'Oh, Magda,' she said. 'I didn't realise.'

Magda turned to her with tearful eyes. She took Melanie's wrists in her hands and raised them to her lap, looking down at her palms as if she were going to read her fortune. 'May I ask you for a favour?' she said. Melanie assented. 'May I kiss your hands? It would be kind of you to let me. Then I can think that next time you touch your lover you will be passing on my love too. Please. I think you are a good and kind lady who will do this for me.'

Melanie was immensely touched. 'But Magda,' she said. 'It has long been over between us. He ignores me now. I'm history. That's why I have to come sneaking in here to catch even a ghost of him in the scent of his silk shirts. I thought you realised that.'

'Him!' exclaimed Magda. 'You think I mean Mr Drew? No, not him. Kirsty. I mean Kirsty. She is your lover now, isn't it so? She told me so after the filming. Isn't it so?'

Melanie gasped with astonishment. Of course! It was crystal clear now. Magda, who had responded to Kirsty's direction with visible delight, had fallen head over heels for her. Kirsty had misunderstood, thinking it was Melanie she was attracted to.

'Kirsty! Yes, she is my lover now. Of course she is.' Melanie lifted her hands towards Magda's lips. 'Kiss them, Magda,' she said. 'Kiss them and I will pass on your love.'

Magda kissed them and moistened them with her tears. 'You are so kind,' she mumbled. 'I am happy for Kirsty that she has such a lover as you.'

Melanie pulled the disconsolate girl to her and pressed her head to her shoulder. Yes, she would be very happy to pass on her love to Kirsty. She would be very happy indeed. But would two moist kisses on her hands be enough to convey such a momentous message from one heart to another? Surely a message like that had to be written in a bigger, bolder font.

'Kirsty will love your kisses, Magda,' she said. 'Kirsty loves to be kissed. She loves to be held, too, like I'm holding you now.'

Magda put her arms around Melanie's neck and clung tightly, still weeping. Melanie stroked her head and neck. Then she kissed her on the neck. Then she kissed her again. Eventually, Magda began to return her kisses, brushing her neck with dry lips that contrasted starkly with her tear-soaked cheeks. Then those lips were on Melanie's own and Melanie moistened them with her tongue. Then the two tongues were entwined.

Magda slipped off her grey skirt and cardigan and laid them to one side. Then they both lay back onto the bed. Melanie took a boyish thigh in her hand and stroked it through the light satin underslip. Magda looked into her eyes and spoke.

'I will give you all the love I have so that you can give it to Kirsty,' she said, 'and maybe, when you do, I will feel it in my heart and will know what it is like to have her in my arms. Or maybe I will be able to forget, knowing that I've given her all I can give.'

Melanie wondered if she was taking unfair advantage of this poor girl, but she couldn't bring herself to feel any guilt. Lust had come upon her as she breathed in Phillip's scent from the silk of his shirts, and lust would have its way, if not with its primary object, then with his housekeeper. Besides, the girl needed comforting. She reached up under Magda's slip to her hips, the point where boyishness gave way to the most delectable feminine grace.

'Be brave, Magda,' she said. 'Some things work out fine, and some things work out not so fine. But in either case there's good times to be had along the way. And anyway, I've a feeling things might work out better than you think.'

Then she pulled down the plain cotton panties and bent over her, bringing her face up under the slip until

149

her nostrils thrilled to the warm musky scent she had so recently and irrevocably come to adore. She kissed each soft thigh in turn. Then she kissed the tender folds of pussy-flesh. And then, as she felt Magda's hands on her head, pushing her face into her, she extended her saliva-moistened tongue and reached in for a clitoris that proved to be as prominent and responsive as her own. Kirsty's going to love this, thought Melanie. Kirsty's really going to love this.

14

A Hard Day's Night

The work went on without respite throughout the afternoon and into the evening. The catering team, having departed with the remains of lunch, returned at six with fresh supplies, hot dishes this time, though still not quite up to Marje's standards. 'They ought to have them all sitting down to a proper dinner, Dulce,' she said. 'A buffet lunch is one thing, but you've got to sit down to dinner, haven't you?'

But nobody listened to her. They filled the compartments of their plastic trays and took them back into the library, sitting on half-unpacked cases or convenient props as they hastily ate noodles, beef stew and sautéed vegetables before returning impatiently to their respective tasks. It was after nine o'clock when Kirsty, satisfied that the progress she'd scheduled for that day had been abundantly achieved, ordered a halt. Then the wine began to flow as the entire team sighed and flopped into relaxation mode.

They looked around them to take in the effect they were creating. Half of the library was now a stage, raised about six inches above floor level. The spaces behind and to the sides of the stage, not yet hidden by the backdrop and side screens, were crammed with equipment and props, some of it still being assembled, most of it ready for testing the next day. Although it would have looked chaotic to a casual observer, the professional eyes that viewed it could already see it in action: the animation effects, the smooth scene changes as props slide out of sight while others take their place on-stage, the precisely synchronised light and sound elements. Those with parts to play were already imagining themselves up there performing and had to hold themselves back from reciting their lines out loud. There would be time enough for that. They would have Sunday evening and Monday morning to perfect their performances before the final critical event on Monday evening.

Victoria poured Tony a glass of wine and took one herself. They were sitting against the far wall of the library, looking across to the stage. Victoria, who knew next to nothing about the Castadiosa campaign, had watched the structure taking shape with growing curiosity.

'What exactly is this play about?' she asked her man.

'It's not exactly a play,' said Tony. 'It's more of a tableau, a protracted sketch, a bit like a TV advert, only longer. About half an hour, in fact.'

'If it's an advert, I'm dreading to think what it's supposed to be selling,' said Victoria. 'Some of those props look rather dubious to me.'

Mike Heppenstall sat near them and couldn't resist joining in. 'Dubious isn't the word for it,' he said. 'If you'd read the script, Vic, you might think "disgusting" more appropriate.'

'Oh! That's way over the top, Mike,' protested Tony. He was anxious for his woman's approval and didn't want Mike, whose attitude seemed to have progressively hardened against the whole business as the week went on, poisoning her mind. 'It's a bit erotic, I grant you. But you couldn't call it disgusting.'

'A *bit* erotic!' said Mike. 'I'll tell you what it's selling, Vic. It's selling this company to an outfit called Castadiosa, and what they're in the market for is dirty minds. So this play, or sketch, or advert, or whatever you want to call it is designed to prove that we in Bermont and Cuthbertson have got the dirtiest minds in the business. That's what it's about.'

'If you feel like that,' said Tony, who was eyeing the worried expression on Victoria's face with apprehension, 'I don't know why you're sticking around. I reckon you're missing the point, but if I felt the same as you I'd have pulled out before now.'

'I'm paid to do a job,' said Mike, 'and I'll do it like a professional. I won't be here for the performance, though. I can tell you that for nothing.'

Victoria was more than a little swayed by the passionate distaste that spluttered and fizzed in Mike's voice as he spoke. She looked curiously at her partner, then at Mike. 'Are you saying it's pornographic?' she asked.

Before Mike could answer, Tony stepped in. He couldn't let her follow that line of thought. 'Of course it's not pornographic,' he said. 'Don't listen to Mike, Vicky love. The Castadiosa people are setting up a media network for women, and we're just trying to show them that we've got the talent and imagination for the job. If Mike wants to close off his imagination, that's his business, but for the rest of us, this past week has been a real tonic, and I for one hope we win the contract. Just keep an open mind, Vic, and you'll see for yourself what it's really about.'

'Well, okay,' said Victoria hesitantly. 'Only I wouldn't be happy if you were involved in anything that exploits women.'

'If anyone's getting exploited,' said Tony, 'it isn't women. You'll see.'

Victoria gave him an affectionate peck on the nose as a token of her trust, but that trust was conditional, as the increasingly anxious Tony was well aware.

* * *

153

Adrian and Dean found themselves together at the edge of the stage. Dean was tired. Adrian, by contrast, seemed full of beans still.

'I don't know how you do it,' said Dean. 'Here's me knackered as a costermonger's carthorse and you look like you could scale the Matterhorn before bed.'

'I put it down to clean living,' said Adrian.

'Sure!' said Dean. 'Anyway, what do you think of this campaign we're busting our guts over? I've been meaning to ask.'

'Well,' said Adrian. 'It's not for the likes of us, Dean my old duck. This is Kirsty's bag. As far as I'm concerned it's just a splendid bit of high camp, but as to any deeper significance . . .'

'I don't think Kirsty'd be too pleased with that "high camp", Ade,' said Dean. 'You know how serious-minded she is. It seems to be some sort of statement for her.'

'About what, though?' asked Adrian. 'When you boil it down, it's all about winning this contract. If it takes a spiel about lust and liberation to do that, then obviously she's going to give the client what he wants. Doesn't mean she hasn't got her tongue in her cheek.'

'In Melanie's cheek, more like,' said Dean.

'What *do* you mean?' asked Adrian.

'Haven't you noticed? Those two have kept so much distance between them in public this week, I can only suppose they make up for it in private. And Kirsty's stopped all that moping and drooling all of a sudden. She's so cheerful and confident she's practically a different person.'

'But Melanie's straight,' said Adrian. 'Isn't she?'

'Was,' said Dean. 'I reckon our Kirsty's fairy godmother has granted her dearest wish. I reckon Melanie's gone pink.'

'Hmm,' murmured Adrian. 'Well, nothing wrong with that, I suppose.'

154

'Bit rough on us, though, don't you think? Bad enough with a woman boss. At least we could pretend to flirt with her now and then. Well, *you* could anyway. Now we've got a dyke and her doxy in charge. There's no leverage in that for the likes of us.'

'I see what you mean,' said Adrian. 'Still, it doesn't bother me. As long as the work's interesting and you're not getting on my tits, I'm happy.'

Dean sighed wearily. Why did their conversations always have to degenerate into pointless spiteful banter? 'Oh, don't let me spoil your bliss,' he said. 'I'm too knackered to fight with you tonight. Anyway, I expect you'll be going off in a minute to look for that driver chappie. I saw you eyeing him up this morning.'

'Yeah, and I saw you looking daggers,' said Adrian. 'If looks could kill! Ruined any chances I might have had, you did. Poor chap was a bag of nerves. Didn't even stay for lunch. What business is it of yours, anyway? That's what I want to know.'

But Dean didn't know how to tell him.

Steve was under no illusions. She wasn't interested in men, not even a man like him – good looking, sexy, an exciting lover who'd give her a good time but wouldn't hang around long enough afterwards to become a bore. Yes, he was perfectly aware of that, but still he wanted her. Those tits! Fantastic!

He'd tried to get into conversation with her several times during the week, but she'd proved elusive. She hadn't ignored him. She hadn't been rude, either. On the contrary, her responses, when he said hello or commented on her appearance, were at least polite and often quite friendly. But somehow they always seemed to close the door to further conversation. But, despite all that, his groin ached with longing. Normally, he steered clear of lesbians. Waste of time. Kirsty, for instance. He'd sussed her out on her first day at B&C. Pretty little thing, but not really his type in any case, so it was just as well. Made working life easier when you're not tempted by your colleagues. Pity Melanie wasn't like that. A real prick-tease that one. Always flirting, flaunting her sexy bum at the boys. He'd like to put one up there, and no mistake. You can't do that with the boss, though, can you? He'd learned that in his last job. Oh, but it'd be worth a few months on jobseeker's allowance to get his hands on that Arlene, if he ever got the chance. Still, at least he'd get an eyeful when she did her stuff on Monday. Even reading about it in the script gave him a hard-on.

Funny kind of thing, this presentation. Not the way B&C generally went about things. No complaints, mind. Much more interesting than the usual bid procedure. The women seemed to be taking it very seriously, though, as if there were more than just a contract at stake. Probably trying to prove something to themselves. Very insecure, women. Need to convince themselves they're as good as the men. Trouble is, they tend to believe the guff they come out with. What's the betting Kirsty believes all this Castadiosa stuff about freeing woman's libido, integrating her intellect with her desire, unifying love, lust and duty? Crap, that's what it was. Pretty horny all the same, and if Arlene was really going to do what it said in the script – Wow!

'Been a hard day, Arlene,' he said brightly. The object of his affection was walking past him on her way out of the library.

'Oh! Hi, Steve,' she said, stopping momentarily. 'Feeling the strain, huh? You're looking a little peaky, too, if you ask me. Have an early night. Plenty more work to do tomorrow.'

There you go, he thought as she vanished through the doorway. Does it every time.

Kirsty sat in the drawing room with Melanie and Magda, sipping wine and discussing the schedule. 'It's all going brilliantly,' she gushed.

'We have you to thank, Magda,' added Melanie, 'for putting the house so much at our disposal, and for the excellent organisation.'

'Not at all,' Magda demurred. 'My part is so little. I just have to keep out of everybody's way, that's all.'

'Oh, don't do that,' laughed Melanie. 'You're the star of the show, after all. Of the opening sequence, anyway.'

'That's right,' enthused Kirsty. 'We've edited the tapes and put in some effects, and it looks fantastic. You wait till you see it, Magda. You look absolutely gorgeous in it.'

Magda sighed. She glanced down at her dowdy grey housekeeper's attire. 'If I look gorgeous,' she said, 'I will not recognise myself. I have almost forgotten that day already. It seems so long ago, like a sunny day of childhood.'

She really is a miserable thing, thought Kirsty. She was so radiant and lovely when we put her into that shift and got her playing the nymph. Why is she so glum now? Is she love-sick for Melanie?

'I'll let you see it tomorrow morning,' Kirsty said, 'as soon as the projection equipment is up and working. It'll cheer you up, I'm sure.'

For Kirsty, the opening sequence was the best part of the show. It encapsulated for her all the romance of the Castadiosa concept, as she understood it. The rest of the show was too physical, too corporeal, with real props and real people on stage. The video was nothing but light and shade. She was sure it wouldn't have been half as good if they'd gone along with their original plan for her to take the role of nymph. Magda had really been a godsend. Her slimmer boyish figure contained more of the ambiguities Kirsty had envisioned than did her own. Her pale face with its big dark eyes was more suggestive of the unfathomed depths of the forest and of the spirit. Her performance too was better than anything Kirsty could have achieved. Her gestures, so perfect in their

157

innocent awkwardness, were exactly what the part called for. It was almost as if Kirsty had known Magda before that day and had created the role especially for her. That was impossible, of course. She'd never set eyes on the girl before seeing her standing in the doorway of Huntscroft just three days ago. And yet, there had been a kind of recognition in that moment, hadn't there?

Magda was speaking. 'Maybe it will cheer me up,' she said. 'But sometimes the good, happy things can be the most painful. Isn't it so?'

Oh! Do shut up, Magda, Kirsty thought. It was disconcerting to have your ideal wood nymph looking and sounding so thoroughly miserable. If there was one thing that could ruin things for Kirsty now, it would be losing faith in her wood nymph. She wished she could arrange a showing right then and there, just to let that wonderful creature of light and shade prevent her faith being eroded by the lugubrious flesh and blood version sitting in front of her. She couldn't do that, so she decided to speak her mind instead.

'Oh, do shut up, Magda!' she said.

Magda started. Melanie looked up in amazement. Kirsty pressed her lips together and slapped her hands onto her thighs. 'You were wonderful on Wednesday, and it's there to see in the video. The image of you as the Nymph of the Rhododendron is what's kept me going through the week. It set the standard I've been aiming at for the entire show. Don't spoil it for me now! Don't make me lose my inspiration now that we're almost there!'

Magda sat silently staring at the girl she adored. A tear appeared in the corner of one eye. Her face, already pale, became steadily paler, as if the burden she carried was becoming far too great for her to bear. When she spoke, her voice was almost inaudible.

'I'm sorry,' she said. 'I didn't realise it was so important to you. But you see, I was happy then, and now I cannot be happy. But I will take your kind words with me and try to take hold of the good feelings you intend me. Please think of me as you saw me then. Please don't lose your inspiration.'

She got up and walked slowly out of the room. Kirsty wanted to jump up and stop her, but Melanie restrained her with a gesture.

'She'll be all right,' said Melanie when Magda had gone.

'I didn't mean to hurt her,' said Kirsty. There was frustration and incomprehension in her voice. 'I know I was abrupt, but I thought it would cheer her up to know how brilliant she was in the video. Has something happened to her? Has she had a bereavement or something?'

'In a manner of speaking, perhaps,' said Melanie. 'But believe me, she'll be all right.'

'How do you know?' asked Kirsty. A flicker of suspicion arose within her and gave birth to a bitter pang of jealously. 'I was right, wasn't I? She's in love with you. What happened? Is she trying to take you from me?' Kirsty was beginning to panic.

'Calm down,' said Melanie. 'No one's trying to take me from you. Magda is in love, but not with me. It's Mr Drew she's in love with. It's quite hopeless, of course. She means nothing to him. Just a housekeeper. Just a cheap domestic servant.'

'Oh!' cried Kirsty. 'The poor thing! And I was so brutal to her just now.' She blenched as white as Magda at the thought of the pain she'd caused, her face creased up in remorse. 'Oh! My poor little wood nymph,' she wept. 'She must think me so cruel! I must go to her and say how sorry I am. Please let me go, Melanie. I can't bear feeling like this. Please let me at least try to comfort her.'

'I guess you'd better at that,' said Melanie, as if persuaded against her better judgement, 'if only for your sake. You won't be able to function while you're so upset.'

Kirsty rose to leave the room. She stopped before she reached the doorway and turned to Melanie.

'You're wondering where she went?' said Melanie. 'Well, I don't know. She might have gone back to her quarters, wherever they might be. But you could try the last bedroom on the left on the first floor. It's Mr Drew's room. If I were her, that's where I'd go.'

Kirsty disappeared through the doorway.

Well, thought Melanie, that's the two of them completely miserable. They'll sink together in a sea of tears and then, if I'm not completely wide of the mark, come bobbing back to the surface like a couple of champagne corks. She drained her wine glass and headed for the library for a refill. She met Arlene on the way.

'What if you're wrong?' asked Arlene after listening in silence to Melanie's tale.

'If I were wrong,' said Melanie, 'Kirsty would be back by now giving me a hard time.'

'Okay. So what about you? How do you come out of this?'

'Smelling of roses, I hope,' said Melanie. 'Everybody's friend, and some people's ex-lover.'

'How do you feel about it is what I meant,' said Arlene.

'Lonely,' said Melanie after a pause.

'I know what you mean,' said Arlene. 'When that girl comes into your life, demanding everything you got, you just got to give it, and you love giving it, too. But you know all along you can't keep it up. You know it ain't going to last. Then, when she moves on, you feel desolated. But don't worry, hon. That don't last too long either.'

'That's reassuring,' said Melanie.

'And if you'll accept a little home comfort from your auntie Arlene, it'll pass all the quicker.'

Melanie smiled. It was an offer she couldn't refuse. There was no virtue in postponement, so they left their glasses of wine half finished and made their way to Melanie's room and the double bed she'd expected would rock to a different refrain that night.

'I'll give you a tip,' said Arlene as they undressed in the subdued light of a single weak bedside lamp. 'When she offers to give you all those drawings she made of you, accept the offer. Then, when she asks if she can take just one back to keep on her bedroom wall, say no. Those women on her bedroom wall are history. Don't join them, or you'll be history too.'

'Thanks,' said Melanie. 'That's a really good tip.'

'Yeah,' said Arlene. 'And I've got a couple more good tips for you tonight, Melanie my girl.' She unfastened her bra as she said this and let her beautiful sculpted breasts bounce free. Melanie thrilled to the sight of the large dark nipples slowly recovering their form after the restraint of clothing. 'I love your tits, Arlene,' she said in a quiet husky voice. 'I just love your tits.'

Arlene already knew this. She lifted a breast with her hand, making the nipple stand out further and creating in Melanie an irresistible desire, a lust for female flesh. 'Come on, now,' said Arlene gently. 'Don't hold back. They're bursting with comfort and it's all for you.'

They leant back on the bed as Melanie took the soft nipple between her lips. It sprang to life, hardening and enlarging under her kisses. Melanie moaned. Then the emotional stresses of the day, stresses she'd been holding back for so long, suddenly descended on her, and her eyes filled with tears.

'That's right,' said Arlene. 'Let it come, Melanie my honey. Let it come.'

Melanie sank into her friend's warm bosom and wept copiously. She felt the sadness of loss, the solitude of abandonment, the joy of past love and the pride of selflessness, and it was all too much. But as her tears flowed over the firm brown flanks of Arlene's breasts, her head began to clear, her spirits, relieved of the congestion of thought and responsibility, began to lighten and, by the time the flow had stopped and she felt Arlene's soft lips mopping her eyelids and cheeks, she felt cleansed and empty, as light as air and helpless as a kitten in Arlene's tender caress.

'That's better,' she heard Arlene say. 'You've had a roller coaster ride this week, haven't you, Melanie? It's been harder than you realised, hasn't it? And you've been so, so good for Kirsty. And she knows that well enough. Even as she's screwing Magda, she knows how good you've been for her. But tonight, you're auntie Arlene's little girl, and auntie Arlene is going to look after you. She's going to hold you and squeeze you, to comfort you and thrill you. Tonight, you're going to forget everything and lose yourself in her big brown bosom. You're going to melt between her thighs, drown in the sweet honey of her soft pink pussy. You've given so much this past week, so tonight you're going to receive, just receive. And then you'll be a big strong girl again, won't you, Melanie? You'll be a tough beautiful boss-bitch again. And tomorrow you'll know exactly what you want and exactly how you're going to get it.'

And Melanie relaxed, totally and completely, in Arlene's arms. She let her jaw slacken and droop under Arlene's hot lips, then melt away in the sweet wine of her breath. She let her arms flop around Arlene's neck and shoulders until they sunk into them like water-logged branches in a woodland pond. Her legs, wrapped around by Arlene's longer, stronger limbs, seemed to evaporate. Soon, she was nothing but the throb in her belly that welled up and expanded, absorbing into itself the tingle in her nipples, the moist warmth of mouth and tongue, and all the other sweet sensations Arlene was visiting on her. So when the time came for Arlene to ease her long fingers into her, Melanie felt them in her entire being and submitted to them with all her soul. And when her body began twisting and trembling in the paroxysms of a protracted orgasm, it was like being tossed on the rippling ridges of an erupting volcano. And then she was floating on a river of magma, racing down the slope of the world, cast this way and that as the current tore at her limbs and her loins until she came to rest with her face once again cushioned between those ample breasts. And then she clutched at those breasts like a baby, sucking comfort from a fleshy nipple until sleep overtook her.

15

Sweet Sunday

Tony was acutely conscious of his partner but was trying not to look at her directly. After Mike's unhelpful intervention the day before, he knew it wouldn't take much to fan the flames of Victoria's suspicions concerning the true nature of the event they were preparing for, and he was afraid that some of the tests they were carrying out might do just that. The motions they were putting some of those props through might well come across as lewd when seen out of context. It didn't help either for some of the lads to be clowning around with them like that. What Adrian was doing with that candle, for example, was definitely not in the script. At a pause in the proceedings, he suggested they take a coffee break, just to get her away for a while. They strolled out of the library towards the drawing room where the coffee was in continuous supply.

Tony was always nervous about Victoria's opinions on the delicate matter of sex, and if she hadn't insisted, he would never have suggested she join him this weekend. She deeply disapproved of pornography, as well he knew. She'd found a girlie magazine of his once at his flat and it almost brought an end to their relationship. It was probably the semen stains on the centre-fold that did it, he reckoned. He could remember that photo now, a close-in spread shot, just thighs and bush and pink, pink pussy. Lovely it was. She said it made her sick to think of him with his dick in his hands, leering at that photo, spraying it with his come. Did you imagine it was me? she'd asked him. Is that all our relationship means to you? He'd tried to deny it, but that seemed only to get him into hotter water. Who then! she'd screamed.

They'd got over it, eventually. He'd apologised for his lapse and sworn that his true attitudes towards love and sex were all she might wish from a well-balanced sensible considerate man, and that was when he'd settled down to a life of sexual restraint for the sake of the girl he loved. He'd done it gladly enough, but how he wished he could let lust have its head once in a while. He always felt it necessary to cuddle her and kiss her when they made love, even when what he really wanted to do was get his face down between her legs or buttocks. Keeping up the conventions she seemed to require had become something of a strain. The skin magazines and hard-core videos he indulged in at Steve's place from time to time were a relief, but it was worrying how sex, which should have been cementing their relationship, was pushing them inexorably apart.

There was no one in the drawing room when they got there. He poured their coffee, indulgently spooning the correct amount of sugar into hers and adding just a swirl of cream, the way she liked it. He was conscious of being suspiciously attentive and hoped she wouldn't see it that way.

She did. Poor Tony, she thought. He had something on his conscience, that was clear. What she'd seen so far *was* quite titillating, and she was curious to see how it would all come together in the show. It was bound to be interesting, as well as erotic – those girls clearly knew what they were doing – but however it turned out, she was sure Tony wouldn't appreciate it. Not with her there.

It was a shame the way men were always so hung up about sex. Tony was like two separate people in that respect. There was the Tony who loved her and could satisfy her in a somewhat restrained manner. And there was the Tony who indulged the wilder side of his libido furtively, with magazines and videos. She wished the two would come together once in a while. There didn't seem much chance of that happening, though. If anything, the split seemed to be widening.

Victoria suddenly realised it had been a mistake to come. Her presence was just putting him under a strain. Perhaps it might help if they were to split up, work in different groups.

'Aren't you tired of having me on your sleeve all the time, Tony love?' she asked. 'We don't have to work nose-to-nose the whole weekend, do we? I wouldn't mind helping Steve with the projection equipment for a while.'

Tony didn't like the idea of her working with Steve. Steve wasn't to be trusted. Kirsty and Arlene would be doing the costumes soon, though, so perhaps she'd like to help them instead. She agreed. It seemed like a good idea.

'So she didn't care, then,' said Kirsty bitterly. 'She didn't mind at all when I didn't come back.'

'For fuck's sake, Kirsty!' yelled Arlene. 'You know that's not what I said. Of course she cared, goddammit!' Arlene turned to Victoria and said, in calmer tones, 'Sorry about the language, Vic. You know how it is when someone just refuses to understand.'

Victoria stood with her mouth open and a black robe in her hands. It was the same black robe she'd picked out of the packing case ten minutes before when she'd joined them in the dining room with the costumes. Although Kirsty and Arlene had warmly welcomed her help, they'd practically ignored her after that. They were engaged in a conversation of their own that had Victoria baffled at first. She was getting the drift of it now, but the more she understood, the more astonished she became.

'But why didn't she come looking for me? Why did she let me spend the whole night with Magda? If it'd been the other way about, I'd have found them and scratched Magda's eyes out.'

'She didn't come looking for you because she knew you'd be happy with your pretty little wood nymph,' Arlene replied. 'She *wanted* you to get together with her. That's how much she cares about you.'

'But she told me Magda was in love with Mr Drew,' said Kirsty. 'I wouldn't have gone to her otherwise. I only went to apologise for what I'd said to her, not knowing.'

'Sure,' said Arlene. 'You only went to apologise, but you stayed to shag her all night. And now you're complaining about Melanie!'

This was the first mention of Melanie's name and Victoria, who had been wondering who this mysterious female could possibly be, was dumbstruck all over again.

'Well, I could hardly leave her alone, could I?' pleaded Kirsty. 'Not after she told me it was me she loved.'

'Nobody's saying you should have,' said Arlene. 'That's the point. Melanie knew the situation and she was happy for you. It don't mean she don't love you, though. It just means she's a very generous person.'

'But all night!' said Kirsty. 'How could she bear it? How could she bear to think of me with Magda, and her all alone. She couldn't have! Not if she loved me.'

'Grow up, Kirsty,' said Arlene. 'She didn't have to think of you all the time. I saw to that. And anyway, did you think of her? Eh? Did you?'

Kirsty probed her memory. 'Yes,' she said. 'I did.'

167

'Sure!' said Arlene. 'For about two seconds. Face it, kitten, you've moved on. You're in love with Magda now. Admit it to yourself, and then you can go and tell Melanie and get her blessing.'

Kirsty was silent for a while. Victoria took the opportunity to remind them of her presence. 'Hrrm,' she coughed. 'I'm terribly sorry. If I'd realised you had so much private, er, business to discuss, I'd have stayed out in the library. I hope you don't think . . .'

'No sweat, Vic,' said Arlene. 'I reckon the kid's getting the message now. That cloak goes with the pointy hat over there. You know. Witches.'

'Oh, yes,' said Victoria, but she made no move to get the hat. 'I was just thinking. Er, Melanie. I mean, Mark . . . I mean, isn't she . . .'

'Straight?' supplied Arlene. 'Sure she's straight. At least, she was. But this little kitten introduced her to the pleasures of pussy, didn't you, kid?' She took the little kitten's chin in her hand and kissed her on the pouting lips with a loud smack. 'And believe me, that's a hard habit to crack once you get the taste.'

'Oh,' muttered Victoria. 'I see. I think. So she's split up with Mark then?'

'Maybe she has. Maybe she hasn't. A taste for pussy doesn't preclude the other thing.'

'But what would Mar . . .' began Victoria.

'Probably been dreaming about it for years,' said Arlene. 'Never known a man who didn't do she-on-she fantasies. Anyway, if Mark don't like it, he'll have to lump it. Melanie's got some good friends now, and we ain't gonna leave her go hungry, are we, kid?' She put her arm around Kirsty's shoulder in a complicit hug. 'Listen, Vic! You waiting for a flock of vampire bats to fly out of that cloak or what?'

Victoria jumped into action and folded the cloak neatly under the hat. She was enthralled by the complexity of the relationships she'd just been made party to. Even more enthralling was the simple straightforward attitude these girls took to it. They loved, it seemed, with abandon. If Kirsty seemed for the moment to have a problem about who exactly she loved, it obviously wasn't going to stay unsolved for very long. And love for one didn't seem to stop them having sex with the others. It all sounded wonderfully refreshing. Such a contrast to her situation, where love seemed to get in the way of sex, to oppose and obstruct sensuality.

When she'd finished with the hat and cloak, Victoria returned to the packing case, which was nearly empty by now. Arlene was examining something that looked like a nun's cowl and Kirsty was stitching a loose button onto something pink. Victoria stood watching them and biting her lip.

Eventually, Arlene noticed her and stared into her face. 'Say, Kirsty,' she said, without turning her head. 'You think you could manage without us two for a little while?'

'Sure,' replied Kirsty laconically.

'Let's take a stroll, Vicky,' said Arlene.

They left the dining room. Kirsty continued working on the costumes and thinking about the events of last night. Did she love Magda, her little wood nymph? She'd told her she did, over and over again. She'd held the poor tearful little beauty in her arms and swore she'd fallen for her the day of the filming and, as she'd said it, she'd believed it was true. But afterwards, she'd thought of Melanie. And then she'd been afraid to face her. Afraid of her anger. Afraid of hurting her. Afraid of how painful breaking up with her might be. And afraid more than anything, she had to admit it, of her forgiveness, of reconciliation, of renunciation.

But Arlene seemed to be saying that it would be all right, that Melanie knew and accepted her love for Magda, that she'd known of it even before she herself had. So there was nothing to be afraid of. She would go and find Melanie now. She didn't quite know what she would say to her, but that didn't matter. Melanie would know what was right. Kirsty folded the last garment from the packing case and placed it with its relations on the side table. Then she left in search of Melanie.

Victoria was visibly nervous as they sat on the edge of Arlene's bed. She was biting her lip so hard, Arlene began to worry about her drawing blood.

'I guess all that girl-talk down there was a bit of an eye-opener for you, huh?' said Arlene.

Victoria nodded.

'Appeals to you, though, doesn't it?'

Victoria nodded again.

'What you got to understand is that it ain't nothing casual, nothing gratuitous. Okay, so Kirsty's found a new lover, but that's just one more for the pot. Four female friends instead of three. It ain't fickleness. It's growth.'

Victoria indicated that she'd already understood this was so.

'But you see, it ain't like a club anybody can join, turn up one or two nights, see how they like it, maybe come regular, maybe move on.'

'No,' said Victoria. 'I understand what you're saying. Love is the admission fee.'

'Well, I'd prefer to say gift,' said Arlene. 'Love is the gift you get when you join, and the gift you give also. When Melanie joined, she didn't need to be told that. And Magda, she's wept buckets for the love she feels for Kirsty, and we'll all of us get a good soaking before too long, you can be sure of that.'

Victoria nodded again and bit her lip even harder.

'What I detect in your case, Vicky, isn't love. It's curiosity. Oh, I don't mean to trivialise it. There's something missing in your life, isn't there? Something that you're afraid you might never find. Maybe what you're thinking of now will help you find what you're missing. But it's a means to an end, and anyway, you ain't sure.'

'You're right,' said Victoria. 'It all sounded so attractive downstairs. It sounded so fresh and light. I love Tony, but our life together is getting stale, and hearing you and Kirsty made me fully aware of that for the first time. I thought I could partake of that freshness, that lightness. I thought it might make a difference for Tony and me.'

'Well,' said Arlene, 'it might at that. But if your heart's not in it, it won't work. And there's Tony. You'll have to freshen him up, too.'

'Yes,' admitted Victoria. 'Though, if I'm honest, I wasn't really thinking about him. I was thinking more of a double life for myself. You know, a loving man at home and . . .' She coughed nervously.

'. . . A bit on the side,' said Arlene. 'And was that to be my role in this scenario?'

'Well, I hoped you might, er, –' she hunted for the appropriate expression '– get me started.'

Arlene laughed gently. 'I could mail you a list of my services and fees if you like,' she said.

Victoria put her hand to her mouth. 'Oh! I didn't mean to suggest . . .'

'No offence taken,' said Arlene. 'I just want you to understand what you're talking about, because I don't think you really do. You've got a problem with that man of yours and you're trying to run away from it. That's easy to do. Too easy.'

Victoria nodded, then stared ruefully at her toes.

'Look, Vicky,' Arlene said. 'I'll tell you what we'll do. You're a nice-looking girl and, even though you're not one of the club, you're kind of one of the family since you're involved with our little show. So I'm going to do you a favour. I don't know where it will lead, but let's not worry about that for the moment.'

171

Arlene stood before her as she sat on the bed. 'Stand up,' she said.

Victoria stood up.

'Now,' said Arlene, 'I want you to take off your clothes, starting with your blouse.'

Victoria bit her lip again, then started to undo the top button of her blouse. Her fingers were shaking and she had to concentrate on the task. She was on the second button, still fumbling and frowning in her concentration, when Arlene suddenly lunged forward. Grabbing her around the waist, she deftly undid the fastening of Victoria's skirt, then swept skirt and panties to the floor with a single movement of her arm. Even before that move was completed, she was twisting her body again and stripping off the upper garments. Then she threw the astonished Victoria onto the bed and was on top of her before she was aware of her nakedness.

'What did you think?' hissed Arlene. 'That it would all be sweet as sugar candy? Well, I'm going to show you what it's really about. I'm going to make your heart thump till you think it's gonna burst. I'm going to make you feel like you just been flayed. I'm going to take out every bone in turn and put it back in the wrong way round. And if you don't want me to do all that, holler "chicken", but do it now, 'cause you won't get another chance.'

Victoria tried to struggle but was firmly pinned by Arlene's weight and superior strength. She panted heavily, but said nothing. Arlene grasped her hair in one hand and pulled her head to one side. Then she bit her on the neck. Grasping a thick fold of skin and muscle firmly between her teeth, she sucked hard to draw the blood to the surface. Victoria made a croaking sound that was growing towards an agonised shriek by the time Arlene released her grip. The love-bite shone like a bloody brand, though the skin was not broken.

'Now,' said Arlene, 'just think how you're going to explain that away. Just ask yourself, while I'm fucking

you, how you're going to explain that to your man.'
And she reached down to Victoria's sex and pushed her
fingers deep inside her, as far as they would go. She
ignored Victoria's cries of fear and pain. But when those
cries turned to spasms of arousal she worked with them,
bringing them slowly up, step by step. The body
underneath her squirmed and struggled, but that was
only natural. This woman, for whom sex had become a
dull and boring thing, had a lot to learn and it would
be a steep learning curve. And Arlene wasn't going to
ring the bell until the lesson was over.

Melanie had expected to see Kirsty at breakfast but,
having glimpsed her disappearing through a doorway,
she quickly realised that the girl was avoiding her. So
now, when she saw Kirsty approaching, a sheepish
expression on her face, Melanie took no chances. She
immediately stopped what she was doing and took her
by the arm, leading her away to somewhere private.
They found a corner of the kitchen and perched on a
work surface side by side.

'I'm sorry, Mel,' said Kirsty softly.

'What for?' said Melanie.

'I don't know,' said Kirsty. 'You knew it was me
Magda was in love with, didn't you?'

'I realised it yesterday afternoon,' said Melanie. 'I
couldn't leave you in ignorance. I knew how taken you
were with your little wood nymph and I had to give you
a chance to see how you felt.'

Kirsty sighed. Melanie was so good to her. It had
been wonderful last night, different, and special. Perhaps Arlene was right and she was in love with Magda
now. But there was something she needed to know.

'Did you want me to fall in love with her?' she asked.
'Did you want to get rid of me?'

Melanie put her arm around her shoulder. 'Listen,
Kirsty love,' she said. 'This past week with you has been

173

wonderful. I wish it could just repeat itself every week for eternity. But we are both different people now, at the end of it, than we were at the beginning. We both have to decide how we want to go forward. If you love Magda, as I think you do, make her your choice. You don't have to stop loving me, and I don't think there will ever come a time when I stop loving you. Don't talk about "getting rid". Talk about new experiences, new emotions, new joys and passions. And we'll share many of those, you and I, for a long time to come.'

Kirsty was satisfied with this exposition. Melanie was such a wise person. She turned her face to her friend and kissed her on the cheek. 'You've been so good to me, Melanie,' she said. 'I couldn't have borne it if you'd got tired of me. I don't know if I love Magda because I can't bear the thought of not loving you.'

'I think you love Magda because you know she needs you,' said Melanie. 'You're a strong girl, Kirsty. You're the kind of girl who can give Magda what she needs, and that's a wonderful kind of love, isn't it? Ours is a different kind. There's no conflict. No either-or.'

Kirsty saw that it was true. She kissed Melanie again. 'She reminds me of you, you know,' she said. 'I think of you when I'm with her.'

'I know,' said Melanie. But Kirsty didn't understand how she possibly could.

16

Raw Recruits

Melanie and Kirsty were still in the kitchen when the catering staff arrived. Kirsty, at ease, now, with the dictates of her heart, and assured of her friend's continuing love and support, took the opportunity to slip away to find Magda and declare her love all over again, even though Magda hadn't the shadow of a suspicion that it had ever been in doubt. Melanie stayed behind and offered to help the two Plumtree ladies.

'That's very nice of you, love,' said Marje. 'Isn't that nice of her, Dulce? Not many youngsters would do that these days, would they.'

'It *is* nice of her, Marje,' said Dulcie. 'It's very nice of you, love. But it's just taking stuff out of boxes and putting them on trays. We'll only be left with time on our hands if you help us. You run along, dear, and leave it to us.'

Melanie explained that time on their hands was what she had in mind. 'You see, we're putting on a bit of a show here on Monday, and we could do with a few extras. I wanted to ask you if you'd like to take part. It wouldn't take too much of your time, and there wouldn't be any lines to learn. I think you'd enjoy it, too, of course. Otherwise I wouldn't even suggest it.'

There were loud ooohs and aaahs as the ladies contemplated sudden stardom at such a late stage in

175

their careers, but neither dared be the first to answer. They tossed little quips and exclamations between themselves until, a 'no' having failed to emerge of its own accord, a simple prompt from Melanie was all that was required to settle the matter.

'There'll be some nice costumes to wear and there'll be plenty of people on stage with you so you won't be on your own. It'll be more like a fancy dress party, really.'

They agreed to spare a few minutes then and there to go and meet some of the others and find out about their parts. After lunch, they'd delay their return to base to try on their costumes and run through the parts. There'd be more time for rehearsals that evening and around lunch the following day. Melanie would square it with their boss, Miss Plumtree, and, although there wouldn't be any payment for their time, they would each get a copy of the video of the show as a memento of the occasion. They were delighted with that, and followed her to the library, skipping and chattering like a pair of schoolgirls on their way to their first disco.

'It's *symbolic*, Mike,' said Tony. He wasn't happy to be reprising this conversation with Mike, who was fairly getting on his nerves by now. And what had happened to Vicky? He hadn't seen her since she went off with Arlene and Kirsty after coffee.

'Symbolic!' spluttered Mike. 'I understand symbolism, Tone, as well as anybody. A cauldron would be symbolic. You know, a good old-fashioned bog-standard witches' cauldron, like you see in any amateur production of *Macbeth*.'

'It *is* a cauldron,' said Tony wearily.

'Shaped like that?' said Mike. 'And with all that fleece around it?'

'Okay, so it's a bit obvious what it's supposed to be symbolising. But it wouldn't work if it just looked like

176

an ordinary cauldron. What's the point of symbolism if nobody gets the point?'

'Fat chance of anybody not getting the point,' said Mike. 'I don't mind telling you, Tone, I'm seriously thinking of moving on. Some guys I used to work with are setting up a new firm to handle media for sports organisations, and they've been dropping hints about an opening for me there. I'm tempted, I can tell you. It'd be like a breath of fresh air after B&C, the way it's been going lately. Don't tell anybody, though, will you. Nothing's arranged yet.'

'You can trust me,' said Tony. 'Anyway, it's time for lunch, I reckon. I'd better go and find Vicky. See you later.'

But Tony failed to find a trace of his beloved Victoria. Kirsty was no help. She'd seen Vicky and Arlene go off together, but had no idea where to. They were probably still together somewhere, Tony thought, assembling some scenery or something. She should have told him where she was going, though. She ought to have realised he'd be worried.

Giving up for the time being, he had lunch with Steve. If Mike had been a bore, Steve was little better. He kept going on about Arlene, who was obviously affecting his blood pressure.

'It's being here in this country house that's doing it, Tone,' he was saying. 'Half those flicks we watch are set in country houses, aren't they? In France, mostly. There's so many of them you imagine the entire French countryside must be bristling with camera equipment and naked porn stars shagging each other stupid. Anyway, I keep thinking I'm in one of those flicks, and every time I see Arlene or Melanie about the place I can't understand why they've got their clothes on. Then I get a hardie imagining them taking them off and flashing their fannies at me. It's more than flesh and blood can stand, mate.'

Tony was sympathetic. 'Still no dice with Arlene, then?' he said.

'Not a sniff, mate. It was too much to hope for, I suppose, her being a voracious lezza. You'd have thought she'd be just a bit bi though, wouldn't you?'

Tony thought of his Victoria in the safe-keeping of this 'voracious lezza' and his worry intensified suddenly. But Vicky'd never go along with that sort of thing. Would she? Nah!

'And this Castadiosa show just makes it worse,' continued Steve. 'Now that the props and costumes are coming together, you can begin to get the flavour of it, and that flavour is pure pussy, ain't it? It doesn't help. Anyway, Tone! How come you're so cool? Isn't it getting to you as well?'

'I've got Vicky here, though, haven't I?' Tony said. 'Puts the damper on it for me.'

Steve knew how things were between Tony and Victoria. 'Well,' he said, 'I think I might just envy you for once.'

They munched their sandwiches and sucked at their tea. After a while, Steve decided he could stand it no longer. 'Look, Tone,' he said. 'I can't stand it much longer. I'm even starting to lust after those two over there.' He indicated Marje and Dulcie with a slight nod of his head. Marje noticed his gesture and misread it. 'More tea, love?' she called out. 'I'll bring it over. Two sugars was it?'

Steve didn't disabuse her and she poured the tea.

'What you going to do, then, Steve?' asked Tony.

Marje came up with the tea and handed it to him. 'Thirsty work, isn't it?' she said. 'We're in it now, you know. Me and Dulcie. We're going to be witches.'

'And nuns,' shouted Dulcie.

'Ooh yes! Nuns too,' said Marje. She walked back to the drinks table.

178

'Can you believe it, Tone? That old biddy just gave me a hard-on. You see how desperate I am! You got to help me out here, buddy.'

They quickly finished their lunch, leaving sandwiches half eaten and tea half drunk, and went out into the hall. They didn't know where to go, but chose the small door behind the stairs that led out to the service area. They found a small room next to the kitchen and went in. It was apparently used for temporary storage and maintenance. It would do.

Steve unfastened his belt and unzipped his fly so that his jeans hung open from his hips. He reached down into his underpants and, with a slow cherishing movement, lifted out his aching tackle. He exhaled deeply with the relief of it.

Tony felt uncomfortable. He'd 'helped out' his friend before and, although he never quite understood this foible of Steve's, he more or less accepted his friend's explanation that doing it himself always left him 'a few spurts short of a good orgasm'. As Steve liked to say, 'I'm just not a natural born wanker like you, Tone.' But normally, there would be a porn flick on the telly and an entire top shelf's worth of skin mags spread open on the floor. Here, there was nothing to excuse the stirrings he felt within himself as he looked down at that familiar prick, as red and swollen as he'd ever seen it.

'Come on, Tone,' said Steve. 'Don't leave me hanging about in agony.' He massaged his scrotum and groaned again. The prick throbbed gently at Tony, willing him to take it in hand.

Tony swallowed hard and tried to think of something deflating as he reached out for Steve's pulsating member. Steve groaned as Tony's sweaty fingers closed around his hard hot shaft. He massaged his balls again and made little thrusting movements with his pelvis

179

while Tony ran his hand slowly up and down from root to tip. Steve voiced his gratitude.

'Oooh! You're a real mate, Tone. Oooh! That's great. This is going to be a full packet, I reckon. I'll owe you a big one after this, old mate. Oooh!'

Tony watched the clear droplets of pre-ejaculate ooze from the little pink eye on each upstroke. He tried even harder to turn his mind to other things, but it was no good. He was undeniably aroused.

'Now hit the helmet, Tone,' said Steve hoarsely. Tony loosened his fingers and slid his hand up to the glans, tightening his grip again so that his fingertips rubbed against the sensitive underside as he worked. Steve was grunting now, and both his hands were busy, holding his scrotum and squeezing the root of his shaft. His pelvic movements reduced to a shudder as Tony rubbed harder and faster, and his face began to contort as if he were having trouble holding onto his lunch. Tony knew that expression, however, and wasn't worried. The contortions would increase quickly now until, just when it looked as though he was going to vomit, he would ejaculate instead, shooting his come across the room in a wide arc. Tony made sure he wasn't in the flight path as he raised the tempo, then, as Steve spectacularly came, almost came himself as he traced those milky gobbets through the air and watched them cling to the wall and drip stickily onto the furniture. And there was nothing in this dingy functional little room to account for his arousal except for that familiar sight, the sight of Steve's long straight prick shooting come all over the place.

'Fantastic,' gasped Steve. He was recovering rapidly. 'Tony, my old mate, you just don't know how much I needed that. I couldn't have done it without you. Like I said, I owe you a big favour. Tell you what! Why don't I get in a fresh stock of videos and we'll have a session when we get back to town? Just you and me.'

Tony was trying to hide his erection, but Steve, tucking himself away, noticed.

'Hey, Tone!' he said. 'You've got it and all. I knew this fucking place must be getting to you, same as me. Go on. Give yourself a treat, mate. No use hanging onto it. I'd offer to do it for you except I know you don't like that. Go on, mate. Face it, we're neither of us going to get a screw in this god-forsaken hole, are we. Not unless those two lunch ladies come across, eh!'

Tony laughed nervously. 'Yeah. It does sort of get to you, doesn't it? Mine isn't as bad as yours was, though, so I guess I'll just save it. Vic might get the urge later and she'll get suspicious if I can't give her full measure.'

'Suit yourself mate,' said Steve. 'Anyway, we'll do what I said, okay? Next Saturday?'

'Great,' said Tony. 'But don't think you have to. Always happy to help you out.'

They tidied themselves up and left the little room, ignoring the streaks congealing on the wall and cupboard.

'It's the waste, Dulce,' said Marje, after Steve and Tony had left the drawing room. 'If he didn't want it he shouldn't have asked for it. It's an extra cup to wash for nothing.'

'He wouldn't do that at home, I bet,' said Dulcie. 'His wife would make him drink it after he'd put her to the trouble.'

'I don't think any of them's married, Dulce,' said Marje. 'That's probably the trouble with them.'

Melanie chose that moment to catch up with her new recruits to the campaign. 'Everything all right?' she asked brightly. 'Did they take good care of you this morning? Did they explain everything to you? The parts?'

'Ooh yes,' said Marje. 'We're going to be witches.'

'And nuns,' said Dulcie.

'Yes, and nuns,' said Marje.

'Good,' said Melanie. 'Let's go and try the costumes, shall we?'

They glanced guiltily at the lunch debris on the serving tables, but were easily persuaded to follow Melanie to the dining room where all the costumes for the show were laid neatly out on tables, scene by scene. Dean and Adrian were making some last-minute alterations. They'd been cursing Melanie for making casting changes at this late stage, but went quiet when they saw her coming.

Melanie led the ladies to the table reserved for the witches scene and showed them their costumes, which were labelled 'Witch #3' and 'Witch #4'.

'Try them on,' said Melanie.

The ladies looked around for changing cubicles as if they were in Debenhams choosing a new autumn outfit. Melanie waited, nonchalantly flicking dust from a nun's cowl. 'Oh! Sorry,' she said at last. 'I forgot for a minute you're not used to this sort of thing. It's just that we theatrical types don't worry about privacy when we're getting changed. Just carry on. Nobody will mind.'

Dean and Adrian exchanged quizzical glances. Theatrical types? What's she getting up to now?

'Oooh!' said Marje. 'I don't like to.'

'Not in front of these young men,' said Dulcie.

'Oh, don't worry about them,' said Melanie. 'You'll only be going down to your underclothes. And anyway, these two fine gentlemen aren't interested in us girls, are you, lads?' She mouthed the word 'Gay' in Marje and Dulce's direction.

'No, don't mind us,' said Adrian sarcastically. 'You couldn't get a rise out of us if you were Claudia Schiffer and Julia Roberts. Isn't that right, Dean?'

'That's right,' said Dean. 'Mind you, there *is* a passing resemblance there, don't you think, Ade?'

'Ye-es,' drawled Adrian. 'Now that you come to mention it. A perm and a highlight or two, and they'd be dead ringers.'

The ladies were tickled pink. 'Ooh, boys!' they said. 'You're having us on.' They were almost disarmed, but still hesitated.

'We'll just go over here in the corner,' said Melanie, shepherding them to one side. 'The boys will turn their heads, won't you, boys?'

'They want to turn our heads now,' said Dean.

'You'd have to look like Hugh Grant and Russell Crowe for that, ladies,' Adrian said.

The ladies responded with more chuckles and disclaimers, but their inhibitions receded further. Shielding each other and hiding behind Melanie as much as possible, they eased themselves out of their Plumtree overalls and into the gowns, which hung long and loose over their well cushioned figures.

Melanie congratulated herself. The first step had been easier than she'd thought. She wondered if she could find these ladies attractive, now that women were such a fixture in her sex life. She remembered some of the sketches on Kirsty's bedroom wall. If Kirsty could be attracted to older women, why not Melanie? She led them back across the room to where a large mirror stood between two tables. They peered at themselves with pride as they made the dresses swirl.

'Hmm,' said Melanie thoughtfully. 'They're not hanging quite right, are they?'

'It's us, love,' said Dulcie. 'Not exactly fashion models, are we, Marje?'

They giggled, but Melanie didn't look convinced.

'No, I think it's the underwear,' she said. 'What do you think, boys?'

'They weren't designed to go on top of anything,' said Dean. He could have told her that from the start if she'd bothered to ask.

183

'Perhaps if you take those slips off,' said Melanie.

They exchanged nervous glances.

'You can do that without taking off the drapes. Don't worry about the boys, you can't shock them.'

They shuffled out of their underslips, withdrawing one arm at a time into the loose sleeves of their gowns, then letting the slips tumble around their ankles.

'I think you're going to have to do the same with your bras,' said Melanie. 'It hasn't made much difference.'

They looked at Dean and Adrian, who just carried on with their work. Melanie seemed to take it for granted that they'd do as she said, offering them no opportunity to protest. They'd managed everything so far, and it had been quite fun, quite exciting. This was just one more little thing, wasn't it? A few more discreet wriggles and their bras appeared from their sleeves.

'Oh, that's much better,' said Melanie.

And they could see she was right. Their images in the mirror looked more witch-like, but graceful, too. The fact that their bosoms drooped a bit more than they had – well, quite a bit more, actually – only seemed to enhance the effect. And the feeling of freedom and release as their breasts settled and brushed against the satin interior of the drapes was quite exhilarating.

'Ee, I reckon I look like a witch now, Dulce,' said Marje. 'Just let me get that pointy hat on and I'll get straight to work on a spell.'

Excellent, thought Melanie. Not far to go now, but it'll get harder from here on.

'We have these special slippers for you, ladies,' said Melanie. 'You won't be able to work on the stage in your shoes. Too noisy.' She pointed to a separate table on which lay a large mound of soft satin slippers with thin wash-leather soles. 'Find your size and put them on,' she said. 'And another thing. Take your tights off first or the static will build up as you move and your gowns won't hang right. Once you get static it can be the devil of a job getting rid of it, believe me.'

They had been about to move towards the slippers, but now they hesitated. They were afraid to build up static, but they were also afraid to take off their tights. It was such an ungainly process, for one thing. Why did those young lads have to be here? It wouldn't be a problem if they'd just disappear for a minute or two.

Silence reigned as they pondered what to do. Their misgivings deepened. It had been like a game up to now, but was beginning to feel more serious. If she can ask you to take your tights off in front of people, what else can she ask you to do?

Melanie seemed oblivious of their problem. She asked them their sizes and rummaged in the pile of slippers, picking out a size six for Marje and a size eight for Dulcie, then handed them to the ladies. The next thing she did astonished them out of their indecision.

'I'm going to be witch number one,' she said, 'so I'll just change now and we can all go through for a rehearsal.'

She pulled off the trim little suit and blouse with complete insouciance. She had only bra, panties and tights underneath. Next, she slipped her witch's gown over her head and removed her bra from her sleeve just as the ladies had done. Then, without giving it a second thought, she hitched up her dress and pulled down her tights, showing a lot of leg and a flash of blue knickers. The boys didn't even glance in her direction.

'That's better,' she said casually. 'I can feel the static dissipating already.'

Melanie sought out a pair of slippers for herself and put them onto her bare feet, giving a little pirouette and stretching on her points like a ballerina. She looked so charming that the Plumtree ladies completely forgot their apprehensions of a few minutes before. They grinned at each other sheepishly and shuffled out of their tights, taking care to show as little as possible in the process.

'Right,' said Melanie when they were all safely shod. 'We're ready for action, I think.'

'Oh no you're not,' said Dean.

Melanie turned to him with a quizzical expression.

'Panty-line,' said Dean.

'But this is just a rehearsal, Dean,' protested Melanie. 'You don't want us to take our panties off for a rehearsal, do you?' She turned to the Plumtree ladies. 'I'm sure we won't mind taking them off for the performance, will we, girls?' She turned back towards Dean. 'But it surely doesn't matter for a rehearsal!'

Dean and Adrian looked at each other. This wasn't like Melanie at all. She would normally be the first to insist on such details, trivial though they might seem.

'We didn't go to all that trouble with these sets and costumes so that people can ruin the effect by showing their panty-lines,' said Dean. 'Besides, if you go in there and Kirsty sees you, there'll be hell to pay. Proper little tyrant that one's become since you put her in charge.'

'Oh, no one will notice,' essayed Melanie.

'Not if you stand stock still and spread your skirts out, they won't,' said Adrian. 'But once you start bending and stretching and things, it'll stand out a mile.'

It looked as if this was going to develop into an argument. The ladies felt that they were somehow responsible. They didn't believe Melanie herself would have any problem taking her knickers off, not after the peep show she'd just given her indifferent male colleagues, and they assumed she was trying to protect them. They appreciated the gesture – after all, a woman couldn't feel secure without her knickers, could she – but began to wonder if it was worth getting Melanie into trouble over. They exchanged nervous glances for the umpteenth time since following Melanie into the dining room.

186

'It's all right, love,' said Dulcie at last.

'Yeah,' said Marje. 'We don't mind. If it'll make things easier.'

Melanie looked at them as if they were betraying her into giving way on a matter of principle. Then she stared at Dean malevolently as she flipped up her skirts once more and pulled down the pretty blue satin panties they'd glimpsed earlier. She twirled them in the air on her finger.

'There!' she said. 'Satisfied now?' She flung them to Dean, who caught them and folded them neatly, placing them with the rest of her clothes.

'You'll live to thank me when Kirsty sees you,' said Dean.

Meanwhile, the two Plumtree ladies were taking advantage of the distraction to wriggle out of the last vestiges of the clothes they'd come in with, pushing them down with their hands through the cloth of the gowns, then letting them drop to their ankles and stepping out of them, finally picking them up with a discreet genuflection and swoop of the hand, and folding them away with their other clothes, and all without lifting their hemlines by more than an inch or two. Nothing to it really. And it didn't feel at all bad. Pleasant, in fact. Exciting.

Melanie and the Plumtree ladies were finally ready to rehearse their roles. They trooped from the dining room across the hall to the library, where Mike and Kirsty were fitting the backdrop and side-screens to the stage.

'You can use the stage,' Kirsty conceded, 'but don't touch any of the props.'

'No problem,' said Melanie. 'We can just run through the main aspects of your parts, ladies. I'll put my hat on the ground and we'll pretend it's a witches' cauldron.'

And so they began to go through their routines, first squatting around the cauldron, then bringing imaginary objects from the wings to cast into it, and finally dancing around it with sinuous rhythmical movements that increased in speed and intensity.

Melanie seemed very satisfied with their efforts. She explained each sequence to them and illustrated the kind of action or movement required, and it wasn't at all difficult, really, to get the hang of it. It wasn't exactly hard work either, but they were breathing rapidly at the end, and their faces were a little flushed, their eyes a little bright. It had been fun, and Melanie was such a nice girl, wasn't she. They were looking forward to the evening, when they'd do it with the full cast and all the props.

A few minutes later they were changing back into their own clothes. This time, Melanie took them up to a first floor bedroom, after collecting all their clothes from the dining room, so they had complete privacy. They'd expected to have to dress in the dining room as before, in front of Dean and that handsome tall one, but Melanie hadn't even suggested it. They were pleased about that – it had been a bit of a strain, after all – but they also felt a hint of regret for the excitement of it, the feeling of being part of the company. Still, you could take your time here, and there was a bathroom attached – 'In case we fancy a pee,' Melanie had said. So direct these theatrical types, weren't they?

They laid their piles of neatly folded clothes on the bed and watched spellbound as Melanie, without the slightest hesitation, pulled the black gown up over her head and stood naked in front of them. Gosh! So uninhibited. But such a lovely youthful body.

'It was getting quite hot under all that material,' Melanie said. 'It seems so light and flimsy, but it's surprisingly warming, isn't it?'

They agreed. They were watching her as she rummaged for her panties amongst her clothes. When she found them, shiny and blue and pretty, she held them out, re-shaping them in her hands. They began to look away then, not wanting to be seen to stare as she put them on, yet not wanting to miss the sight either. But Melanie didn't put them on straight away. It seemed she was thinking about something. Still holding up the panties, she spoke.

'Look,' she said. 'I hope you don't take it the wrong way, but there's something I ought to explain before rehearsals this evening.'

They exchanged frowns with each other. Whatever it was, it had to be serious to distract a naked woman from covering herself up.

'It's the show,' said Melanie. 'You see, we're all quite used to it ourselves, so we tend not to see it as other people might. It occurs to me now that you might be . . . well . . . you might find it a little bit . . .'

It seemed she couldn't find the right word to describe it to them. Her hands, still holding the panties were clasped together in her anxiety, and her upper arms were pushing her breasts together, making them heave and roll as she struggled to express herself, making the nipples stand out pink and round.

'What do you mean, love?' asked Marje.

'A bit saucy, you mean?' suggested Dulcie.

Melanie smiled gratefully. 'Yes, I suppose that's what I'm trying to say. A bit saucy. Perhaps even a bit, er, spicy,' she said, pursuing the culinary metaphor she'd been given.

'Ooh!' Dulcie chuckled. 'Marje and me don't mind a bit of spice, love. Do we, Marje?'

'Not a bit,' Marje corroborated. 'You get some pretty spicy acts on at the club we go to of a Saturday night. Some of those comedians . . .! Just a good night out, though, isn't it, Dulce? No harm in it.'

'I'm so glad you see it that way,' said Melanie, letting her arms drop and her breasts bounce free once more. 'It's just that some people can be a bit . . . a bit . . .' She was having trouble with her words again.

'Particular?' ventured Marje.

'Prudish?' essayed Dulcie.

'That's right,' said Melanie, apparently accepting both offerings. She was so pleased that they were not to be counted in that category that she gave each of them a peck on the cheek. 'I hope you didn't mind me mentioning it,' she said, 'only I wouldn't have forgiven myself if you'd come to the full rehearsal tonight and been shocked.'

'Don't you worry, love,' they said. 'It'd take a lot to shock us, so it would.'

They were so pleased to have cleared this little matter up for the lovely young girl that they didn't stop to consider how little she had actually told them, how inadequate their expectation was of what they would see on the stage that evening. They scarcely noticed, too, how unusual it was to be talking like this to a completely naked woman whom they hardly knew, a woman who had, furthermore, just kissed them on the cheek and brushed her firm, naked, young-woman's breasts against their older, more flaccid, but mercifully covered ones. All the same, their colour was visibly heightened, and the gleam in their eyes was even brighter as they looked shamelessly on while Melanie stepped into her panties and pulled them slowly up, with much twisting and turning, to cover that neat bush of glistening black and those tear-drop buttocks with the faint pink marks that looked as if she'd been leaning too long against a radiator with horizontal bars. It wasn't until she was fastening her bra that they broke out of their reverie with a start and began their own toilette.

'Let me help you,' said Melanie.

Marje had picked up her warm white thermal knickers, but Melanie didn't give her the chance to step into them. She took hold of her gown near the waist and hauled upwards. Marje, taken by surprise, instinctively co-operated, and a second later stood as naked as

190

Melanie herself had been a moment before. She hadn't intended it this way, but it was too late now.

'You have a lovely body, Marje,' said Melanie casually. 'How do you keep in such good shape in your job? You must be tempted to nibble all sorts of fattening things all the time.'

Marje laughed nervously as she hastily slipped on her knickers. 'I wish it looked like yours,' she said. 'Now *that's* what I call a lovely body.'

Melanie was helping Dulcie, who had already pulled on her knickers to avoid her friend's predicament. 'We're old and fat, love,' said Dulcie. 'Aren't we, Marje?'

'No you're not!' said Melanie. 'You're gorgeous. Both of you. Do you think I'd have chosen you for my little show if you weren't?'

They giggled. They were feeling more at ease with their knickers on. In a moment their bosoms would be covered, too, and all would be well. But there was still a surprise to come.

'You have such shapely breasts,' said Melanie, cupping the nearest pair – Marje's – in her hands. She lifted them gently, spreading her fingers to augment their natural volume and lend them a form their owner barely recognised. Then she let them down again gently. 'I noticed the moment you took your bra off, even under the witch's gown.'

Marje was blushing like a schoolgirl. Melanie's touch had been so tender, so nice. For an instant she'd been made to see her own body in a different way, and to admire it more than she'd done for a long, long time. She lifted her bra and let the breasts fall into the cups, then fastened it behind and pulled up the shoulder straps. Melanie was still talking.

'Breasts are so important, don't you think? I know I can't feel right if they're not comfortable, or if I think the bra I'm wearing is the wrong fit. And other people notice, too. Even if they're not fully aware of it.'

191

Marje wondered if her bra was doing her justice and decided it probably wasn't. Dulcie went through the same thought process as she sheathed her own sagging orbs and envied her friend the touch of Melanie's hands. Without conferring, both Plumtree ladies determined that they would be wearing their very best underwear by the time they returned to Huntscroft.

17

In the Heat of the Afternoon

Dean, Adrian and Kirsty were the only ones still working at three o'clock. In truth, there was little enough left to do, but these three seemed driven to try out the various pieces of stage machinery for the third or fourth time, just to make sure there were no hidden snags, no lurking gremlins. Arlene appeared from somewhere and stood watching them for a minute or so. Then, her presence barely noticed, she went to the back of the stage and picked up one of the props, a long black leather whip. Unfurling it, she made it crack loudly in the dusty air of the library. It made them start.

'Your work's done for the day,' she said. 'Anybody still fussing about here in thirty seconds' time gets this across their rump.' She cracked the whip again.

They knew she was right. They'd be more likely to introduce faults and glitches than get rid of them now. They looked at each other and smiled, relaxing visibly.

'Okay, folks,' said Kirsty. 'We'll call a halt for the afternoon. Let's all enjoy some downtime while there's still daylight.' She put down the screwdriver she'd been toying with and left the room. If there was downtime to be enjoyed, she knew who she wanted to enjoy it with.

Arlene studied the two remaining faces. These guys looked so much at a loss she almost regretted stopping them working. They needed taking in hand, evidently.

'Why don't we three take a walk in the grounds?' she said. 'We're in the middle of a vast acreage of the finest English parkland, or so they tell me, and I haven't seen a yard of it yet. Come on. It'll clear our heads.'

Dean and Adrian shrugged their unenthusiastic acquiescence, and a minute later the unlikely threesome found themselves blinking in the afternoon sun, breathing the perfumed warmth of the still, September air. There was a green lawn in front of them that swooped down towards a grove of trees and a hazy hollow that looked as if it might conceal a small lake. They headed for it.

'Back in a minute, Tone,' said Steve. 'Have to pay a visit.' He and Tony were supposed to be discussing what to do with themselves for the next couple of hours, but Tony was preoccupied. He hadn't seen Victoria since morning coffee and no one seemed to know where she might be. It just wasn't like his Vicky to go off without telling him. Something must have happened to her.

Steve headed for the nearest bathroom. Inside, he relieved himself with force, fingering his flaccid penis and enjoying the slightly bruised feeling occasioned by his mate's un-tender ministrations. The first piss after a good wank was always a bit special. It hadn't been half bad, that wank. Good enough to see him through this weekend, anyway. At least he could look Arlene in the eye now, as long as he didn't dwell too long on those fantastic tits. Could do with a proper screw, though. Nothing doing around here, unfortunately. All spoken for, or lezzas, or both. Too bad.

As he left the bathroom, he saw Victoria slowly descending the staircase. There was something odd about her appearance, a strange look in her eye. He waited until she reached the last few steps. 'Where've you been, Vic?' he whispered. 'Tony's doing his nut. Been looking for you all day.' She wasn't answering him, just smiling. 'He's in the drawing room on his tenth cup of strong tea – as if he wasn't wound up enough already! If you want my advice, you'll have a good story ready before you go in.'

When she finally responded, her voice was soft and rasping, but oddly self-assured. 'Thanks, Steve, I'll join him in a minute. But first –' there was a barely discernible pause '– what would you say to a quick fuck?'

At about the same time, Melanie was helping the Plumtree ladies reload their little van with the remnants of lunch. Having got them safely dressed, Melanie had kept up her solicitude non-stop, flattering them with her attention, treating them like intimate friends. Indeed, by the time they were ready to leave, Melanie found it quite a wrench to see them drive off, even though they would be returning in only a couple of hours. The truth was, she'd become engrossed in the task she'd set herself, the task of exploring in reality some of the ideas they'd put into the Castadiosa presentation, of liberating the repressed womanhood she'd glimpsed beneath those Plumtree overalls. Now she was eager to continue what she'd started, to see it to a conclusion.

At the same time, she realised that it wasn't something to be rushed. She'd already made a lot of ground and a break now would do no harm; it would help the ladies assimilate their recent experiences. She'd stood naked with them, touched them, kissed them on the cheek, and they had glowed. How they had glowed! She would see that glow again, and soon. The deal she'd negotiated with Craig would see to that.

Melanie made her way back into the house. The place seemed deserted as she wandered from room to room on the ground floor. From a window, she saw three figures crossing the lawn in the distance: Arlene, Dean and Adrian. From another, she saw Kirsty and Magda sitting on a bench in the dappled shade of a red-leafed maple. They were holding hands. Melanie felt suddenly very lonely and very tired. It was so exhausting, this Castadiosa business. She decided to go to her room and lie down for a couple of hours. Perhaps it would clear her head, help her to see where all this was going to end. She directed her weary steps towards the main staircase, her mind already visualising the comfortable double bed on which she would soon be resting in peaceful solitude. It was all she wanted in the world. But it wasn't to be. She was hardly across the hall when she heard a loud cheerful feminine voice calling her.

'*Hola* Melanie! *Que tal*? How are you?'

Melanie turned in surprise. 'Arancha!' she exclaimed. 'I thought you weren't due until tomorrow.' Her fatigue was forgotten as she turned to greet the woman in whose hands her career now rested.

The two women embraced like old friends, Melanie returning the kisses to each cheek as if this was the way she always greeted professional acquaintances. Arancha explained her early arrival with colourful language and graphic expressions. The others would fly from Barcelona the next morning, but she had spent several days in the USA and had come to Huntscroft directly from there.

'Ernesto say me, "Why you need to go? You made your mind up already. Stay in United States" he say. "Plenty of business to do in United States". But I tell him no. I tell him: Ernesto, I am artist. You are bean counter. You need me to tell you what is good and what is only expensive.' Arancha laughed heartily. 'So I am here,' she said. Then she took Melanie by the arm and whispered confidentially in her ear. 'Also I wanted to see you before they come. I did you a favour, yes? Now I want you to do me a favour. I want to know what you are going to present so I do not get a big surprise tomorrow.'

Melanie saw no problem with that. They would be rehearsing in a few hours, she said, and Arancha would be welcome to watch. Ernesto and her other colleagues need never know about it. Arancha showed her gratitude and pleasure with another kiss on the cheek.

Half of the lake was already in shade from the tall trees on the far bank, but the near side still glistened brightly in the declining sun. They were seated beside a large weathered stone that might have been deposited there by a receding glacier thousands of years ago. In fact, it had been placed there by man much more recently, an integral part of the same plan that had caused the lake to be dug and lined, the woods to be planted, the gentle slopes behind them to be profiled. The rock was a suntrap. Pale in colour, it caught the afternoon sun and reflected it onto the tiny sheltered beach of gravel and sand that lay between it and the water's edge. It was the perfect place for a summer picnic, or for sunbathing, or just sitting to watch the damsel flies flashing like electric needles amongst the reeds and half-submerged boulders.

Arlene watched as Adrian stretched his arms and shapely torso before lying supine onto the sand, his hands pillowing his head. She watched his eyelids flicker under the bright sky, then close shut. She saw that Dean was watching him too, and she understood the expression on the latter's face.

'Great spot, huh, Dean?' she remarked. 'You could forget all your troubles in a place like this. Until the sun goes down, anyway.'

'Sure,' said Dean. 'Then you could just walk into the lake and drown.'

'Hey!' exclaimed Arlene. 'That ain't no way to talk!'

'Relax, Arlene,' said Dean. 'I wasn't being suicidal. It's just the ethos of the place. Typical late 18th century romanticism; an escape from the brutality of the industrial age and a last refuge for its innocent victims. If you

197

look into the water for long enough you'll see the bloodless limbs and drifting hair of all those dishonoured maidens from the tuppenny novellas.'

'I was forgetting,' said Arlene. 'You guys are professionals. I guess you can't look at a cherry tree in blossom or hear a bird sing without putting it into some stylistic context or other. Don't you ever just enjoy?'

'Given half a chance,' said Dean. 'It's new ideas we enjoy, though, not overcooked clichés like this piece of Regency kitsch.'

'Speak for yourself, ducky,' piped in Adrian. 'Warm sun on my gorgeous body is a cliché I can enjoy any time, any place.'

'I'm with Adrian on that,' said Arlene. 'But say! How come you've still got your clothes on, Adrian? You weren't sparing my blushes, were you? Strip off and give the sun a sporting chance.'

Adrian raised his head and squinted at Arlene after flashing a sidelong glance towards Dean. 'I was tempted,' he admitted. 'But it wasn't *your* blushes that were holding me back.'

'What's the matter?' said Dean, an edge to his voice. 'Afraid I might lose control? Go ahead. You can dance naked on top of this rock if you like. I won't pay the slightest attention.'

There was no movement for several seconds. Then Arlene broke the impasse. 'Well,' she said, raising herself to her feet, 'I'm going to follow my own advice. This sun is too good to waste.' Without ostentation or ceremony, she peeled off her jeans. The rest of her attire quickly followed. Her bra came off last, and the two men looked on admiringly as she released her lovely breasts from its support.

'Hmmm,' she breathed. 'I can sure recommend it, boys. Come on. You can't let a lady go bare-assed all by herself. It ain't gentlemanly.' She sat down on a smooth boulder that straddled the water's edge, stretching out her arms and legs, letting the sun and air get to every part of her body.

Adrian stood up. 'Come on, Dean,' he said. 'Let's do it. In half an hour it'll be too cold.'

Dean's reluctance was evident. 'It's all right for you fine specimens,' he said, 'but some of us are better staying covered up.'

Adrian went over to him. Taking him by the arm, he gently raised him to his feet. 'Better for whom?' he asked. 'Come on. Show me that little round backside of yours. I've got a sudden urge to see it, and your soft flabby belly. We can play at being Romantics, escaping the dark satanic mills, getting back to nature till the sun goes down.'

Dean was almost ready to capitulate. 'And what then?' he asked. 'Do we walk hand in hand into the lake and drown?'

'Oh, we drown, all right,' said Adrian. 'But not in the lake, Dean, my old duck. Definitely not in the lake.'

Arlene tucked her legs underneath her and posed like a siren on her rock as she watched the two men undress. She admired the contours of Adrian's tanned athletic figure as he shed his T-shirt and jeans. She felt the tender vulnerability of Dean's pale padded shape as it saw the light of the sun and of his colleague's gaze. Then she saw them embrace, and glowed inwardly with the passion of it. She wondered if she ought to creep away quietly and leave them to each other, but she didn't want to go. Arlene loved to watch people fucking. She had watched Melanie and Kirsty that first time in her Chamber of Correction. She would watch Adrian and Dean now.

She was conscious of her engorging vulva as Adrian's hands pushed into Dean's underpants and drew them down. The penis that sprang into view was as neat and dapper as the man it belonged to, and the sight of it gave her a thrill. And when Adrian's much longer, thicker rod appeared soon after, partly shielded by Dean's admiring hands, it so much added to her mood that she could no longer prevent her own fingers from reaching for her sex to massage the sudden flood of silky moisture into her labia. But it was to her nipples she turned a little later, when the two men knelt on the hard ground, Adrian pumping into the little round backside he had coveted. It was her nipples that would bring her to a sweet gentle climax, so appropriate in this romantic sheltered nook into which the sun poured all its heat and all its desire. She fingered them and licked them one by one. She nipped them with her strong white teeth until they smarted. Then, as Dean shuddered and gasped in Adrian's all-enveloping grip, she felt her own little shudder, heard her own inward gasp. And then they all three stopped moving for a while, breathing deeply, letting the approving sun restore their strength, their energy, their appetites.

Steve and Victoria were in one of the first floor bedrooms. Steve had wrestled with his conscience all the way up the stairs. Vicky was his best mate's woman. They'd been together for years. What kind of a louse would do a thing like this to his best mate? Despite these thoughts, his feet had never faltered as he led her upwards, anxious to get her out of sight before his best mate chanced to poke his head around the door of the drawing room and see them. By the time he'd closed the bedroom door, he'd convinced himself that there was, after all, nothing reprehensible in what he was about to do. He imagined himself explaining it to his mate and receiving, after some initial scepticism, his benison. 'You see, Tone, you're my best mate and I'd do anything to oblige you, as a best mate should. Victoria is your other half, so obviously I'd do anything for her as well. Of course, I'd never have tried it on in a million years, but when she came and begged me for it, how could I refuse? It would be like letting *you* down, Tone, and I'd never do that.' 'I reckon you had no other recourse in the matter, Steve,' he heard his friend ruefully acknowledge. 'I ought to thank you, to tell the truth.'

If something in that imagined scenario sounded a little contrived and unlikely, Steve didn't dwell on it. A fuck was a fuck, after all, and you had to grab your opportunities in a place like this, surrounded as you were by raving lezzas, every one of them intent on giving you a balls-ache.

When he turned from the door towards Victoria, he was excited to see her already on the bed with her panties around her ankles. This wasn't like her at all, but he wasn't going to make enquiries as to what might have occasioned the transformation. The glimpse of pussy under her skirt told him all he needed to know for the present. She wanted it. Simple as that. She wanted it as badly as he did, and she wanted it now. He practically tore at his belt and flies in his eagerness to oblige.

And Victoria certainly did want it. What's more, she knew exactly how she wanted it: lewd and crude, that was how. She'd had enough of the decorous love-making of her long-term partnership. She'd had enough of discreet advances, of modest caresses, of bashful penetrations under cover of sheets and darkness. She knew it would take time to break these conventions with Tony, and she knew she wouldn't be able to wait, so it had to be Steve. One quick and dirty fuck with Steve and she'd be fully equipped to tackle her partner and cut through all those self-imposed shackles one by one. Arlene had shown her the route she wanted to take. Now Steve would give her a test drive.

With her panties still hanging from one ankle, she got up on all fours and hitched her skirt up over her buttocks, flashing her fanny at the incredulous Steve, who struggled all the more frenetically to free himself of his pants. She wiggled her hips at him as she unfastened her bra strap with one hand. 'What's keeping you, Steve?' she moaned. 'Can't you see I'm gagging for it?'

It was like something out of one of those rented videos. His fingers kept missing the tab of his zipper as he watched hers thrashing at her labia and spreading open her already slack and moist vagina. 'Get it up, Steve,' she was saying. 'Just get it up!'

Steve finally managed to get his jeans and underpants down to his knees. He almost toppled onto the bed, clasping her hips to save himself. His face brushed against her buttock and he caught the pungent scent of the sex she had so recently enjoyed with Arlene. It caught him unawares and went straight to his head, and to his loins. Grunting loudly, he plunged his face between her buttocks and licked and gnawed hungrily. She pushed back into his face, encouraging him into a frenzy. Then, feeling himself about to come, he climbed hastily onto her. Clasping her around the body, his hands enfolding her hanging breasts, he let his stiff, sore penis find the path of least resistance into her, then groaned and grunted as she worked him with her pelvis, her coarse expressive cries now muffled by the bedding her face was half buried in. He came less than a minute later.

Not long afterwards, Melanie and Arancha encountered a rather uneasy-looking quartet in the drawing room, namely Steve, Tony, Victoria and Mike. As she poured a coffee for Arancha, Melanie came to the realisation that they'd interrupted some kind of scene. 'Is there something wrong?' she asked, addressing no one in particular. There was no answer. 'It's a full rehearsal tonight, don't forget. If anything's happened that puts that at risk, I want to know about it.'

Mike tried to reassure his boss. 'Tony's a bit worried about Vicky, that's all. Personally, I can understand her

202

wanting to get away for a while, from all this . . .' he took his time selecting a diplomatic word, though did nothing about the sarcasm in his voice '. . . symbolism.'

Tony amplified Mike's explanation. Apparently, Vicky had developed a headache and had gone to lie down, then had slept for several hours. Melanie could tell from Tony's voice that he didn't believe the story, while Victoria's expression indicated that she didn't care whether he believed it or not, and there was conscience-stricken complicity in Steve's downcast gaze.

'Well, I hope you're feeling better now, Vicky,' said Melanie. 'Thanks for all the help you've given us, but I suggest you take it easy from now on. When Magda gets back, I'll ask her to get you something from the medicine cabinet, just in case you're catching a cold. Have you a sore throat?'

Melanie's question was prompted by the chiffon scarf swaddling Victoria's neck, an accessory its wearer didn't seem entirely at ease with. Victoria understood the reference and her hand went up to the scarf, checking that it was securely in position over the telltale love-bite. 'No,' Victoria stuttered. 'That is, not really. Just a little discomfort.'

'First sign,' said Melanie, vaguely aware that she was fuelling some conspiracy but certain that it was for the good of the enterprise to do so. Whatever was afoot had better not come to light before the contract was in the bag. If that meant making an invalid of Victoria – and there was nothing like an ailment for postponing retribution – then an invalid Victoria would have to become. 'You should keep warm and have plenty of hot drinks. Tony, perhaps you would fetch Vicky's thickest sweater from your room? That blouse is totally inadequate.'

The authority in her voice overcame Tony's scepticism, at least for the moment, and he rose to obey her command. When he'd gone, Melanie scanned the remaining company with a suspicious eye. 'Everything all right otherwise?' she queried. 'Steve. Is all your equipment working and ready for action?'

The exchange of glances between Steve and Victoria filled in some of the blanks in Melanie's assessment of the situation. Steve eventually gave an affirmative nod.

'Good,' said Melanie. 'So just leave everything in place until the appropriate time. It's everybody's responsibility to keep cool and avoid trouble. Understand?'

Steve understood. It occurred to him that he might just take the opportunity before dinner to inspect the Huntscroft collection of expensive automobiles. He announced this casually, then left the room.

Victoria understood too. She gave a little shudder, as if with cold, and left to intercept Tony with the sweater. It would do her good to keep to her room for an hour or two more.

Mike did not understand but was full of consternation. He wanted to tell Melanie of his intention to leave the next morning and so be absent for the performance but he realised this wasn't the time to give her another thing to worry about. He decided to wait until after the rehearsal, when she'd appreciate that everything was working perfectly and that he was quite dispensable. He too left the room.

Arancha, having taken a ringside seat to watch the scenario unfolding, looked up at Melanie with mischief in her eyes. 'You are the big boss, no?' she said. 'You are like the headmistress putting all the naughty children in their places. But some problems are like lumps in a mattress, isn't it so? You can push them down, but they come up somewhere else.' She laughed, and her brown eyes shone like a tiger's.

18

Dress Rehearsal

The evening started slowly. Kirsty and Magda, looking flushed and happy as schoolgirls after a winning hockey match, returned to the house and began to turn their minds from each other to the rehearsal. Arlene came back alone from the lake and was quick to monopolise Arancha, about whom she'd heard so much and with whom she was sure she had so much in common. After her, the Plumtree ladies drove up to the rear entrance exactly on schedule, looking smart and shapely, as Melanie didn't fail to notice, lightly but flatteringly made up and with their best underwear beneath their Plumtree uniforms. It was the Plumtree ladies who occupied Melanie for the next hour until dinner.

'I can't tell you how much I appreciate your help with our show, girls,' she told them. 'You're a couple of darlings, you really are!'

'We're looking forward to it, love,' said Dulcie, 'Aren't we, Marje? It's you we have to thank, really.'

'That's right,' said Marje. 'It's you we have to thank. And you're helping us do the dinners as well. Such as they are. Little better than snacks, if you ask me.'

Melanie looked at her watch anxiously, as if expecting someone who was overdue. Just then, the door opened.

'Excuse me, Ms Brooks, but I was just going into town and I wondered if there might be anything I could get for you and your colleagues.' It was Craig, resplendent in his full chauffeur's uniform.

'Oh, thank you, Craig,' replied Melanie. 'I don't think so, but wait here a minute while I check with Kirsty.' Melanie went out of the kitchen and headed for the library, where she carried out a slow tour of inspection, exchanging a few encouraging words with those present, before making her way back to the kitchen. The ladies were laughing pinkly at some joke when she entered. As for Craig, he was seated provocatively on a work surface, his muscular thighs well parted, stretching the fabric of his blue serge trousers. No one could fail to notice that he was a very well endowed specimen of youthful masculinity.

'Nothing required, Craig,' said Melanie. 'Thanks for asking.'

Craig slithered off the work surface, momentarily straining his flies even more, then tipped his cap back onto his head and headed for the door. 'Right you are, Ms Brooks,' he said. 'Cheerio, ladies. Drive carefully.' He winked at Melanie as he left.

It took Marje and Dulcie several minutes before they could continue with their respective tasks. Melanie looked from one to the other. 'Has he been teasing you?' she asked with a smile in her voice. 'He's quite a lad, that driver. A girl has to watch herself when he's around.'

'He was only joshing us about our little Plumtree van,' explained Dulcie. 'Pretending to be envious. Saying how he'd swap his boss's BMW for it any day.'

'Quite a card, he is,' added Marje.

'You weren't flirting with him, were you?' pursued Melanie. 'From where I was standing, he looked rather pleased to see you. Unless that was a hernia truss he was wearing.'

'Oooh!' they squealed in unison. 'What a thing to say!'

'I may be getting on in years,' laughed Marje, 'but I know that wasn't no hernia truss.'

'Couldn't help noticing, could we, the way he was sitting,' contributed Dulcie.

'You don't get many of them to a pound, do you?' concluded Marje.

The two ladies were still under the impression that it was all a joke, a bit of play-acting. It would be necessary to disillusion them, but gently, gently.

'He must have taken a fancy to you, girls. That's what I reckon,' said Melanie.

'Oooh!' they squealed again.

'A lad like that!'

'Half our age!'

The thought had crossed their minds, though, Melanie could tell. Craig had used his few minutes to good effect. 'Some men *like* older women,' she mused. 'They like maturity, experience. And you *are* rather attractive, you know. I could quite understand a hot-blooded chap like Craig showing an interest.'

The ladies had barely stopped laughing since Craig's departure, but now they turned to her with puzzled expressions on their still-flushed faces. Was she serious? Could she really think Craig would be interested in them?

'I'm only sorry I came back so soon,' Melanie went on. 'Another five minutes and who knows what I might have butted in on!'

Marje looked at Dulcie and Dulcie looked at Marje. They weren't sure now whether they'd been flirting with Craig or not. Each imagined it might be the other the lad had fancied, but each also hoped it had been herself. Oo-er! The evening had barely begun and exciting things were already starting to happen.

Melanie remained with the Plumtree ladies while they served the dinners, giving her a chance to interact briefly

207

with everyone else and to assess the general morale of the crew. She soon discovered that morale was, in fact, a little patchy. Magda and Kirsty were in fine spirits, as was Arlene, who had found a true kindred spirit in Arancha and was making the most of her. Dean and Adrian, too, seemed more relaxed and at ease with each other than usual. On the other side of the balance, Mike was excessively lugubrious, while Steve, Tony and Victoria were still smouldering dangerously, like a volcano. Melanie took what opportunities she could to remind Steve and Tony of their duties. As for Victoria, who had no further part in the proceedings, Melanie would have liked to ask her to stay away from the library that evening. If the volcano were to erupt, she would be the trigger. She couldn't think of a diplomatic way to do it, however.

Towards the end of the dinner session, Craig made another appearance. The ladies blushed when they saw him, but vied shamelessly with each other to offer him the best of the remaining provender. Craig declined the food, but, being off duty – and dressed now in slacks and a form-fitting, soft silk shirt – accepted a glass of wine.

'You're looking very chic this evening, Craig,' commented Melanie. 'Have you got a date by any chance?'

Craig savoured his wine before answering. The ladies hung in suspended animation, waiting for his reply.

'Can't say that I have,' he drawled. 'But the night is still young.'

Melanie heard two exhalations of breath behind her. 'Such a romantic, aren't you,' she teased. 'But if you've nothing better to do, you could stay to watch our rehearsal. Marje and Dulcie –' she indicated the Plumtree ladies with a sweep of her hand '– are going to be in it.'

'Er, yes,' said Marje. 'We're going to be witches.'

'And nuns,' said Dulcie.

'That's right. And nuns,' said Marje.

'In that case,' said Craig, 'I don't see how I could refuse.' He beamed at the ladies, who smiled nervously back. The silk of his shirt shimmered as he flexed his pectoral muscles. 'A more spell-binding pair of witches would be hard to find, I'm sure.'

'There,' whispered Melanie as Craig sauntered away with his glass of wine, his slacks straining over his buttocks, 'I knew you were flirting with him. Take care, girls. Don't start anything you wouldn't want to finish.'

The girls blushed even redder. Melanie smiled a cheeky smile that suggested she well knew what they were up to and approved heartily. They looked at her with moisture in their eyes and strange half-smiles on their lips. What had been nothing more than fantasy a short while before was starting to emerge into the realms of the hypothetical, if not yet the possible. It wasn't only their eyes that were moist now.

The lights of the library dimmed as Kirsty called for the rehearsal to begin. They were to run through the whole thing once, scene by scene, with short intervals between the scenes for reactions, postmortems, etc. It wasn't too late to make changes if necessary.

Mike switched on the projector for the opening sequence. It shone onto a large white screen that covered the front of the stage. Kirsty called for silence as the soundtrack of orchestra and cello grew from silence and as the dim blotchy pattern of light on the screen slowly intensified and resolved itself into the dark dense foliage of the rhododendron grove. The wraith-like figure of the wood nymph could be dimly discerned, cowering in the shadows.

As they watched, the wood nymph emerged hesitantly and began to move, pushing the hanging leaves as she went. The camera followed her. A faint susurration crept into the soundtrack under the music: the rustle of leaves in the wind, or the sound of something reptilian threading its way across the leaf litter towards her, to tempt her, like Eve, from her innocence. Then a light appeared in the distance. As she moved towards it, the light grew and the branches surrounding her writhed and twisted in the wind as if trying to reach out to her. The soundtrack grew also, until the hissing sibilants and muted vowels of the name 'Castadiosa' could be discerned. The nymph's movements now became hesitant, as if there was something to fear. She looked around, showing an anxious profile to camera: the beautiful, ardent-eyed profile of Magda in as yet unrequited love. The sound grew inexorably, chanted by many voices overlaid on each other: *Castadiosa, Castadiosa*. The wood nymph, no longer moving forward, seemed to want to escape but was unable to. *Castadiosa, Castadiosa*.

Suddenly, the light flared like an exploding star. It shone through the wood nymph's flimsy shift, effectively stripping her naked. There were gasps of admiration and desire from the watchers as her boyish silhouette turned and twisted under the glare; *Castadiosa, Castadiosa*. Then the camera swung forward to view her from the direction of the light, closing in on her face as her expression changed from fear and awe to one of acceptance and welcome. And the chant still grew – *Castadiosa, Castadiosa* – as that look turned to an ecstasy that seemed to draw the viewer into her very soul. And then, with a final, curt *'DIOSA'*, so loud that it threatened their eardrums, the chant abruptly stopped, the light went out. The opening scene was over.

There was awed silence in the room, then Kirsty asked for comments. 'Remember,' she said, 'the video will end, tomorrow night, with the screen blazing away to expose the stage behind it. We only have one screen, so we have to rely on that working on cue.'

'It'll work,' said Mike laconically. 'The current went to the right place at the right time just then. All we have to do is connect one wire to the charge and the screen will melt from the centre out in a ring of blue light.'

'It'd better,' said Kirsty. 'Anyway, what about the clip? Don't you think Magda's performance was brilliant? Absolutely brilliant?'

There was general agreement about that. Melanie said nothing, however. She was listening for Arancha's opinion, but Arancha was holding her fire.

Four women undressed in the dining room. Melanie and Kirsty stripped unselfconsciously to the buff, chatting as they did so about Magda's stellar performance as the wood nymph. The other two, Marje and Dulcie, after removing their outer garments, hesitated, watching with fascination as their fellow performers released their youthful curves from bras and panties, but still uncertain about exposing their own. However, it took just a glance and a word from Melanie, bare and lovely to their eyes, to overcome their inhibitions. 'It's nuns for this scene,' she said with the sweetest of smiles. 'You'll need the cowls and the waistbands.' After that, the ladies joined the other two in nakedness, and felt brave and sexy for doing so.

The stage was lit by a dim reddish light, as it would be on the night immediately after the screen had burned away to nothing. The viewer's eyes would take a little while to get accustomed enough to the gloom to see the figures kneeling on the ground: Melanie, Kirsty, Marje and Dulcie, dressed in black robes belted by white ties and with black cowls with white bands across the front. They looked like nuns, though of no recognisable order.

The light was flickering softly, as if cast by a candle or lantern. As it flickered, shapes against the sides and backdrop revealed the scene to be a kind of crypt. There were statues in niches, some painted on, some in three dimensions, these latter being made of polystyrene foam but looking like weathered marble or granite. Here and there stood large candlesticks containing unlit candles. The scene was accompanied by a soundtrack of murmuring voices. They might have been uttering prayers, but no words could be distinguished.

After a time, one of the kneeling nuns stood up and walked to the front of the stage, where stood a lectern. On the lectern was a closed book, large and dusty. The nun – it was Melanie herself – produced a light from somewhere and with it lit a candle that was attached to the lectern, the better to read by. Simultaneously, the ambient lighting increased, allowing the people and objects on the stage to be seen more clearly. A murmur arose from the audience at this. Understandable. The large candles in the candlesticks were shaped like phalluses, and the statues depicted couples discreetly copulating in a variety of positions.

Melanie opened the book.

'What is Castadiosa?' she intoned. 'Castadiosa is the life of every woman. Not the life she leads, but the life she wants, in her heart, to lead. Castadiosa is all around her. It informs her. It inspires her. It indulges her dreams. Most of all, it liberates her. Sometimes, Castadiosa is her guide, her mentor. Sometimes she herself is the *casta diosa* – the chaste goddess. She is a goddess because she is strong, she is powerful. She is chaste because she is woman, and woman is pure; woman can do no wrong. To the pure, all things are pure.'

Melanie paused and looked up from the book. Her expression registered a faint theatrical anguish that might have been caused by inner conflict. 'Ah! But where is Castadiosa? Who will bring her, incarnate, before us? Who will release us from the prison of our timid conventionality and re-unite our sundered personae: our hearts, our minds, our bodies? Who will make us whole?'

The murmuring soundtrack began again. Melanie closed the book, took the candle from the lectern, and

212

went around the stage, lighting each of the other candles with it. One phallus after another took flame, white phalluses, pink ones, black ones. When she reached the last candle, she did not light it. Instead, she put aside the one she carried, then took the other from its holder. The lighting now intensified and picked her out, revealing all the details of the large red wax phallus she held in her hand. She pressed it to her bosom, forcing it between her black-clad breasts, then pushing it up towards her lips. She spoke again.

'We are driven by our desires, and yet, we cannot satisfy them without sacrifice. We allow that which should make us strong to weaken us. Castadiosa! Teach us to take nourishment from our appetites, to grow with our desires and our lusts, to blossom with our orgasms. Castadiosa! We beseech thee!'

As she spoke, she stroked the head of the phallus with her hand. When she stopped speaking, she lowered it slowly from between her breasts, letting it slide down to her lower belly. There she held it close as the lighting slowly dimmed and the murmuring chant returned. When the stage was almost dark, there was a loud crack, as of a whip. The murmuring voices turned into shrieks and squeals. There was another loud crack, and the voices seemed to disperse in all directions, still squealing and shrieking, until they faded to nothing.

'Okay,' said Kirsty as the room lights were raised. 'We'll have a break now. Any comments anyone?'

Melanie joined the Plumtree ladies as they got to their feet and began to leave the stage.

'I nearly had a fit when I saw them candles,' said Dulcie.

'Me too,' said Marje. 'And them statues.'

Melanie smiled impishly. 'I told you our show was a bit spicy, didn't I?' she said. Then, with sudden concern, 'You didn't find those things offensive, did you?'

They were quick to reassure her. 'Mind you,' added Marje, 'I did wonder for a minute or two what you were going to do with that candle at the end. Looked ever so sexy as it did, when you had it between your . . . your . . .'

'My boobs,' Melanie helped her out.

'Your breasts, dear,' said Marje with a giggle. 'They're so lovely, "boobs" don't do them justice, I reckon.'

Melanie smiled. Her conversations with her new friends were reaching the levels of intimacy she'd been aiming for. 'That's so sweet of you,' she said. She placed her hands under the objects of their admiration and lifted them gently. 'That's a nice compliment coming from two ladies with such fine figures as you have.'

Melanie left them protesting their inferiority as she joined her team-mates to discuss the technicalities of the next scene.

The next scene was the witches' coven. The four nuns had already transformed themselves by the simple expedient of removing their waistbands and exchanging their cowls for the witches' hats – low backward-raked cones and round brims – that gave them as much an air of elegance as of mystery. They were joined on the stage by a fifth witch, Arlene, who had just changed into her costume in the dining room. Arlene was obviously the head honcho of this particular coven. Already taller in stature than the others, she wore a taller cone, and her robe had flashes of fiery red in it.

Compared to the previous scene, the stage itself contained little visual interest. The backdrop and side sheets were bare and dark, denying the eye any focal point, like the night sky on an open moor. But in the centre was a cauldron, nestling in a thick bed of dark wiry fleece that might have been intended to represent a campfire but didn't quite succeed.

Marje and Dulcie were too preoccupied with finding their positions and bending their joints to pay much attention to their surroundings at first, but as they got comfortable, they began to realise that the cauldron was of a very unusual shape. Melanie watched them out of the corner of her eye as they squinted and peered at it. Then Dulcie gave a little start and put her hand over her mouth. She turned to Marje, who started in turn. They had finally deciphered that elliptical shape, those sculpted double walls, and that thick bushy fleece.

It was cleverly done. At first glance, it looked like a fire-blackened metal pot. You had to think a little to come to the alternative interpretation. You had to ask yourself what could be the significance of those unconventional features. Then, once you saw it, you could never see it as a pot again. Especially when you fixated on the bright pink interior.

Melanie explained the scene to the ladies, making no bones about the nature of the thing before them. She told them that the witch's cauldron of legend was in any case a female symbol so, by making that more obvious in this sketch, they were only capitalising on a long tradition. She assured them it was artistically justified, as they would be certain to realise as the rehearsal progressed.

The ladies nodded, accepting her explanation. They had seen enough already not to be too shocked. If you could have candles that looked like penises, why not a cauldron that looked like a . . . well, a . . .

'I should warn you in advance, girls,' said Melanie. 'At the end of the scene, the whole thing throbs and glows, and a long pink clitoris pokes out at the top end. It's quite funny, really. It has a serious message as well, of course.'

The ladies were grateful for the permission to find it funny, and they tittered together for a second or two. 'Got any more surprises for us?' asked Dulcie. 'You said it was spicy, but we didn't expect a great big . . .' she hesitated, then took the plunge, '. . . front bottom.'

'I promise you there'll be no more front bottoms, girls,' said Melanie. 'But you'll see a fine pair of boobs in the next scene, and, if you don't blink and miss it, a bare backside.' All three laughed quietly together. Satisfactory, thought Melanie. The Plumtree ladies were as ready now for what was to come as they would ever be.

The scene began to the sound of low dark music. Arlene stood behind them, looking across them and the cauldron to the audience. She began the recitation that would establish the theme and give them their cue to begin the dance.

Sisters of the stormy night,
Gather round the campfire bright,
Bend your wills and form your minds
To summon our infernal friends.

The four squatting witches, eyes closed, began to sway gently, moaning as they did so.

Sisters wicked, sisters swart,
Let your lusts of every sort
Crawl up from their hideaway,
Steal your hearts and have their day.
Heed not those who'd say you nay.

The swaying increased in amplitude, from side to side and round and around. The moaning grew insidiously. It began to look as if the witches were being taken over by demons. A dull reddish glow appeared deep within the fleecy campfire.

When the spark of lust is lit,
Who would dare extinguish it?
Feed it sisters, make it burn,
Let it sear you from within.

A whisp of steam – dry ice, in reality – appeared above the cauldron as the witches rose to their feet and began their dance. The music intensified and acquired a hard pulsing rhythm of the kind that, should it take hold of a person's mind, wouldn't easily let go. The dim stage lighting began to modulate to the same rhythm, and the dancers, having barely moved from their positions up to now, began to turn and sway into and out of the shadowy margins of the stage. Arlene crossed to stage left out of their way, and continued her exhortation.

Feel the surging demons rise
In your belly, 'twixt your thighs,
Feel their hunger at your core,
Hear them shriek from every pore
From your delta's slavering maw.

The dancers now began to swoop and glide across the stage, almost vanishing in the darkness of the wings, then returning to make obeisance to the steaming cauldron. Following Arlene's commands, they brought objects with them as they re-emerged, and dropped them into the cauldron, not eyes of newts and toes of frogs but more familiar, everyday objects, the appurtenances of any woman's daily life.

Feed it sisters, feed the pot
Till the brew gets good and hot.
Wooden spoons and kitchen ladles,
Balls of wool and knitting needles,
Flask of wine for recreation,
Jar of cream for lubrication,
For a charm of powerful trouble
Like a hell-broth, boil and bubble.

The double walls of the cauldron began to extend and spread outwards as it received the offerings, revealing its

217

pink interior to the audience. Still the dancers pranced and swooped, bringing more and ever more various objects to feed its hungry maw.

Bring it fruit and bring it bread,
Bring it meat to keep it fed,
Bring the stuff of daily life,
Bring the implements of strife.
Feed it quick and feed it right
For none can stay its appetite.

As each object disappeared into the cauldron, its interior glowed a little redder until the entire stage and its occupants were illuminated from this single source, turning the faces of the dancers into grotesque Halloween masks. At the same time, the cauldron began to pulsate to the rhythm that still dominated the soundtrack. From one end of it, a new excrescence made itself apparent. Shrouded at first in folds of cotton, it slowly increased in size until its pink glossy beak-like tip broke clear.

Now the charm is made at last.
Feel the rhythm's seismic blast.
Let it rise and take control,
Let it ripple through your soul.

An intense shuddering bass entered the soundtrack to underlie the now frenetic beat, ebbing and flowing between the tall high-wattage subwoofers so that the sound felt like seismic waves passing from one end of the room to the other. At each passage, it threatened to shake the cauldron to pieces. It took hold of the dancers, too, so that they shuddered and shook like victims of some cruel fever, their unrestrained breasts wobbling under their flimsy robes, their thighs and buttocks trembling in spasm as each wave of sound

218

washed over them. Arlene stood silent and immobile, as if she alone were immune from the turmoil on the stage before her. Slowly, she raised her arm, held it high for some moments, then let it drop. In that instant, the cauldron closed in on itself, cutting off the light. The dancers dropped lightly onto their haunches and stopped moving, and the soundtrack changed abruptly from its complex of ear-splitting rhythms to a single high-pitched tone which, although not loud, seemed to fill the hearer's skull as water fills an overflowing cistern. As the sound faded slowly away and the ambient light rose once more to reveal a scene little different from that at the start, Arlene uttered the concluding lines of her monologue.

And when the hurly burly's done,
When your souls are lost, and won,
Acknowledge Castadiosa's sway,
Let her strength show you the way,
And heed not those who say you nay,
And heed not those who say you nay.

'It didn't seem like that when we did the other rehearsal,' said Marje. She and her fellow dancers had flopped onto the edge of the stage to get their breath back. 'I don't think I ever got so worked up just dancing, not even when me and my old man used to do the Twist for half the night down the Palais, before it was turned into a bingo hall.'

'You certainly entered into the spirit of it,' said Melanie. 'You were fantastic, both of you.'

'Yes,' agreed Kirsty, still gasping. 'I'm so glad you agreed to take part. It wouldn't have been half as good with just Melanie and me. You were terrific.'

A masculine voice joined in the chorus of praise as Craig appeared, towering above their prostrate bodies, the bulge of his manhood conspicuous between his slightly parted legs. 'Great stuff, ladies,' he said, 'but you should have issued a health warning, I reckon. So much gorgeous female flesh jiggling and fluttering like that! More than a mortal can take.'

They laughed.

'Turn you on, did we, Craig?' queried Melanie. 'And us so demurely draped from head to foot! My! You must have a low arousal threshold.'

'You may well be right about that, Ms Brooks,' said Craig deferentially. 'However, the sheer erotic power these two lovely ladies packed into their every movement, drapery notwithstanding, was enough to pump the testosterone level up to overload in the veins of any red-blooded male.'

'I quite see what you mean, driver,' replied Melanie, ostentatiously examining Craig's swollen crotch. 'I just hope you can withstand the pressure till you find an opportunity to relieve it discreetly. We don't want to frighten the horses, do we?'

'I wouldn't know about horses, ma'am,' said Craig. 'It's cars I deal with. Big fast powerful cars. Cars that can take a passenger, or, as it might happen, more than one, and, in the hands of a skilful and considerate driver, give them the ride of their life.' He was addressing Melanie with his words, but his eyes were devouring Marje and Dulcie. For their part, they were gazing at their hands and biting their lips. Nevertheless, they perfectly understood that they were being propositioned.

Craig left the group immediately after this exchange. Melanie slid along the edge of the stage towards her two friends.

'What are you going to do after the rehearsal, girls?' she murmured. 'This whole show is a turn-on, isn't it? If it hasn't turned you on yet, it's a complete flop. So what are you going to do? Will you go straight home, rouse hubby from the armchair in front of the telly and nag him into giving you satisfaction?' She paused for a few seconds to let the improbability of that scenario sink in. 'Or will you stay on here a while longer and take what's on offer?'

The ladies, silently chewing their lower lips, exchanged nervous glances. Their cheeks were pink and their eyes sparkled like champagne, but neither dared be the first to speak.

'Think about it,' said Melanie. 'There's another scene to rehearse before you have to decide.'

The final scene was again the convent crypt. The only thing different about it was that the lectern had moved from front stage right to centre stage left, and it was facing the wings instead of the audience. An observant spectator of the earlier scene might have noticed the iron fittings at either side of the lectern and wondered what function they might serve. That viewer could hardly fail to notice now the gaudy red leather thongs that hung limply from those same fittings.

The same four nuns as before took up their kneeling positions, and the dim reddish light began to increase. Melanie rose to her feet and faced the audience. She began to speak about desire and duty, lust and guilt, the conflict that society foisted upon womankind in spite of herself. She spoke of how Castadiosa could resolve this conflict, how the chaste goddess, for whom all things are pure, all desires holy, could sweep away guilt and unify the soul of woman. But how to let her in? How to cast off the shackles and kneel before her? Who could frail woman call upon to purge her of false guilt and give her the strength to prostrate herself before the goddess?

As Melanie was finishing her speech, the light shifted almost imperceptibly so that a niche at the rear of the stage, hitherto in complete darkness, now began to reveal its contents. That it was a human form was soon apparent, but it was unclear, since it did not move, whether it was another statue or a living breathing person.

'Who can free us from our chains?' intoned Melanie. 'Who can cleanse us of our stain?'

Barely had she finished when the figure stepped suddenly forth and, jettisoning the black cloak that had covered it, raised its arm. A long snake-like whip uncoiled into the air, its knotted end almost grazing Melanie's ear as it hissed over her shoulder, then it retracted with a loud *CRACK*. Arlene stepped into centre stage behind Melanie. Melanie did not turn to look at her, but all other eyes stared as if they were seeing a vision. Arlene was clad only in a G-string and that harness that had aroused Melanie so much on their first meeting. Her brown oiled body reflected the red light from thighs, from belly, and – most incredibly – from those magnificent breasts which, emphasised by the harness, seemed impossibly large, impossibly round, impossibly tumescent at their tips.

The whip cracked again. The red spotlight was entirely on Arlene now, leaving Melanie encased in a cylinder of silvery white light all to herself.

'Could I but cast off this shame,' Melanie whispered, 'I would make my body a temple for the chaste goddess herself. My breasts, my thighs, my belly would be her altars. My orgasms would be as offerings to her. My come, sweet nectar to nourish her.'

The whip cracked once more, and again. Arlene's velvet voice answered as if from a deep pit.

'Let the fire of the whip cleanse you. Let the force of the lash snap your chains. Let the lacerating scourge strip you of your skin of shame as a butcher flays a stuck and bleeding hog.'

More whip cracks followed this. Melanie, still without looking at her temptress, moved slowly to the lectern. She stood against it with her arms hanging loosely at the level of the thongs. Arlene deftly tied the thongs to secure Melanie's wrists, then took up her position behind her captive. As she did so, she took hold of a fine cord – invisible to the spectators – that hung from Melanie's robe. The audience gasped as she raised the whip. Then, in a single motion, Arlene tugged the cord sharply with her free hand, flexed her entire body, and began her stroke. Melanie's robe cascaded to the ground just as the white spotlight went out. Then, before the audience could recover from the microsecond's glimpse of naked white flesh, the red spotlight went out. All that could be perceived was another loud whipcrack and a piercing scream. When these sounds died away, Melanie's voice was heard for the last time. 'Castadiosa,' it said, in tones of rapture. 'Castadiosa'.

19

Postmortem

When the lights went up again, Melanie and Arlene, both respectably draped once more, descended from the stage to the acclaim of the audience. Melanie made a bee-line for Arancha, as did Arlene and Kirsty.

'Well, Arancha,' said Melanie. 'What's the verdict?'

'Hmm,' said Arancha. 'Is very good, but I feel I need more. I feel like something started and didn't finish.'

'You think we're holding back?' Arlene queried.

'You show what you mean,' replied Arancha, 'but in symbols, metaphors. You have the imagination for Castadiosa, is clear, but have you also the courage? That's what my colleagues will be asking themselves.'

Kirsty was following the implications in her mind. 'You mean you want a real whipping?'

'That would be very nice,' agreed Arancha. 'I like very much to see whipping. But it is not me who should tell you what to do. I think you understand Castadiosa and will know yourselves what you must do. Courage, that is all. I go to my room now.' She left.

'We need an editorial meeting,' said Melanie. They agreed to meet in Melanie's room at an appointed time, then they too left the room, not noticing that Victoria, who had been hovering close during the debriefing, watched them go with a thoughtful expression.

There was no point in asking the Plumtree ladies what they'd decided. Their rosy complexions sufficiently conveyed their anticipation, and if not their complexions, their moist eyes, hungry and expectant. Melanie found them waiting at the edge of the stage and gathered them up with a maternal arm around each waist, then led them out of the library and up the broad staircase.

The door of a room on the first floor was already open, and Melanie guided her charges through it. Craig was inside, stretched out on the big double bed, though fully dressed. He beamed up at them.

'Ah, Sisters!' he said, for they were still in their nuns' costumes, 'At last. I thought you'd given me up as an irredeemable sinner.'

'And that you are,' said Melanie, 'but even irredeemable sinners have their uses.'

Melanie closed the door. Craig got up from the bed and stood before the two older women, who were silent and nervous. Aiming to put them at their ease, he took a hand in each of his and looked into their eyes, dividing his attention as equitably as he could between the two of them.

'And what do you think, ladies?' he asked in gentle tones. 'Is there no hope for me? Or do you think we three could share some tender pleasures together? Could you find it in your hearts to bless a poor working lad like me with the joy of your sweet embraces?'

The problem with a double seduction is finding an approach that works for both. In this case, Craig was some way off the mark. His words touched Marje's soul and brought a tear to her eye. It would be a few minutes before she would recover. Her friend Dulcie, in contrast, was somewhat niggled by his faux sentimentality. Up until then she'd been the more nervous of the two, but now her irritation vanquished her timidity and it was she who took the initiative.

'Never mind all that nonsense,' she said. 'Me and Marje are nekkid under these shifts, and if you've still

225

got those fancy pants on in twenty seconds we'll tear 'em to shreds and have your balls for gobstoppers.'

Moments later, Craig and Dulcie were on the bed. The loose black gown was up around her waist and her legs were spread wide. Craig, now clad only in the silk shirt which barely covered his muscular buttocks, was massaging her inner thighs with his hands as her hands massaged his scrotum and the long shaft of his penis. Marje remained standing near the door. She had watched her friend take control of the young stud and help him off with his slacks and underpants. Now Melanie embraced her from behind and whispered in her ear.

'Don't worry, Marje. There'll be plenty left for you.'

Marje relaxed back against Melanie's body as they witnessed Craig's slow entry into Dulcie's open vagina. 'Doesn't that look good?' said Melanie. 'Let's you and me watch together. Let's watch that gorgeous prick sliding in and out of Dulcie's juicy quim. Let's watch her come. I don't think we'll have to wait long.'

Melanie heard a faint 'Oooh' from Marje's lips and felt her weight as she relaxed further. She let her hands press gently into Marje's plump tummy and up into her unsupported bosom.

'We'll watch her getting it good,' Melanie continued. 'And then I'm going to watch you getting it, Marje. I'm going to watch his naked buttocks pounding into you, and I'm going to hear your sweet moans as he takes you all the way to orgasm and beyond, again and again.'

Dulcie's head had disappeared into the folds of her robe, and her hands were clutching at her bare breasts and nipples. Craig had hitched her ankles over his shoulders and was fucking her long and slow, withdrawing his shaft to the tip before plunging it back in, right up to the hilt, with a loud slurping sound. Dulcie groaned deeply at each stroke, her body contracting as if it was trying to wrench his penis off to keep inside her

226

for good, but then relaxing as it slid easily out, ready for the next stroke.

Melanie's hands were moving now, massaging the soft contours of Marje's yielding body. She had wondered before if she could fancy an older woman, and had already decided that, in Marje's case, she could. She wondered how far she could go right here and now. Their bodies were as close as they could be, and Marje seemed to appreciate it as much as she did, but was there a point beyond which she would find resistance, or worse, rejection? She pushed herself against the twin round buttocks and moved her leg forward to embrace the soft warm thigh. Was that a response in kind she felt? Was that an invitation to advance?

'She's loving it, Marje,' said Melanie. 'She's loving it, just as you're going to love it in a little while.'

Marje moaned gently and took hold of one of Melanie's hands, the one that had been massaging her tummy. She squeezed it tenderly but urgently. Melanie brushed aside Marje's hair with the other hand and put her lips to her neck. Marje turned her head into the embrace, just enough to let Melanie feel the pressure against her cheek. Melanie gave the neck a little kiss.

Craig had unhitched Dulcie's legs and was lying on top of her, pressing her thighs together with his own, squeezing her love-hole tight shut so that the slightest movement of his prick inside her would give her the strongest sensation. With the most subtle variations of rhythm and amplitude, he was bringing her slowly up to the brink, then drawing her back. Her face, finally freed of the encumbering robe, registered the ebb and flow of her orgasm with rolling eyes and gaping groaning mouth. Watching, Melanie stroked Marje's buttock through her shift with her free hand, then gently gripped the yielding sensitive flesh. 'And I'm loving this, Marje.' She said. 'I'm loving the feel of your body against mine, the scent of your hair and skin, the softness of your curves under my fingers.'

227

Marje moaned again and drew Melanie's other hand down towards her delta. Melanie pressed her fingers into its softness, registering, even through the cloth, the texture of pubic hair and the tumescence of the flesh beneath. In a moment, her fingertips registered too the wetness that seeped through the flimsy black material.

'Dulcie's coming now, Marje,' said Melanie. 'It'll be your turn in a minute. I want to see you getting fucked, Marje. I want to see that more than anything right now. Then I'll have to go, and you will too. But tomorrow, I want you for myself, just you and me alone together. Don't say anything. Just nod.'

Marje nodded.

'Tomorrow then,' said Melanie, and they watched as Dulcie shuddered and shook to her climax under Craig's sweating muscular back.

Melanie got to her room with just time enough to change into jeans and jumper before the editorial meeting was scheduled to start. Arlene and Kirsty turned up exactly on time. Dean, whom Kirsty had called in to advise on technical issues, appeared within a minute or two. Arlene had brought some glasses and a bottle of wine, which she distributed as they all settled around the edge of Melanie's bed and prepared themselves for some serious work.

Melanie reminded them of what Arancha had said about the need to demonstrate courage to the Castadiosa directors. They reviewed the opening video and the three stage scenes one by one, asking each other where the weaknesses lay. They quickly homed in on the last scene.

'I never really liked that ending,' said Arlene. 'Pardon me if I say "I told you so", but I felt all along it would be a bit of an anticlimax.'

'Okay,' said Kirsty petulantly. 'You were right. I suppose it's all my fault. I wanted symbolism, you wanted hard-core. No contest. I should have realised that.'

The last thing Melanie wanted was a blaming session. 'We all agreed the script,' she said. 'Besides, if anyone's to blame it's me. I ruled out anything too explicit because I was afraid of embarrassing Charles, our buttoned-up boss. That was a reasonable approach to take at the time, but a week is a long time in sexual politics, and our boss isn't nearly as buttoned-up now as he was then. So let's just open our minds and see how best we can remedy the situation.'

An earnest but focused discussion ensued. The problem, as it turned out, wasn't too hard to solve. Within a few minutes they had agreed the essentials of a new ending to the final scene. They were moving on to the technicalities of how to implement it when there was a gentle tap on the door.

'Come in,' called Melanie.

The door opened and Victoria sidled in. The words poured out of her in a torrent. 'I'm sorry if I'm disturbing you, but I heard what the Spanish lady said and I want it to be me.'

They exchanged perplexed glances with each other.

'You want what to be you?' asked Melanie.

'Whatever,' said Victoria, then, seeing that they still didn't seem to understand her, 'The Spanish lady said there was something missing, and I figure you're going to put in something explicit and, well, sexy. I want to volunteer for that. Whatever it is.'

There was silence as they weighed this up. During the pause, Mike Heppenstall, who had chosen this moment to try to find Melanie in her room to ask to be excused staying for the performance, arrived at the open door. Seeing a meeting in progress, he was about to creep away again but, sensing something interesting was afoot, he sidestepped instead into the shadows, out of sight but well within earshot.

'Are you sure you're ready for this, honey?' said Arlene, addressing Victoria and peering intently into her eyes.

'Yes,' said Victoria, nodding her head for emphasis. 'I don't mind the pain, if it's whipping. I don't mind what it is. I want to do it. I have my reasons.'

'There won't be any pain,' said Arlene. 'What they'll see tomorrow will be the gentle loving side of Mr Whiplash. But you'll be buck naked in front of all those folks, Vicky hon. Buck naked and bent over with the spotlight shining full on your fanny. First, Mr Whiplash will bring your nipples to attention. You'll like that. Everybody does. Then he'll reach into your slit and caress your little love-bud till your juices are running down your legs. You'll like that too. Maybe you'll even forget everybody's looking at you. But then, when he's had enough of your clit, Mr Whiplash will tickle and tease your butt-hole till it opens so wide the people in the front row will see what you had for breakfast. And then – oh, my dear, sweet Vicky – and then you'll get butt-fucked with an absolutely mega strap-on. Auntie Arlene will fill you so full your lights'll be trying to escape through your eyeballs. And I happen to know for a fact you've never been butt-fucked before. I've seen your sweet ass, remember, and a shitter that tight has to be a one-way street. So let me ask you again. Are you sure you're ready for this?'

There was silence for a while. Kirsty looked enthusiastic. 'It'll be much better if Vicky does it,' she said. 'You can stay on your spot, Melanie, in the cylinder of white light while Vicky gets it under the pink flood. It'll be like you're imagining it and she's your alter ego. That was what I really wanted from the start. That's what the whole thing is really about.'

Victoria, having digested Arlene's deliberately brutal account of the ordeal she was letting herself in for, took a deep breath and dived in. 'I'll do it,' she almost shouted. 'You must let me do it. Please. But I have a suggestion. If you agree. If you think it will work better . . .'

They were all looking at her, some with puzzled, worried expressions on their faces.

'I want Tony to butt-fuck me. For real. My Tony. Naked. On the stage . . .'

She ran out of steam and took on a forlorn look, as if she thought she'd blown it by asking for such a radical change. Kirsty, however, perked up.

'That's even better,' she enthused. 'The show is too female as it is. Having a man in there would balance it out. Don't you think?'

Dean interposed with a cautionary note. 'Aren't we getting a little carried away?' he asked rhetorically. 'The idea of Tony agreeing to Vicky getting screwed on stage is absurd enough; the idea that he'd agree to do the screwing is completely off the planet!'

'I think he'll agree,' said Victoria. 'I *hope* he'll agree. I thought I could be patient and work on our relationship over time, but I realised today I can't. I'm fed up with the way things are. I want to open myself up to life, to the world, and I want to do it now. I think I can persuade Tony, but if I can't, it'll be all over between him and me. That's why you've got to let me do it. It's our only chance, Tony's and mine.'

She was breathing heavily with the passion she felt. Then, realising she had at least to try to cover all eventualities, she added: 'If Tony won't, I'm sure Steve would.'

Arlene grunted. She didn't doubt that Steve would be willing and, considering that Kirsty was so favourably disposed, agreed in principle. She and her strap-on would stand in reserve in case of need.

Dean still looked sceptical, but had no real objection. 'We can get the extra costumes sorted out in the morning. I suppose Vicky and Tony – or whoever – will

231

join the nuns in the crypt. It'll give the audience a nice little frisson when the habit comes off to reveal a rampant male underneath.' He smiled enigmatically at the thought.

After that, Melanie had only to ratify the decision. 'I like the idea,' she said. And that was that. There would be work to do in the morning, but now it was getting late. 'Time for bed, folks,' said Melanie. 'Sleep well, and be on top form tomorrow. We've got a great show, and we'll have fun presenting it, but don't forget what's riding on it. Your job, my job, Bermont and Cuthbertson.'

As the meeting broke up, Mike Heppenstall tiptoed silently down the stairs.

20

Curtain Call

Alone in her room, Melanie stripped and showered. She was tired, but not so tired that the idea of climbing into that big double bed and sleeping soundly till dawn held any appeal. The events of the day, and the anticipation of what was to come tomorrow, had awakened all her deepest appetites so that, even if her body cried out for rest, her spirit was ravenous for sex. Besides, a deal was a deal.

Still drying herself with a large fluffy towel, she picked up the house phone and pressed the button marked 'driver'. Craig answered immediately.

'Hi, Craig,' she said. 'I'm ready to deliver my side of the bargain, that's if those two didn't entirely exhaust you.'

Craig laughed. 'Not entirely. Not for lack of trying on their part, mind. They're insatiable. If they hadn't started getting worried about their husbands, we'd probably still be going strong. But never fear, I've kept something in reserve to surprise you with'

'I'll see you here in, say, fifteen minutes then, huh?' said Melanie. 'My room's the one on the second floor landing.'

'I've got a better idea,' said Craig. 'How about we meet up in the master bedroom? It's the last on the left on the first floor. Question of atmosphere. I like to do things in style when I get the chance.'

Melanie already knew where the master bedroom was. She liked the idea, and it wasn't just a matter of style or atmosphere either. No, what appealed was the idea of making love to Phillip's driver in Phillip's bed, surrounded by the trappings of Phillip's most private moments, then sleeping in his arms until dawn, dreaming that they were Phillip's arms. That would be very nice indeed. She agreed at once.

''Strewth, Tone! You look as if you've seen a ghost! What's up, mate?' Steve was so shocked by Tony's pallor he forgot the guilt that had prevented him looking his friend in the eye a short time before. Tony crossed the drawing room to the drinks cabinet and reached for a bottle and a glass. Steve rescued both from Tony's shaking hands just in time to avert a catastrophic spillage of good brandy. He poured a suitable measure into the glass and handed it to Tony. The latter gulped it down. It seemed to help. 'It's Vicky,' he said eventually. 'I think she's gone mad!' He explained, with long pauses and excruciating facial contortions, the ultimatum his woman had just socked him with. 'In front of all those people!' he kept repeating. 'She wants to do it in front of all those people!'

Steve sucked his teeth contemplatively as he listened. 'And your problem is ...?' he said. Tony looked at him uncomprehendingly. Steve administered another measure of brandy and sat his friend down in a large soft armchair, like a father about to tell his teenage son about the birds and the bees.

'Sounds to me like you're onto a good thing here, Tone,' he said soothingly. 'For years you've been grumbling about how dull your sex life is with Vicky. Now, all of a sudden, she wants to spice it up big-time. What more could a fella wish for? Wake up and smell the pussy, old son! Get up on that stage tomorrow and get stuck in. You'll never look back.'

Tony still trembled weakly, but his friend's calm insouciance had already taken the edge off the shock, and his thoughts began to turn to the potential advantages. One thought in particular rose out of the chaos of his mind and fluttered about in his skull like a banner at a World Cup final. If he were to do this for her now, she would never be able to refuse him any indulgence in the future, never be able to make him feel ashamed of his own impulses and fantasies. Whatever he wanted, she'd have to go along with it. And there were so many things he wanted. So many.

There was a long silence as the two men mused over the scenario from their different perspectives. Tony, calm now, sipped the last drops of his brandy and aired the one remaining obstacle that stood in his path. 'There's just one snag, Steve,' he said.

'And what might that be, Tone?' asked Steve solicitously.

'I'd have to dress up as a nun.'

Steve sucked his teeth again. 'Nice,' he said. 'Sexy.'

Melanie didn't wait until the appointed time before slipping on a pair of jeans and a blouse, then creeping down to the first floor and quietly padding along the corridor to the master bedroom. She tapped lightly on the door, just in case, but there was no one there. This magical room would be hers for the entire night. Hers and Craig's. Entering, she closed the door and breathed in the cool sweet air. She looked around, taking in the sights that so often greeted Phillip's own waking eyes. Then she went into the dressing room to savour again the scents of his wardrobe, scents that would fire her lust as no others could.

Five minutes later, her cheeks brushed by cashmere, her nostrils wide, she heard the bedroom door quietly open and close. 'I'm in here, Craig,' she said in a well judged whisper. 'I'll be with you in a minute.' She didn't want to tear herself away too abruptly. She breathed deeply, as one who might not get the opportunity again for some time to come, then she became aware of a looming presence in the dressing room doorway.

'There's something appealing about other people's wardrobes, isn't there?' said a calm masculine voice. Melanie's blood froze. It wasn't Craig's.

Kirsty couldn't wait until the next morning to finalise the plan for the last scene of the show. It was she who'd sent Victoria – who would have preferred to broach the subject more tactfully and in more intimate circumstances – to put her demands to Tony straight away. Now, with an impatient Magda in tow, she'd found Victoria again and was pressing her for Tony's answer. It was vain for Victoria to explain that Tony had simply turned pale and run away without a word.

'I've got to know now,' Kirsty insisted. 'I can't go to bed with this uncertainty hanging over the whole thing. Can't you find him and get an answer, one way or the other?'

Magda looked at Victoria with pleading eyes, as if begging her to satisfy this one simple request and release Kirsty to her own aching loving arms. That was when Arlene and Arancha, who happened to be passing on their way to Arancha's room – which had a double bed and on that account was the preferred venue for the night of mutual exploration they had hastily planned – joined in the conversation.

'Relax, Kirsty,' said Arlene. 'It'll sort itself out in good time. Let Vicky handle it her way.'

'Too late for that,' said Victoria bitterly. Tony's evident shock was probably terminal as far as their relationship was concerned. Poor decent Tony. How could she have imagined he'd tolerate even seeing his woman on stage in a porn scene, let alone participate in it himself! He's probably packing his bag and calling a taxi right this minute. How she wished she'd stayed at home this weekend.

Arancha poured oil on troubled waters. 'Arlene is right,' she said, addressing Kirsty. 'You must go now and give comfort to your beautiful *chabala*, your lovely nymph of the wood. You must forget about Castadiosa until tomorrow.'

And, miraculously, Kirsty obeyed. She smiled a bashful smile at Arancha, then turned to Magda to take her hand and lead her from the room. Their light tread could be heard on the parquet of the main hall as they headed off to Magda's quarters. Then silence.

Arancha now turned to peer into Victoria's furrowed and tearful face. 'You have lost nothing,' she said. 'No one who looks into her own heart and accepts the challenges she finds there ever loses. You were alone before. You will not be alone ever again.' She touched Victoria's cheek with soft fingertips. 'Your man is already more of a man than he was. You have made him so by your challenge. Is he man enough for you? Maybe. Maybe not. You will know very soon.' Then Arancha and Arlene left, leaving Victoria to her thoughts.

Melanie practically fell out of the wardrobe. When she looked up at the shape silhouetted against the dim light of the bedroom she was trembling too much to focus on it. Only when he spoke again could she be sure of the identity of the voice's owner. 'Or perhaps those particular scents and sensations remind you of our times together. If so, I'm flattered that you seem to treasure those memories so much.'

It was Phillip. Melanie wanted to run, but her legs would not support her even to stand up. She wanted to cry out, but her lungs refused to function. She could only stare as he took a step forward and towered over her as she sprawled on the dressing room carpet.

'I'm afraid my driver won't be keeping his appointment tonight after all,' Phillip said. 'He has other duties to perform.'

Melanie made a dull croaking noise. Had she managed to get Craig into trouble with his boss? 'It . . . It was all my idea,' she stammered. 'It wasn't Craig's fault. Really, it was . . .'

'What nonsense!' said Phillip angrily. He helped her roughly to her feet. 'You're behaving like a naughty schoolgirl caught doing something forbidden after lights out. Did I teach you nothing? What kind of business-woman is it that crumbles like a freshly baked scone at the slightest provocation? Really! I'm disappointed in you.'

Melanie tried to compose herself, with indifferent success. 'I'm sorry,' was all she could say.

'Sorry!' His voice was still hard and unforgiving. 'You're sorry! A week ago I gave you my fullest co-operation in your endeavour to win a critical contract, and what do I find on my return? My good friend, Charles Bermont, transformed from depression and slow decline back into the outward-going enterprising person he used to be; my pretty but lugubrious house-keeper deliriously happy in the arms of your talented young subordinate, and my excessively image-conscious driver acquiring a taste for older women and discovering the joy of giving! And you say you're sorry!'

Melanie was slow to understand that her unladylike reaction to the surprise of seeing him was the sole cause of his irritation. She felt she had to redeem herself in his eyes somehow. But how? 'I've been very, very naughty,' was all she could say.

When Mike Heppenstall slunk into the drawing room, the look on Tony's face told him that the cat was out of the bag. 'What's your worry, Tone?' Steve was saying. 'So they want you to dress like a nun! Afraid it might turn you off? I don't think so. You'll have Arlene up there flashing her tits, Vicky flashing everything else, the smell of pussy juice in your nostrils. You'll have the

238

biggest hard-on you've ever had in your life. You won't even notice you look like a randy Mother Superior with a candle up her cunt.'

Mike took it for granted that Tony wouldn't stand for the new arrangement. 'You have my sympathy, Tone,' he said. 'It's disgusting, what they're asking you to do.'

'He doesn't need your sympathy, Mike,' said Steve. 'And if you're so disgusted, why don't you piss off and let him get on with it?'

'Just because *you* think flagellation and anal intercourse on stage is high art,' said Mike, 'it doesn't mean Tony thinks the same.' He turned to Tony. 'I'm on your side, Tony,' he said. 'I'm sorry about Victoria and I hope she comes to her senses before it's too late, but I applaud your resolution not to give in to her, even if that means they get Steve to do it instead. They won't have to ask *him* twice, you can be sure of that.'

'What did you say?' asked Tony.

'Come again!' said Steve.

Melanie managed to get to her feet in spite of her still unsteady limbs. Phillip turned and walked into the bedroom. She followed, musing on just how little she really knew of this man. They had spent many (well, several) nights together, and their unions had seemed complete, with no apparent gaps, no lacunae between his being and her own. But then they were student and tutor. Now it was different. The knowledge she'd had of him then was useless now. The memories she had of him, of his body, of his mind, could only hinder her if she were to fall back on them. Only the desire she felt – as strongly now as then – could help, and the next few minutes would be critical. She mustered all her resources.

'What do you want?' she asked. 'A full confession? Do you want me to tell you how I seduced Charles for

239

Jeanette, how I shagged your housekeeper on that very bed, then handed her over to the girl she loves so madly? I could tell you, too, how I made your chauffeur polish your Ferrari twice, and how I used him to seduce the caterers. I could tell you all that and more.' She paused, watching him, waiting for a sign.

'I'm sure you could weave a charming tale from so much raw material,' Phillip said, 'but you ought to be aware that I already know everything that's happened.'

Melanie had already begun to suspect as much. To hear it confirmed now was oddly reassuring, comforting. She felt her self-control returning. 'Ah yes,' she said. 'Your famous managerial philosophy: delegate, yield responsibility, but stay informed.'

He gestured her to sit on the bed, then pressed a button on the dressing table. It seemed only seconds before the door opened and the butler appeared pushing a small trolley. The butler placed the trolley against the wall and unfolded the lid to expose a bottle of champagne in a chiller, and a tray of canapés. He deftly opened the champagne and replaced it in the chiller. From below, he produced two frosty glasses and placed them on the tray. He would have filled the glasses, but Phillip dismissed him with a word, and he went. When the door closed behind him it was as if he had never been there, as if the champagne and canapés had appeared by magic.

'She said that!' yelled Tony. 'Victoria said *he'd* do it if I wouldn't!' Mike, realising his mistake far too late, cowered against the wall as Tony exploded in front of him. 'And did she say how she could be so sure about that?' Tony was remembering how oddly she and Steve had behaved earlier that day when they'd finally re-appeared together. Had she been shacked up with him the whole time? The fact that Steve had been with him for nearly all the time Victoria had been absent seemed

240

insignificant in the face of this new evidence. Steve – his guilty conscience rising up again – didn't help.

'Easy, Tone,' he soothed. 'Don't get yourself in a state. Vicky was just stating an opinion. Any woman would say the same about yours truly. I'm that kind of bloke.'

'Oh yeah!' shouted Tony. 'So what you're saying is, you'd fuck my woman up the arse no questions asked. Is that what you're saying, Steve?'

'Easy, easy!' winced Steve, a little deeper in than he'd expected to be. 'All I'm saying is what *she* might think. It don't mean I'd do it. You're my mate, after all.'

'She *knows* that, Steve,' said Tony with venom. 'She knows I'm your mate, but she still thinks you would. How do you account for that? Mate!'

'You're making too much of this, Tone,' said Steve, but he was losing control of the situation. He'd never seen Tony in this mood before, and it scared him. He didn't like the way this was going.

Phillip poured two glasses of champagne, then waited for the bubbles to settle before topping them up. 'Quite,' he said. 'More than that, I know what is going to happen. For example, I know you'll win the contract tomorrow. And after that, I know you'll be offered a partnership in Bermont and Cuthbertson. Why don't we drink to that.'

Melanie was taken aback, but only for a moment. She had known these things too, in her heart of hearts. But there were other things she did not know. What had happened to Mark? Where was he now? These questions loomed suddenly very large in her mind. This was strange because Phillip had completely dominated her consciousness since the sound of his voice had first jolted her out of his wardrobe. Now, as she found herself groping, step by step, towards some kind of accommodation with him, it was Mark who came to her mind to fill the emotional vacuum her receding panic was leaving behind.

Mike didn't know what to do. Tony and Steve were almost at blows, and it was his fault. He wasn't physically strong enough to hold them apart, and they weren't even listening to his pleas for calm. He was beginning to panic when Dean and Adrian appeared from nowhere. Thank goodness! Perhaps they could do something.

'What's this?' said Dean. 'You look like a couple of puppy dogs squabbling over a bone. If you're going to start punching the lights out of each other, wait till Ade and me are sitting comfortably with a drink in our hands.'

Steve, relieved at the interruption, took the opportunity to explain and hopefully defuse the situation. 'Just a misunderstanding, Dean,' he said. 'Tony's got it into his head I've been sniffing round his woman, that's all. Couldn't be further from the truth. He's just upset about what she's asking him to do in the show.'

'Oh, that,' said Dean. 'Ade and me are looking forward to that, aren't we, Ade? We were thinking of opening a book on which one of you will do the honours. Ade reckons Tony'll come up trumps, but I think he'll cop out and leave it to you, Steve.'

Tony was horrified, but his aggression was both blunted and re-directed. 'That's my woman you're talking about!' he wailed. He cast about in his mind for a course of action. 'I'm going to find her right now and get her out of this place. I don't care if we have to walk back to town, she's not going on that stage tomorrow. No way! Over my dead body!'

'I wouldn't be too sure about that, if I were you,' said Dean. 'She looked pretty determined to me. Anyway, you can ask her yourself. Here she comes now.'

Sure enough, Victoria appeared in the open doorway at that moment. She surveyed the group of contentious males and sniffed the odour of masculine stress that hung in the air. There was something about that odour, something that spoke to a woman's deepest instincts.

Melanie squatted on the bed and leaned back against the dolphin-carved headboard. She took the glass Phillip offered her and watched as he sat on the edge of the bed, within glass-clinking range.

'To success!' said Phillip.

'Success?' queried Melanie. 'To whose success? Mine, Bermont and Cuthbertson's?' Her eyes narrowed. 'Or yours?'

'Mine?' He laughed. 'What part did *I* play? Only to delegate, to yield responsibility.'

'As a chess master yields responsibility to a pawn,' said Melanie sardonically.

'Oh, not a pawn!' Phillip responded. 'Certainly not a pawn. A queen, more like.'

They drank. Melanie savoured the metallic tang of the effervescent wine and marvelled at the throng of tastes and textures that leaped and played like dolphins from her lips to her throat, the opening ceremony of the festival of the senses that she had already determined would soon follow. Back then, when she was the student and he the lecturer, she would have waited for him to make the next move. Now – how things had changed – she knew the next move had to be hers. It surprised her, this knowledge. It displeased her too, in a certain way. Phillip, beautiful, wise and wonderful though he was, was no longer the awesome figure he'd been then. But if something had been lost, was not something new about to be gained?

She reached forward to kiss him on the mouth, guiding his face towards hers with her long fingers. 'Thank you for those times,' she said. He would understand from this that they were over for her, just as they were for him. He would understand that her confusion at their first re-union a week before, and her panic of a few minutes ago, had been aberrations, hangovers from an age of youth and inexperience, and would never be repeated. He would understand too that the book now lay open at a new chapter in their relationship, that the page stood blank and empty, and that they had the choice either to leave it that way or to write upon it what they would, anything at all, except that it had to be bold and novel and exciting to be worth the expense of ink.

Victoria stood in the middle of the group of men, all of whom were on their feet and looking at her. Tony had begun to tell her to pack her things, but she'd stopped him before he got to the main verb in his sentence. 'You listen to me!' she'd said. She took a deep breath, not out of nerves but for the power of oxygen in her arteries and of male pheromones in her nostrils. They were listening, and she was going to give them something to listen to.

'Yesterday, I was your woman, Tony. Tomorrow, you might be my man. But not today. Today, I tore up the contract. I tore it to little tiny shreds.' Tony looked hurt and she felt sorry for him, but there was no turning back now. 'I didn't like the terms any more. I'm not blaming you; we laid them down together in our mutual fear and ignorance of ourselves and of each other. They were bad terms, Tony. They were killing us.'

Tony was nodding. That was good. The others were exchanging looks of wonder, admiration, expectation. That was good too.

'I realised that today. I think you must have realised it long ago, and perhaps you should have been the one to do the tearing. But you didn't, so I did. Now, we have a new blank page, Tony. We can fold it up and put it away, or we can draw up a new contract. It's entirely up to us. It'll take courage I didn't know I had until today. I think you have the courage too, but I've got to be sure.

That's why I want us to perform on stage tomorrow. You and me, Tony. If we can do that, we'll never need to doubt each other or ourselves ever again.'

She stopped talking. She heard someone say 'Bravo!' in an awed stage whisper. She looked quickly around the company to gather strength from their admiring faces, then at Tony.

Tony raised his eyes to hers. He knew she was right and that there was no other way, but his anger still glowed within him. In the faces of his male colleagues he saw not the pity or *schadenfreude* he might have expected but only adulation for her and expectation for himself, and that would make it easier for him. That would make it all right, as long as he didn't lose their respect by doing the wrong thing now.

'So it's over between us, for today,' he began. 'That's what you're saying, isn't it? All our times together – wiped clean off the slate.' He gulped, though his throat was dry as dust. 'You say the paper's blank. So I could tell you to toss it in the bin, right? If I wanted to. I could tell you to flush it down the loo, yeah?' There was an intake of breathe at this. Tony gulped again. His residual anger was blowing his fragile vessel dangerously close to the rocks. He could lose his woman *and* his friends if he didn't take care.

'But that wouldn't be what I want, Vic. That wouldn't be what I want at all.' He steered his mind towards the possibilities the future now offered. More sex. Exciting sex. Sex bizarre and sex profane. He saw the faces of his friends begin to lighten.

'So let's leave that bit of paper lying on the table for now. I'm not sure I'd know what to write on it just this minute, anyway. We can pick it up again tomorrow, after I've buggered you on stage in front of all these so-called friends of mine.' The rocks were looming again. 'They're all dying to see it, you know. They're all dying to see me with my prick up your arse. Mike's practically coming in his pants at the thought of it, though he'd never admit it in a million years. And as for Steve, he'd be in there like a shot if he had the chance. That's if he hasn't been there already. That's if he hasn't been preparing the way for his old mate all afternoon.'

Tony's anger dissipated with his words, submerged beneath a deeper emotion as the images they painted played in his mind. That emotion was lust, yes, but a liberating lust, a tolerant sharing lust, a lust that could contemplate his mate coupling with his woman and take joy from it. There was even a laugh in his voice as he finished his speech.

'Never mind what Steve or anybody else has been doing all afternoon,' said Victoria. 'It's no concern of yours. It's what happens now that matters. I may be single again, until tomorrow, but I don't want to sleep alone tonight. I want to sleep as a single girl sleeps. But since I've only got one night, I want to make the most of it.'

The implications of her words sank in slowly. They looked at each other. They looked at Tony. They looked at Victoria. Nothing was said. Everything was understood.

In the Spaghetti Westerns, the anti-hero, outnumbered and outgunned, always goes for the most notorious gunslinger first. That's logical. He's the one who'll get you if you don't get him. Victoria, outnumbered and outgunned in quite a different sense, did the opposite. She went for the most timid and least experienced of the five men in front of her. She went for Mike. That was logical too, because Mike would be the first to make his escape if she gave him the chance. She didn't give him the chance.

'You'll help me celebrate my freedom, won't you, Mike?' She put her hand on his shoulder and kneaded it gently.

Mike shrank under her grasp, but didn't move away. His eyes flashed between her face and Tony's. He seemed to be expecting Tony to protest or, worse, to raise a fist at him as he had to Steve only minutes earlier. But Tony just looked on with a twinkle in his eye.

Victoria moved in on Mike so that her breasts were touching his ribs. 'Don't think about Tony, Mike,' she said, aware of his apprehensions. 'Think about me. Think about what you'd like to do with me. Think about what you'd like me to do with you.'

Mike was clearly thinking. The crotch of his trousers was filling from within. Steve noticed. 'Getting horny, Mike?' he scoffed. 'Go on, you old wowser. Get it out before it goes off.'

Mike groaned as Victoria's fingers wrapped around his swelling tackle. 'I'm going to unzip you now, Mike,' she said. 'Then I'm going to take you into my mouth, and I'm going to suck you and lick you till you come.' She quickly loosened his belt and unfastened his zip. Mike leaned weakly against the wall as she stooped to his groin and eased his prick from his underpants. Reaching in for his balls with her long fingers, she ran her tongue along his stiffening shaft, then licked the clear drops of pre-come from the tip. Unable to control himself, Mike started to come straight away. There was a cheer as the milky drops spurted onto Victoria's shoulder and cheek. Mike could only groan, his face glistening with sweat, even though his exertions had been minimal.

Victoria stood up, satisfied with her first trophy, easy though it had been. She gave Tony a triumphant look. Tony let her see how excited he was. 'Let's all go and find somewhere more comfortable,' she said. 'There are plenty of rooms in this place, with big soft beds. Grab a few bottles, and let's go.' They did as they were told. All of them.

'Tell me,' said Melanie, 'was it really necessary to take my man away from me? Would it have disrupted your game too much to have allowed me the consolation of his loving arms when I needed it the most?'

'Ah,' said Phillip. 'I wondered when you would bring Mark into the conversation.'

'He's never been out of it, as far as I'm concerned,' said Melanie. 'Oh, I admit we were at odds with each other last weekend, but it was really unfair of you to step in and widen the gap between us. I think you owe me an apology for that.'

Phillip made no attempt to deny her accusation. 'Does a chess master apologise for sacrificing a knight at the start of the game,' he said, 'a knight who could only have got in the way of his queen?'

'Not when he's playing with wooden chess pieces,' Melanie replied. 'But a queen of flesh and blood might find a victory bought at her heart's expense a rather hollow one.'

'Indeed she might,' said Phillip. 'But such an enterprising and attractive queen as you would have no trouble finding consolation in other arms, as you've abundantly proved.'

Melanie couldn't deny this, but thought it rather heartless of him to dismiss her complaint so cavalierly. But then a new idea occurred to her, one that, if she were right, would make sense of everything. 'There are consolations and there are consolations,' she said. 'But if I understand the laws of chess correctly, it is quite possible for a sacrificed knight to come back into play later in the game, to serve his queen by his presence, having already served her by his absence.'

Phillip smiled a sweet smile and, crossing once again to the dressing table, pressed the button that had earlier summoned the butler.

Victoria sat at the head of the bed, her legs folded in front of her, her back against the headboard. At the foot sat Adrian, leaning against the wall with Dean reclining between his outstretched legs. The other three men were still on their feet, shuffling about as if unsure what to do next. Steve found an occupation handing out wine glasses and filling them. Mike stood against a wall, his glance oscillating between Victoria and the open door, while Tony hovered by the doorway surveying the scene, apparently waiting for his own role in what was to follow to become clear.

Victoria was in no hurry. It would, she realised, again have to be Mike she'd turn to first, if only to calm his all-too evident nerves, but this time she'd involve the others in the task. If Dean and Adrian could be so conspicuously at ease in each other's arms, she saw no reason why that shouldn't apply to Steve and Tony and Mike also.

Tony closed the bedroom door. Victoria took that as her cue to gesture Mike to her side, where she began to undress him. A nod and a glance brought Tony across to help. Soon, Mike stood naked and trembling before her.

'I want you to stand close to me, Mike, and watch me taking my clothes off,' she whispered. 'Don't touch me, though. Not yet. Just watch and think about my body, how it will feel in a little while when I take you inside me.'

Victoria started to undress. Mike watched. Tony reached around his hips and took hold of his scrotum, startling him, but causing his penis to jerk erect, a fresh drop of pre-come forming at its tip. Victoria smiled. She was going to enjoy her night with these men. She was going to enjoy the sights and sensations they were going to give her, and those she would give to them, also. There was one thing, however, that she would hold back tonight, one step forward she would not take. Tomorrow she would go on stage to be reunited with her man. Until then, she would preserve her anal virginity so that she could give it up to him in a spectacular ritual that would put the seal on their future together. She was suddenly very glad she'd come to Huntscroft this weekend, very glad indeed.

Even before the door opened Melanie knew it would not be the ageing grey-haired man who would respond to the bell this time. She knew it would be an altogether younger taller man. It would be Mark. After what seemed like an age in which the silence hung over her, making her squirm under its dead weight, the door opened and his cheerful 'Hi, Mel!' swept away all her doubt and anxiety as an evening breeze dissipates the oppression of a sultry summer day. And his next action replaced that doubt and anxiety with something else, with a sense of triumph, a deep and satisfying feeling that this tumultuous week had at last reached its destined conclusion and was ready to give way to that new and exciting future she'd speculated about just minutes before. For Mark strode calmly up to Phillip and, taking him in both arms, kissed him fully and sensually on the mouth. And Phillip returned his kiss with evident passion. And all the confusion and uncertainty that had plagued Melanie during the week dissolved in the warm moisture of that kiss. No longer was it Mark *or* Phillip. Now it was Mark *and* Phillip. It was Mark and Phillip, and Kirsty and Arlene, and Craig and Magda, and Arancha and Ernesto, yes, and the Plumtree ladies too. But mainly it was Mark and Phillip, and it would be Mark and Phillip for some time to come.

And Mark and Phillip began to undress. It was for her that they were undressing, and when, once their briefs had been discarded and their tumescent pricks liberated, Phillip drew Mark to him again, kissing him and taking his prick in one hand, that was for her as well. It was Phillip's way of restoring Mark to her with his blessing, with his approval. And Mark's erection, now reaching its zenith between Phillip's caressing fingers, was also for her, and she knew she would soon receive it with rapture, would draw it into herself as a sponge draws in water, and all would be well.

nexus

The leading publisher of fetish and adult fiction

TELL US WHAT YOU THINK!

Readers' ideas and opinions matter to us. Take a few minutes to fill in the questionnaire below and you'll be entered into a prize draw to win a year's worth of Nexus books (36 titles)

Terms and conditions apply – see end of questionnaire.

1. Sex: Are you male ☐ female ☐ a couple ☐?

2. Age: Under 21 ☐ 21–30 ☐ 31–40 ☐ 41–50 ☐ 51–60 ☐ over 60 ☐

3. Where do you buy your Nexus books from?

☐ A chain book shop. If so, which one(s)?

_____

☐ An independent book shop. If so, which one(s)?

_____

☐ A used book shop/charity shop
☐ Online book store. If so, which one(s)?

_____

4. How did you find out about Nexus books?

☐ Browsing in a book shop
☐ A review in a magazine
☐ Online
☐ Recommendation
☐ Other _____

5. In terms of settings, which do you prefer? (Tick as many as you like)

☐ Down to earth and as realistic as possible
☐ Historical settings. If so, which period do you prefer?

_____

☐ Fantasy settings – barbarian worlds

- [ ] Completely escapist/surreal fantasy
- [ ] Institutional or secret academy
- [ ] Futuristic/sci fi
- [ ] Escapist but still believable
- [ ] Any settings you dislike?

_____

- [ ] Where would you like to see an adult novel set?

_____

6. In terms of storylines, would you prefer:
- [ ] Simple stories that concentrate on adult interests?
- [ ] More plot and character-driven stories with less explicit adult activity?
- [ ] We value your ideas, so give us your opinion of this book:

_____

_____

_____

7. In terms of your adult interests, what do you like to read about? (Tick as many as you like)
- [ ] Traditional corporal punishment (CP)
- [ ] Modern corporal punishment
- [ ] Spanking
- [ ] Restraint/bondage
- [ ] Rope bondage
- [ ] Latex/rubber
- [ ] Leather
- [ ] Female domination and male submission
- [ ] Female domination and female submission
- [ ] Male domination and female submission
- [ ] Willing captivity
- [ ] Uniforms
- [ ] Lingerie/underwear/hosiery/footwear (boots and high heels)
- [ ] Sex rituals
- [ ] Vanilla sex
- [ ] Swinging

☐ Cross-dressing/TV
☐ Enforced feminisation
☐ Others – tell us what you don't see enough of in adult fiction:

_____

_____

_____

8. Would you prefer books with a more specialised approach to your
   interests, i.e. a novel specifically about uniforms? If so, which
   subject(s) would you like to read a Nexus novel about?

_____

_____

_____

9. Would you like to read true stories in Nexus books? For instance, the
   true story of a submissive woman, or a male slave? Tell us which
   true revelations you would most like to read about:

_____

_____

_____

10. What do you like best about Nexus books?

_____

_____

11. What do you like least about Nexus books?

_____

_____

12. Which are your favourite titles?

_____

_____

13. Who are your favourite authors?

_____

_____

14. **Which covers do you prefer? Those featuring:**
    (tick as many as you like)

☐ Fetish outfits
☐ More nudity
☐ Two models
☐ Unusual models or settings
☐ Classic erotic photography
☐ More contemporary images and poses
☐ A blank/non-erotic cover
☐ What would your ideal cover look like?

_____

15. **Describe your ideal Nexus novel in the space provided:**

_____

_____

_____

_____

16. **Which celebrity would feature in one of your Nexus-style fantasies?**
    We'll post the best suggestions on our website – anonymously!

_____

THANKS FOR YOUR TIME

Now simply write the title of this book in the space below and cut out the
questionnaire pages. Post to: Nexus, Marketing Dept., Thames Wharf Studios,
Rainville Rd, London W6 9HA

Book title: _____

To be published in September 2006

CALLED TO THE WILD
Angel Blake

Stories of pagan orgies lead a journalist to a remote Scottish village. What he finds there goes beyond his darkest dreams: Miriam, the exotic dancer whose breasts weep milk; May, the wild girl of the woods who must be trained and tamed – both members of an ancient cult whose women debase themselves for their bestial lovers. But when he discovers their shameful secret, he must choose sides between them and their puritan enemies, designers of the most exquisite erotic tortures.

£6.99   ISBN 0 352 34067 3

THAI HONEY
Kit McCann

Mitch, doyen of the London fetish scene, flees his hollow marriage for Thailand, paradise of easy sex. Enchanted by promiscuous Thai girls and ladyboys, he lives a fantasy of erotic adventures, introduces willing partners to deviance, and opens a go-go bar, with thrashing on the menu. Sucked into a vortex of insatiable desire, transvestism and corruption, he finds that behind the smiling masks, perversion is reality. But what is his own reality? A searing exposure of sado-masochism and shifting identity, *Thai Honey* begins where *Platform* leaves off . . .

£6.99   ISBN 0 352 34068 1

THE SECRET SELF
Christina Shelly

Since his teenage years, Adam has struggled with a terrible, inescapable truth: he is hiding the secret of a distinctly feminine self from the world. Following a startling adventure with a much loved and very beautiful Aunt, he has spent twelve years nurturing this self in the privacy of his home. But now he has moved to a new city and been accepted into one of the country's most exclusive transvestite clubs, the *Crème de la Crème*. This, however, is only the beginning of a journey that will see his secret self finally revealed in a series of highly erotic adventures and startling revelations.

The Secret Self is a deeply sensuous and detailed study of the psychology of a tormented and beautiful transvestite and also an exciting thriller. It will enthral cross dressers and their admirers everywhere.

£6.99   ISBN 0 352 34069 X

If you would like more information about Nexus titles, please visit our website at www.nexus-books.co.uk, or send a large stamped addressed envelope to:
  Nexus, Thames Wharf Studios,
  Rainville Road, London W6 9HA

nexus

This information is correct at time of printing. For up-to-date information, please visit our website at www.nexus-books.co.uk

All books are priced at £6.99 unless another price is given.

----------✄----------------------------

Please send me the books I have ticked above.

Name   ....

Address   ....

              ....

              ....

              .... Post code ....

Send to: Virgin Books Cash Sales, Thames Wharf Studios, Rainville Road, London W6 9HA

US customers: for prices and details of how to order books for delivery by mail, call 888-330-8477.

Please enclose a cheque or postal order, made payable to **Nexus Books Ltd**, to the value of the books you have ordered plus postage and packing costs as follows:
   UK and BFPO – £1.00 for the first book, 50p for each subsequent book.
   Overseas (including Republic of Ireland) – £2.00 for the first book, £1.00 for each subsequent book.

If you would prefer to pay by VISA, ACCESS/MASTERCARD, AMEX, DINERS CLUB or SWITCH, please write your card number and expiry date here:

....

Please allow up to 28 days for delivery.

Signature ....

Our privacy policy

We will not disclose information you supply us to any other parties. We will not disclose any information which identifies you personally to any person without your express consent.

From time to time we may send out information about Nexus books and special offers. Please tick here if you do *not* wish to receive Nexus information.   □

----------✄----------------------------